Nickname:	The Buckeye State
Date Entered Union:	March 1, 1803 (the 17th state)
Motto:	With God, all things are possible
Ohio Men:	Neil Armstrong, *astronaut* Clark Gable, *actor* Zane Grey, *author* John Glenn, *astronaut and U.S. senator* Paul Newman, *actor* Tecumseh, *Shawnee chief*
Flower:	Scarlet carnation
Tree:	Buckeye
Bird:	Cardinal
Song:	"Beautiful Ohio"
State Name's Origin:	From the Iroquois Indian word for "good river."

Heroes never give up...

Jay lay partway in the icy water holding on to the boy. He felt Valerie grip his ankles and start to pull him backward. Just as the child he held reached the edge of the hole, Jay felt pieces of ice loosen. This wasn't going to work.

He hadn't felt his arms in a long time. He prayed that his fingers were frozen in a position that still gripped the boy's coat. A large chunk of ice gave way beneath Jay's chest.

"Don't let go of him, Jay. Help will be here. Hold on."

Her voice became the only thing he knew. Scrabbling with his feet, he squirmed back onto more solid ice. He closed his eyes, trying to struggle against the cold. *Hold on Jay, hold on hold on hold on.*

Then someone yanked hard at his feet, pulling him away. He was strapped to something, dragged across the ice. He looked up at the sky. Faces filled it. Valerie. Strangers.

As they loaded him into a rescue vehicle, a man bent over him before the door closed. "Jay, do you hear me? We got him out, Jay. You did good."

American

HEROES

AGAINST ALL ODDS

Linda
MARKOWIAK
Courting Valerie

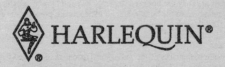

HARLEQUIN®

TORONTO • NEW YORK • LONDON
AMSTERDAM • PARIS • SYDNEY • HAMBURG
STOCKHOLM • ATHENS • TOKYO • MILAN • MADRID
PRAGUE • WARSAW • BUDAPEST • AUCKLAND

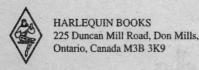

HARLEQUIN BOOKS
225 Duncan Mill Road, Don Mills,
Ontario, Canada M3B 3K9

ISBN 0-373-82233-2

COURTING VALERIE

Copyright © 1995 by Linda Markowiak

Visit us at www.eHarlequin.com

Printed in U.S.A.

About the Author

Linda Markowiak is a former trial lawyer who once argued a case in her state supreme court before deciding that writing romance was even more interesting—and challenging—than her legal career. Linda lives in northwest Ohio with her husband, twelve-year-old son and ninety-five-pound dog.

Books by Linda Markowiak

Harlequin Superromance

Courting Valerie #629
Firm Commitment #717
Motive for Marriage #755
Reluctant Witness #785
Love, Lies & Alibis #819
A Cop's Good Name #846

Dear Reader,

We grow good heroes in the heartland. Here, the earth is dark and fertile, rewarding hard work and effort, and the trees grow tall and sturdy. Our cities are vibrant, yet full of small neighborhoods where you still know and care about your neighbors.

When I began writing *Courting Valerie,* I immediately thought of an Ohio-style hero: tall and sturdy, ambitious and intense, but above all, a man with values and integrity. One who is confident enough to be relied upon, but with a bit of Midwestern humility that is best called compassion.

My hero, Jay, looks far afield in his quest for success. But in the end he knows he'll only find *real* success back home, in a place called Ohio, with the woman he's never stopped loving.

Judy Ann

Please address questions and book requests to:
Harlequin Reader Service
U.S.: 3010 Walden Ave., P.O. Box 1325, Buffalo, NY 14269
Canadian: P.O. Box 609, Fort Erie, Ont. L2A 5X3

CHAPTER ONE

VALERIE BRETTINGER picked up her pen, firmly ignoring the unmistakable flutter in her stomach. This was going to be like any other interview. She looked across the broad conference table and met Jay's steady gaze.

"Well," she began, "your résumé is certainly impressive. Why don't you start by telling us why, after nine years in a big Chicago law firm, you want an entry-level position as an assistant county prosecutor."

Jay Westcott smiled in a way that was both familiar yet different. There was a self-mocking tilt to his smile, that hadn't been there before. "I got tired of the city, and I wanted to come home."

Valerie and her associate, Meg O'Connor, waited, but he didn't say any more. "Would you like to expand on that a little bit?" Meg asked finally.

"Sure, Ms. O'Connor," Jay replied, looking not at Meg, but at Valerie. "I thought I'd like city life, and Rossen, Sebastian and Bowles was a great opportunity. It's one of the biggest law firms in Chicago, and I got assigned to the department I wanted most, litigation. I figured I'd like trial work. But in a big firm, you don't get to go to court, not for a long time. After five years, my managing partner let me argue a municipal court case, and he acted like he was doing me a big favor. It wasn't what I expected after Yale."

The corner of his mouth moved in another half smile. "I had the mistaken notion that if I proved myself, I might be a child star at the firm.

"So I started doing charity legal work, *pro bono*, criminal defense work, to be exact. And I found I liked the courtroom more than anything else about practicing law. I knew I'd be old before I was in charge of a court case at Rossen, Sebastian and Bowles. That's when I started to doubt I had a future at the firm."

Both Valerie and Meg nodded. Lawyers themselves, they understood the lay of the land at a big-city law firm.

"There are some personal reasons, of course." Jay stopped for a second and looked straight at Valerie. She looked back, willing herself not to blush. His personal reasons couldn't possibly have anything to do with her, not after so many years.

"I found I missed a lot of things—the friendliness of a small town like Amsden, the open spaces, knowing that people cared about me. And some things happened in the city that made me realize that living there wasn't all I hoped it would be."

Valerie nodded, relieved. She hadn't expected any personal details—not in a job interview. Her dealings with Jay would be purely professional. She'd made that decision the moment she'd seen his résumé. She needed to be fair, even to Jay Westcott. But still...

"This is a small office," Meg was saying. "Right now, there's just the two of us, and we pretty much divide things up evenly. Valerie's in charge, of course," she added, "but now that she's planning a political career, we need another attorney to cover some of her cases. And the docket keeps growing. Although you are from Amsden, you've been away a long time. In that time, our small town has come up against some big-city problems—drugs and thefts.''

"I can handle it," Jay told her confidently.

"Yes, your résumé certainly suggests you can," Valerie said. She had no concerns about his ability. "But how would you feel working for..." She fell silent, embarrassed. She'd been about to say, "How would you feel working for me," but she'd stopped herself just in time.

"I don't think you're supposed to ask me that in a job interview," he said, laughter in his pale blue eyes, as well as in his voice.

"I wasn't going to ask anything inappropriate," she assured him coolly.

"Valerie, I know what you were going to say. You were going to ask me how I'd like working for two women, weren't you?"

"No," she said quickly. It wasn't what she'd been about to ask. That much was true. A lawyer would know better than to ask a question that implied job discrimination. Meg was looking at her, wide-eyed. Meg knew, of course, what was permissible in a job interview, and she obviously thought Valerie was about to cross that line.

Valerie felt her cheeks growing hot. Her coloring was delicate, and she blushed easily, a trait she considered a definite drawback in anyone with political aspirations.

"I was just going to ask you how you'd feel working for lower pay in an office that doesn't have very many amenities," she said hastily.

Jay shrugged, leaning back in his chair, his hands resting easily on the table. "I don't mind in the least. I'm from Amsden, and even though, as Ms. O'Connor said, I've been away for a long time, I know what to expect.''

Meg spoke. "I want you to understand exactly how the office works. Valerie and I work together, and she doesn't pull rank on me, or anything, but she's the county prosecutor. It's her name and reputation that are on the line, and I work for her.''

"It would be a pleasure working for you, Valerie,'' Jay said quietly, looking at her with that disconcertingly direct gaze she knew so well. "I've always had a lot of respect for your intelligence and your ability to get things done. Before she passed away, my mother used to fill me in regularly on your successes.''

Meg looked quickly from Jay to Valerie, her expressive eyes widening in surprise. Meg was smart, Valerie thought, and she'd noticed something passing between them. Valerie straightened. This was ridiculous. She hadn't seen Jay Westcott in over four years, and he'd left her high and dry years before that. There was no way she was going to allow him to think they could pick up where they'd left off.

Meg had taken over again, explaining more about how the cases were divided and how the office worked. Jay asked about special projects, whether there were any opportunities to work on interesting legal issues. Valerie felt her head spinning. She'd have to do better than this. She was a professional, for heaven's sake, and she'd prepared for this interview, knowing it would be difficult.

"There are some interesting cases, but there are plenty of routine cases, too, like people running stop signs, getting speeding tickets, and things like that,'' she interjected when Meg paused. "Meg and I both hate traffic cases, so we split them right down the middle. The judge doesn't do traffic on Fridays, so I take Tuesday and Thursday mornings and Meg does Mondays and Wednesdays. In fact, I've just come from there."

Jay nodded. "I know I'd have the least seniority. I could do them every morning."

Meg laughed warmly. "You're hired," she joked, reaching over the table and pumping his hand enthusiastically.

"Great. When do I start?"

Watching them laugh together, Valerie felt about a hundred years old. "I wish it were that simple," she said. "We've interviewed several candidates, and we haven't had much chance to weigh their qualifications. Your résumé indicates you're qualified, but we'll need to see your writing sample, of course."

"No problem," he said, opening a leather briefcase and producing a sheaf of paper. Of the four candidates they'd interviewed so far, he was the only one who had brought his writing sample with him. He really must want the job, Valerie thought, and he obviously understood the interview process. The other candidates had been right out of law school, and they had needed a little hand-holding.

"Here's a brief I wrote for the Illinois Supreme Court." He handed her a thick, bound brief. "It's filed in the name of the senior partner of course, but I wrote it. I also have some settlement entries and contracts I wrote but I thought you might like to see how I handled a trial issue."

"Thanks." Valerie accepted his brief and put it on the table next to her. She looked at him and decided it wouldn't hurt to smile. "Did you win this case?"

"Of course," he responded, smiling back, the corners of his mouth turning up impishly.

Her smile had been a bad idea, Valerie decided. When he grinned at her, she was reminded of the man she used to know. He'd changed in twelve years. There were fine creases radiating from the corners of his blue eyes, a certain firm set to his mouth that hadn't been there years before and a few deep lines around it, too. But the black, unruly hair that a good haircut couldn't keep from looking mussed where it fell onto his forehead, was still the same. And there was the same strong jawline, with a bit of a shadow even when freshly shaved, and the powerful shoulders that his crisp, elegant suit couldn't downplay.

The little flutter in her stomach was growing, getting harder to ignore. "I don't have any more questions. Do you, Meg?" she asked in her interviewer's voice.

"None," Meg said, sounding reluctant, but clearly taking her cue from Valerie.

Jay stood up slowly and put out his hand. Valerie took it with professional poise. "We'll be in touch," she promised.

"Valerie, Ms. O'Connor, thank you for this opportunity to interview." He smiled at them both. "If there are any questions I can answer for you, any other work of mine you'd like to see, please don't hesitate to call me. Let me tell you before I leave that I know we'd work well together."

Meg shook his hand then, and in profile Valerie could see there was a little spot of color on her colleague's cheekbone. Well, she thought, sighing, Jay hadn't blown the interview, not by a long shot, and he'd certainly have Meg's vote.

So it came as no surprise that over lunch that day Meg pushed her relentlessly.

"Jay Westcott is clearly the best candidate," she

said for the fourth time, as she dipped her spoon into her soup. To Valerie, Meg was not just an assistant prosecutor. In the year they'd been working together, she had become Valerie's best friend. Valerie looked at her with affection, knowing that the snappy red-head would always speak her mind. "He's the most experienced, by far, and we wouldn't have to train him. We're busy now, especially with you doing all that political work. We need someone who can really do the job, not just go through the motions."

Valerie toyed with her salad, distributing the dressing more evenly. They were in one of Amsden's two restaurants, and she looked around, trying to organize her thoughts. Jay was the best candidate, no doubt about it, but she'd been asking herself the same question over and over in the weeks since she'd seen his résumé. Why was he coming home to this little town, and why did he want to work for her?

They had parted twelve years ago on terms as good as could be expected, all things considered. Jay had never promised her a thing. She had always known he would be going; in fact, at the end, it was all he'd talked about. Getting out, getting away. He'd always had plans, and had never made a secret of them. And he'd never said he cared for her, or anything like that, only that they should stay friends.

Of course, when he'd left, he'd broken her eighteen-year-old heart. She took a thoughtful bite. It had been a very long time ago—too long to be carrying around old hurts and secret longings for might-have-beens.

Coming out of her reverie, Valerie realized that Meg was still extolling Jay's qualifications, and that in her enthusiasm her friend was beginning to repeat herself.

"He doesn't have very much trial experience, or experience with criminal law," Valerie told her.

Meg snorted. "And those kids right out of law school do? Come on, Valerie, he's a great choice. If anything, he's overqualified."

"That's just it. Why does he want a job that must pay less than a quarter of what he's been earning?"

"Because he wants to come back to Amsden, and this little town doesn't exactly have a lot of opportunities for corporate lawyers."

Valerie took another bite and chewed thoroughly. "That's my point," she said after a few moments. "Why does he want to come back here?"

There was a brief silence. "Why do we care?" Meg sounded puzzled. "He'll stay here for a year or two and learn how to do trial law, and then maybe move on to something else in Amsden. Or he could move closer to Columbus." She eyed Valerie thoughtfully. "This isn't like you, Valerie. You're always giving people the benefit of the doubt. Do you know something about him I don't? Is there some reason you don't like him?"

"Of course not."

"Then what's the problem? We need another assistant, and I want Jay Westcott working with me. This guy knows law, and he's a lot more mature than the other candidates. His writing sample was great. It's not really any of our business why he's come back to Amsden, is it?"

Meg was right, of course. From the moment she'd seen his cover letter, Valerie had been giving herself a talk. His letter had been a straightforward bid for a job, but it was also personal and warm. The personal and warm part was irritating as all get out, considering they hadn't talked in years. But she'd scolded herself for feeling that way. After all, was he supposed to pretend he didn't know her? So, she'd been giving herself a lecture about fairness, and judging a job candidate on his merits. It might be hard for her to work with Jay, but Meg was right—he was the best person who'd applied, by any objective standard.

"I want to discuss it with Judge Haskins," she told Meg. "Officially, this is my decision, but I wouldn't think of hiring Jay unless the judge says it's okay."

Meg nodded. "Of course. Jay will be in his courtroom every day. This is a small town, and I know we need to work together." She cocked her eyebrow at Valerie. "And you talk everything over with Judge Haskins, anyway."

"Well, not everything."

"It's okay, Valerie," Meg assured her with a smile. "It's a big help to have a mentor, and I know Judge Haskins is important to you."

"Important enough that I wouldn't be a prosecutor without him. Not yet, anyway. Thanks to Judge Haskins and his political skills, I'm the youngest prosecutor this county's ever had," Valerie said quietly. She hesitated for a second before going on. "But it's more than that, Meg. The judge is like a father to me. I care about him a lot."

She realized Meg knew that. Everyone who practiced law in Amsden, Ohio, did. But Valerie wasn't convinced Meg really knew how much she cared about Judge Haskins. "It's like this, Meg," she went on, trying to explain something she wasn't sure she fully understood herself. "The judge has dreams for me. They're dreams I've hardly dared to dream for myself."

Meg reached over the table and squeezed Valerie's hand briefly. "But you're the one making those dreams come true, Valerie. You're the one working so hard, you're the one who won the election. You're the prosecutor, and in a few years you'll be in Columbus, doing something big.''

Meg was a loyal friend, Valerie thought, and what she said was true. She was working hard, making a name for herself, and she was proud of what she'd accomplished.

Meg lifted her coffee cup to her lips. "If the judge says it's all right, you're going to hire Jay Westcott, aren't you?''

Valerie nodded, sighing a little. "Yes, I guess so.''

Meg smiled. "Good. I didn't want to contaminate our discussion while you were making your decision, but now that it's over, can we really talk about him?''

"We've been talking about him for an hour already.'' She tried to hide her impatience, heartily wishing they could go on to something else. "And what do you mean, 'contaminating our discussion'?''

Meg flipped her red hair over her shoulder. "I mean, by saying something about what a gorgeous guy he is. When you said you used to know him, you didn't mention anything about that. But you must have noticed. Those blue eyes with that black hair...'' She rolled her eyes soulfully. "And I just love that twisted grin of his, don't you?''

"Meg, this is business,'' she warned her friend quickly. "Anyway, he's married, if that's what you're getting at.''

"Oh, I didn't know.'' She sounded disappointed. "He wasn't wearing a wedding ring.''

"But he's married. I've met his wife.''

"Oh,'' Meg said again. "What's she like?''

Cool. Beautiful. Elegant, Valerie thought. Just the

kind of woman Jay *would* end up with. "I only met her once, and I hardly talked to her."

"Well, the best men are always married," Meg observed glumly.

"I take it from all this talk it's not going well with Dave, then." Meg's relationship with Dave Grau had always been stormy.

"No, not at all, especially lately. You know how moody he's always been, but now it's worse than ever. Sometimes he's so up, you'd think he was the greatest guy in the world. But then he gets so depressed.... It's getting to be more than I can deal with." For a moment, Meg's eyes filled with tears, but she blinked them hurriedly away. "I don't think it's generally easy to love a cop, do you?"

It was a question Valerie felt qualified to answer. After all, she'd been engaged to one, herself. "I'm living proof of that," she reminded her colleague, trying to smile about it.

"I'm sorry," Meg said quickly. "I always forget that, forget you had a whole life here before I moved to Amsden. Anyway, your cop is the chief of police, and mine is on the front lines. There's got to be a difference."

"Well, Ellis Campbell and I are still friends, and being a police officer didn't have anything to do with our breaking up. Ellis and I finally realized we were just buddies. It was no foundation for a marriage."

"Ellis is a pretty laid-back guy."

"But ambitious."

"Yes, well, so are you," Meg reminded her with a twinkle in her eye. It was hard to keep Meg down for long.

"Maybe it will work out with Dave yet, Meg," Valerie said encouragingly. "Let's get our check, and

I can talk to Judge Haskins about hiring Jay before the one o'clock arraignments start.''

They paid for lunch, and started up the street, talking over the day's arraignments. There were only two felonies. It was two more than the town had had five years ago. Valerie hadn't been exaggerating when she'd told Jay that times were changing. Still, this town of ten thousand in north central Ohio certainly didn't have the problems big cities had nowadays.

It was a lovely town in a beautiful setting. Wedge-shaped, it fanned out in a broad valley, sheltered by gentle, wooded hills. On the side roads there were still many of the old dairy farms, with lush pastures carved out from the trees, and dotted with the big black-and-white holstein dairy cows that gave so much milk.

Amsden had always been prosperous—originally as a source of supplies for the surrounding farms. Now it was a resort town, a summer community. Amsden Lake was only fifteen miles away, and it brought in a lot of tourists. The stores had changed since Valerie's childhood. Now, instead of the hardware and feed stores, there were antique shops, specialty clothing stores and a little art gallery.

In another season, the town was clogged with summer people. But now, in the early winter, it was just the townsfolk. Valerie had been born here—had lived here all her life—and she knew practically everyone in town. What was it Jay had said? He'd come back for open spaces and friendly people. Maybe he really had come back for those things. They were worth having, after all, even if Jay hadn't understood that twelve years ago. It was out of character for him to want to come back, though, she thought as they crossed the square. A person couldn't really change that much, not even in twelve years, could they?

They were coming up to the elegant Victorian courthouse. Valerie pushed open the hundred-year-old door, above which was a huge, stained-glass window, its jewel tones glowing against the old brick. The window depicted a blindfolded woman with flowing hair, holding the scales of justice. *Justice is blind.* The words symbolized everything Valerie Brettinger believed about the law. The law was about fairness, and doing the right thing. As prosecutor, she had control over what happened to the criminal cases that came up in Amsden County. Her job was a satisfying one, and she believed in doing it right.

"See you." Meg waved, hurrying down the hall to her office. She was doing the arraignments, and needed her files.

Valerie stopped in front of the imposing door of the town's one courtroom. She opened it a crack. There was no court in session, so she went in.

"Hi, Roberta," she greeted the judge's bailiff. "Is Judge Haskins in?"

"He's in his chambers," Roberta told her with a tight smile. "I'll buzz him and tell him you're on your way in, okay?"

"Thanks," Valerie said, glancing at the young woman. Roberta seemed nervous today. She'd seemed nervous a lot lately, very different from the outgoing, eager person she'd been when she'd been hired six months ago. Sometime soon she'd have to find the time to ask Roberta if anything was wrong.

When she closed the door to his inner office, Judge Haskins took one of her hands in both his large, warm ones. "How are you, Valerie, dear?" he asked, twinkling at her.

"Fine, Judge," she said warmly. "And you?"

"Very relaxed, thank you. It was a long morning

for us both. The traffic docket was endless, and I was a bit irritable. I'm sure you noticed.''

Valerie had noticed, but he did seem more at ease now. The traffic docket was mindlessly routine, nothing but paperwork, volume and lame excuses from people. She didn't wonder that it aggravated him.

He poured her a cup of coffee. ''How's politics?''

''Great. The guy you put me in touch with says that in three years the party might have a place for me on the ballot for the state Senate or House. And they'll bankroll me some if I get the nod.''

''Money's certainly what it's all about.''

''And influence,'' Valerie reminded him. ''Which I have, thanks to you.''

The judge smiled, obviously pleased by the compliment, and reached into his pocket for a mint. ''Want one?'' He held out the tube to her.

She shook her head, watching him as he slowly broke the seal, peeled the paper back and popped one in his mouth. Judge Haskins was in his early sixties, with curling, pure white hair, and he was handsome, except for a reddened, puffy face. He was often irritable, and she wondered, not for the first time, if he was in as good health as he claimed. Often, his hands trembled, and occasionally there was something in his manner that made her think he was in pain.

They'd been friends ever since the judge had decided to be her mentor five years ago, right after she'd gotten out of law school. She had clerked for him during the summers, and he'd seen something in her, something he said was special. Valerie hated to think he might be sick, but she knew better than to ask. He had a crusty pride. If he wanted her to know anything, he'd tell her.

''I've come about the assistant prosecutor's position," she told the judge. "I know it's my decision, but I wanted your advice. Meg interviewed him with me, and we think we've found the right person for the job, a man named Jay Westcott. He's from around here originally. His family had a dairy west of town."

"Westcott," the judge said thoughtfully. "Sam Westcott's son?"

Valerie nodded.

"I knew Sam Westcott, years ago. He wasn't a happy man, was he?"

She wondered exactly how well the judge had known Sam Westcott. "Sam was all right some of the time. He died four years ago."

"Yes, I know. It's my business to know, Valerie. After all, I'm a politician, too."

She was quiet for a moment. If the judge knew Sam Westcott and knew he'd died, he must also know he'd had a drinking problem.

"Sam was an alcoholic, Judge, very irrational sometimes, with a nasty temper when he drank." She took a sip of coffee, wincing at both the heat from the cup and the memories. To say Sam Westcott had had a temper was a gross understatement. "His drinking practically ruined the dairy. But I see no sign that Jay has an alcohol problem, and it wouldn't be fair not to hire him because of his father, would it?"

"Of course not," he agreed readily. "We're all sinners, Valerie, each in our own way. You know that, don't you?"

Although it was the sort of cynical thing he said at times, Valerie never liked to hear him talk that way. She was bright enough to know the judge was probably right, but she preferred to look at human nature a little more positively.

"Do you want to meet him before I hire him?" she asked carefully.

"No, my dear, this is your call. If you like him, hire him."

"I'll telephone him today."

VALERIE LAY in bed a few nights later, thinking about Jay. He'd be coming to work in ten days, and he'd be an excellent assistant prosecutor, she knew. He was too good for it, really. She couldn't imagine the work satisfying him for long. That he wanted the job at all still puzzled her, but she might never know why he did. Meg was right, of course; it wasn't any of Valerie's business.

Eventually, she supposed, she'd stop lying awake thinking about him and start seeing him as just a colleague. It was a comforting thought, and she started to relax.

But it was in that half asleep, half awake state that she had the most difficulty controlling her thoughts, especially the emotional ones. And the subject of Jay had once been very emotional. Before she could stop herself, she was right back again to that terrible day, more than four years ago—the only time she'd seen Jay in the last twelve years.

The memory always started with the sickening-sweet smell of flowers. Sam Westcott hadn't been respected, but the town had wanted to show support for his widow, and there had been quite a turnout for the funeral.

She remembered his family standing around Sam Westcott's casket, which was closed. Sam hadn't looked very good just before he died, and the family had made the right choice about the casket.

With her mom and dad in tow, Valerie had done

her duty. Approaching the family, she went first to Jay's mother. Valerie mouthed soothing words to the dry-eyed woman. But she hadn't been able to take her eyes off Jay. He looked quite different from the young man she remembered. He seemed dark. The perfectly cut suit was dark, his hair was dark, his expression somber. But even after seven years, those blue eyes had jolted her.

Once they'd been so close, and she still missed him. In the back of her mind, even as her own life had moved forward, she'd always believed he would return to Amsden. And now he had finally come home, even if it had taken his father's funeral to bring him here. Maybe he'd been as lonely as she'd been. After the funeral, they could talk. She'd lost the thread of her thought as he'd put out his hand and taken hers. "Valerie," he said.

Then a woman had walked confidently up to Jay, and taken her place beside him. She turned toward Valerie, one hand gracefully outstretched. She had silvery blond, impossibly smooth hair, and she was model slim.

"Valerie," Jay said again. "I'd like you to meet my wife, Allison...."

Even now she was embarrassed, thinking about her eagerness to see him that day. Damn, she thought, but that particular memory fragment could still disturb her. She rolled her pillow, putting its cool bottom side against her cheek.

It had taken a long time to get over loving Jay. The funeral had finally put to rest her naive hope that someday he'd come back. That day was a turning point, the day she'd really grown up. She'd realized she needed to get on with the rest of her life, and she had. And finally, when her love for him faded, really faded this time, she'd felt so much better.

She was happy with her life. In these last two years as a county prosecutor, she'd built her reputation, and her percentage of convictions was high. Twelve-hour days had helped make that happen. She'd gotten a lot of publicity when she'd served on the governor's task force for the prevention of child abuse and she was on half a dozen local boards. With Judge Haskins's help, she was building a political career. For a woman of thirty, she was doing very well, and nothing was going to shake her composure or her plans.

JAY OPENED the cardboard box. Inside were mostly mementos of his nine years in Chicago. There were three plaques commemorating his *pro bono* work, his trophy from the Chicago Junior Bar Association softball tournament and his diplomas. He lifted out the paperweights and little brass doodads that secretaries and clients had bought him for Christmases past, the kinds of gifts people gave when they thought they had to give you something but didn't know what to buy.

He pulled out a set of framed prints, all representing the water. Gray water, green water, deep lakes and angry seas. Finally, he reached into the bottom of the box for the small oil depicting some hills. It had reminded him strongly of Amsden County, even though he'd purchased the picture in Chicago. He should have known when he'd bought it that he missed home. But it had taken a long time for him to see that, and he'd made a real mess of his life first.

He hadn't seen or heard her arrive but there she was, in the doorway. He could feel her presence before he looked up. It had always been like that, even when she'd been a girl.

"Hi, Valerie," he said softly, not looking up.

"Hi, yourself. Are you settling in all right?"

He glanced up then. "Of course. Brenda saw to it that my desk was stocked, and I assume that stack of files on the table is tomorrow's traffic docket. I'm just unpacking some personal things." He held up the small painting. "What do you think?"

She came into the room. "It's lovely. It looks like that big hill that overlooks the far side of Amsden Lake, except that there aren't any houses in the painting."

He shook his head slightly. "It reminds me more of my back forty—that place out behind the woods where you can't see the farmhouse or the dairy barn. You come out from the trees, and you climb the long hill. When you get to the top, it opens into the valley, and you can see for miles. It's my favorite place on the whole farm." He paused, his light blue eyes seeing something far away. "You remember it, don't you?"

She nodded.

"We always used to walk up there together after the milking was done."

"I remember, Jay," she said in a flat voice. Her cheeks warmed, and there was an awkward pause. Of course she remembered it; they had climbed that hill together too many times to count. They had also made love there—the one and only time they had. He had been her first lover. No matter how long ago that had been, how could he imagine she would forget?

He also seemed a little embarrassed, as if he'd stumbled into the conversation never really intending to conjure up the old memories. In that moment, Valerie knew he too was remembering, and that was a surprise; she would have guessed those thoughts were something he'd put out of his mind as soon as he'd gotten out of Amsden.

"I'm sorry, Valerie," he told her quietly. "I didn't mean to embarrass you, at least not in the first five minutes after I got here." A faint smile crossed his features, then was gone almost instantly. "It's been a long time since we've seen each other, but I guess old habits die hard. I'm just used to saying whatever I want around you."

There was a polish, a courtesy to him now that most definitely had not been there years before, and Valerie was grateful for it. Quickly changing the subject, she asked, "Are you staying in the farmhouse?"

"For now."

"Does that mean you're going to move into town, then?"

"No, not really." He smiled again, but didn't elaborate.

"I just thought the farmhouse wouldn't hold very many happy memories," she started, then thought better of it. This first conversation was every bit as hard as she'd thought it would be.

Trying to think of something to do to relieve the awkwardness, she walked over to his desk. Picking up the plaques, she read them carefully, then lightly touched the paperweights and the little brass ornaments, one by one. "I thought you'd have a picture of your wife on your desk."

"I don't have a wife," Jay replied softly. "Allison and I were divorced six months ago."

Valerie sucked in her breath, then with a conscious effort let it out slowly.

"Can I tell you about it some time?" he said.

She nodded.

"Over lunch? Can you go today?"

She nodded again, then said hesitantly, "Well, I've got to get back to work. If you want coffee, Brenda keeps a perpetual pot going. We're all coffee freaks here."

She slipped out of his office and went back to her desk. At first, she couldn't concentrate. Of all the things she'd expected Jay to tell her on his first day on the job, she'd never expected that. Somehow, she'd gotten so used to the idea of Jay Westcott's being married that she couldn't seem to shift gears readily enough to think otherwise. She made herself pick up her brief. It didn't matter whether Jay was married or not, she reminded herself. She had hired him, he was here, and she had better get used to the idea, if she didn't want to make a fool of herself.

She turned on the computer. A computer search of the case law was always intense enough to consume her whole brain. Valerie logged on and was almost immediately absorbed in the task.

"Are you ready for lunch?" Jay's voice pierced her concentration.

"What?" she asked, startled. She hadn't realized it was noon already. "Oh, yes, let me just check this case and then log off." In a minute or two, she was done.

"What were you working on?"

"Looking for the latest word on the exclusionary rule. I've got a brief due in the court of appeals."

"You didn't bother her while she was hooked onto Westlaw, did you?" It was Meg's voice, and she was laughing. "Valerie's a computer whiz, in addition to all her other talents."

"I didn't know that," Jay said. "I'm old-fashioned, I guess. I usually compose my briefs on the word processor, but when I do research I prefer the library. All those dusty old books make me feel like a real lawyer.'' He chuckled. ''It's a big part of my self-image.''

Valerie had her coat on her arm, and he took it from her and held it for her.

''Where are we going for lunch?'' Meg asked.

Jay looked at Valerie quickly. She knew he had something private to discuss, but she wasn't going to leave Meg out if she wanted to go along. ''How about the Blue Roof?''

When they got to the street, Valerie told Jay, ''There's only the Blue Roof and Kaiser's, but there are some fast-food restaurants on the west side of town. Both the Roof and Kaiser's are pretty plain, and I'm sure you're used to—''

''The Roof is fine, Valerie,'' Jay said quickly, smiling at both her and Meg. If he minded having Meg along, he wasn't showing it. ''Do we need to drive, or can we walk?''

''It's only a couple of blocks,'' Meg told him. ''It's pretty cold today, but usually we walk.''

Lunch was merry. Instead of serious talk, they told stories of the funny things that had happened in court.

''Tell Jay about the necklace,'' Meg urged Valerie, a twinkle in her eye. It was her favorite story.

It was fun to have a new listener. This was getting to be an old war story by now. ''Well,'' Valerie began, ''you'd like this better if you'd already met Bob Vanette. He's a great guy, but…well, you'll see what I mean. When Bob was first hired at the public defender's office, he was right out of law school, and exceptionally polite. He was assigned a client who was accused of stealing a ruby pendant, and the guy insisted he didn't steal it. Of course, one of the first things a lawyer learns is that you never take what someone says at face value, without checking it out.

"Anyway, Bob believed the guy, and he insisted on taking the case to trial, even though I offered him a decent plea bargain. I had my first witness on—the owner of the necklace—and Bob was cross-examining the witness in this ponderous way he has, getting him to describe the necklace in great detail...you know, how big it was, and how it was oval with diamonds all around the main stone.

"All of a sudden, a woman in the spectator's gallery jumps up and starts berating the defendant. The bailiff's trying to hush her up, and then she yanks something from around her neck, yelling about what a cheapskate the guy is. She tosses something, and it lands right at Bob's feet. There's this pregnant pause...."

She couldn't go on. No matter how many times she told the story, she had to stop here. She and Meg were convulsed with laughter, and Jay couldn't help joining in.

"Tell me the rest," Jay urged Valerie.

She was gasping for air, her pale face flushed. "So, Bob stares down at his feet and suddenly this hush falls over the whole courtroom. You know how it is, like when you're with a crowd of people and you say something really awful, put your foot in your mouth and your words just hang in the air. That's how it was at that moment. In slow motion, Bob bends down and picks this thing up off the floor. You know what it was, of course."

"A ruby pendant."

She nodded, her eyes dancing. "I'd love to see Bob's expression one more time."

"What did you do?"

"What could I do?" Valerie countered. "He was holding it, just staring at it, with the stone dangling from its chain. Still nobody said anything. So into that silence, I stood up and said, 'the prosecution rests.' It brought down the house."

They laughed together. "It's good to hear you laugh again, Valerie," Jay said softly.

Valerie could feel herself blushing. They'd been having such a good time. Why did Jay have to say something like that, and right in front of Meg?

"It was the perfect thing to say, simple and effective," he finally added.

"It wasn't calculated theatrics, or anything. It was one of those moments that happened exactly right."

"Well, I don't know about that. A good lawyer engineers moments that just seem to happen. And if he doesn't, he takes advantage of the ones that do." Jay paused. "Tell me, does Bob Vanette speak to you these days?"

"Oh, Valerie bought him lunch that day, and they worked it out," Meg told him. "Bob's not the kind of guy who holds a grudge. He's sweet, and anyway, you know how lawyers are. You don't usually make it through law school without figuring out you can't take it personally. And Valerie has a knack for making friends with everybody."

"You can meet Bob this afternoon, if you want to," Valerie told Jay on the way back to the office. "I was going to bring you down to meet Judge Haskins today, anyway. There are a couple of pretrial conferences you can sit in on, if you want."

"Sounds great. Tell me about the judge."

"Don't let Valerie go on, Jay," Meg warned him. "When she gets on the subject of the judge, she has a hard time stopping."

"Come on, Meg," Valerie said seriously. She looked at Jay. "He's special to me. He told me I had talent right off, when I was having trouble in law school and wanted to quit. Then he convinced me to start doing political work, even before I graduated, and he watches over my career for me. If he hadn't supported me, I wouldn't be the county prosecutor."

It was a little too much for Jay. "Valerie, you were always talented, and I've heard how hard you've worked. If the judge helped you out, great. But I know you, and I'm sure you deserve your success."

"Oh, no, she doesn't work hard. Only day and night," Meg confirmed. "Valerie does deserve it, Jay. Do you have any idea what her conviction rate is? Or how many committees she's on?"

Valerie shrugged, careful not to look at Jay. It felt funny having Meg make such a big deal of it to him. "A lot of people work hard, and deserve a break. But that doesn't guarantee anything, especially in politics. I'm just saying the judge has done a lot for me, and I'm grateful."

"I'm looking forward to meeting him," Jay said politely.

CHAPTER TWO

"SO YOU'RE Jay Westcott," Judge Haskins said affably, putting out his hand. "I knew your dad."

Jay shook hands. "My dad's gone now. How did you happen to know him?"

"He was around," the judge said vaguely. He held out a paper tube. "Want a mint?"

"No thanks, Judge." He smiled. "Valerie's told me a lot about you, and I'm looking forward to working in your courtroom."

The judge shot Valerie a look of undisguised affection, and the three of them continued to talk together pleasantly. A few minutes into their conversation, the judge's bailiff came in with a stack of papers and placed them on the farthest edge of the desk.

"Hang on, Roberta," the judge directed her, just as she was walking out the door. "I want you to meet someone. Roberta Preddy, Jay Westcott. Jay's our new assistant prosecutor."

Jay stood quickly and held out his hand. Hesitantly, the young woman came into the room and took it. She was a petite, freckled blonde, and her hand felt small and cold in his. She seemed inexplicably nervous, and she didn't say a word.

"I'm glad to meet you," he told her, wondering about her edginess.

Roberta slipped out the door before he had a chance to say anything else.

"What's with Roberta these days?" Valerie asked the judge when the door shut behind the young woman.

"How should I know?" Judge Haskins shrugged. "Well, she is a little flighty, but at least she used to get the job done. Now her work's getting sloppy."

"I'll talk to her for you and see what the problem is."

The faintest tinge of deeper red appeared on his already florid cheekbones. "That won't be necessary, Valerie. I take care of things like that. I'll handle it."

The tone the judge used was quiet, but there was decisiveness in it. For some reason, it made Jay slightly uneasy. When she had described him earlier, Valerie had made Judge Haskins out to be a pussycat, a mother hen watching over her career. This guy was no pussycat. And of course, a county judge was a big shot anywhere, but especially in a little town. This wasn't Chicago with dozens of courts and judges scrapping for reelection. This was Amsden, and here, Judge Haskins probably was used to having things exactly the way he wanted them.

Jay watched him carefully. Whether or not he was happy in his new job might very well depend on how well he and the judge got along.

Valerie helped herself to one of the judge's mints, settling back more comfortably in her chair.

Judge Haskins picked up his oversize coffee mug. "Don't worry about Roberta, Valerie. She'll come around."

SEVERAL TIMES during that day, as he settled in, put his office in order and reviewed his new files, Jay thought about Judge Haskins and how different things were going to be, practicing law in Amsden. Actually, he had a lot of thinking to do these days, it seemed, and most of it was not at all pleasant or easy.

He pulled his coat from the old brass coat tree and put it on wearily. The thought of going home to that dark, empty farmhouse was almost intolerable, but he couldn't put it off forever. Then he saw that Valerie's office light was still on.

Even though her door was open, Jay knocked politely on the doorframe. She looked up to find him lounging in the doorway, filling the space. "When's quitting time around here, anyway?" he drawled.

Valerie glanced at her watch. Six o'clock already. "It was an hour ago," she said ruefully. "I'm sorry, Jay. I didn't realize we hadn't gone over the office hours.... What?" she asked quickly, seeing the broad grin on his face.

"I was teasing you. I don't think you'll need to tell me when to come and go, Valerie." The smile never left his face. "When I was at Rossen, Sebastian and Bowles, the workweek for associates was eighty hours. Saturday was just another workday, and I got Sunday afternoons off for good behavior."

"Sorry. This is awkward for me, Jay. I never expected you to be working here."

"Believe me, neither did I," Jay agreed readily. "Does it bother you that you're my boss?"

It bothered her. "Well, no, not if it doesn't bother you."

"Should it?"

"Of course not." It shouldn't, she knew. But Jay was a man, one she remembered as having a healthy ego. Aside from the fact of their long-ago friendship, or whatever it had been, how would it feel to the average man to work for a woman four years younger than himself, a woman with less legal experience?

He laughed easily. "I know what you're thinking. How will I handle it? How could an egotistical corporate lawyer from a big-city law firm come back and work for a hometown woman? A woman he used to endlessly big-brother when they were kids. Is that it?"

It was close enough. So that's what Jay had thought of their relationship. Big brother, little sister. That he would remember it that way hurt, even after all these years. She faced him squarely. "Yes, that's what I've been thinking."

He lifted his hand to stroke it through his unruly dark hair, attempting unsuccessfully to smooth it. "Look. From everything I hear, you're good at what you do. In my mind, that qualifies you to run this office. I don't think of myself as egotistical, but believe me, I'm self-assured enough to work for you. The question is, are you self-assured enough to let me?"

She looked away, hoping that the silly thumping in her stomach she had been feeling on and off since the day of his interview would go away soon. "This is a small office, Jay. Meg pretty much does what she wants with her cases. I'd rather think of the three of us as working together."

He cracked a smile and strode into the room. "Me, too. That's exactly what I was hoping you'd say."

Suddenly, she smiled a little, too. She couldn't help it.

Jay caught it. "I'm hungry. Would you like to go to dinner? We've got some catching up to do."

Her smile faded. Damn, she thought, he could get to her so easily. He might not think of himself as egotistical, but what would one call a man who came home after twelve years and expected her to be ready to pick up right where they'd left off? He obviously assumed she had no plans, assumed she'd be happy to drop everything and spend her evening rehashing the old days.

"I don't think so, Jay. I've had a hard day, and I'm going to go home and put my feet up."

"Just a quick one?" he asked hopefully. He started to say something, stopped and started again. He chuckled, his eyes dancing. "Think of it as a mercy dinner."

"A mercy dinner?"

"Yes. I'm basically used to it by now, but tonight I don't feel like eating alone."

She couldn't say no. She'd already made it clear she had no other plans, and to refuse him now would be very rude. She'd been outmanipulated. "All right," she agreed reluctantly.

On the street, she said, "We ate lunch at the Blue Roof. That leaves us with Kaiser's, unless you want to drive somewhere."

"If we drive, what are our options?"

"Is pizza still your favorite food?"

"You remember," he said, and in the light of the street lamps, she could see the corners of his mouth turn up.

Keep it light, she thought. They didn't have to share memories of the past, after all. "Well, there's a little Italian restaurant west of Amsden Lake, pretty near your farm, actually. It's about twenty-five miles from here."

"Sounds good," Jay told her, beginning to walk. "We'll take my car."

It wasn't until she was settled into his Porsche that

Valerie realized she was only supposed to be out for a quick dinner. A fifty-mile round-trip didn't exactly qualify.

So he drove a Porsche, she thought, with renewed irritation. She, herself, drove a nice sedate Chevy. Of course, it was important for a future politician to drive an American car, preferably something not too sporty. But she sighed, knowing she'd drive a Chevy, anyway. Nice safe Valerie, everybody's friend.

"I like your car," she said politely.

"It's not very practical, though, is it? Not much room, but it served its purpose. Symbols of success were very important at Rossen, Sebastian and Bowles. The clients were supposed to be impressed that a lot of other clients were paying two hundred dollars an hour for legal services, too. The partners drove big luxury cars, but the senior associates all drove sports cars, as soon as they could possibly afford to." He stopped for a second. "I sounded like a snob just now, didn't I? I don't need to justify my driving a Porsche. After all, you know why I bought it."

She had no idea why he'd bought it. "Why did you, if you don't like it?"

He chuckled. "I do like it, Valerie, that's the point. After all, it's the kind of thing I left home for. The problem is, I thought having it would be something in itself. Now I know it's just a neat, fun little car, and really nothing more than a means to get around."

They were moving out of town, heading west toward the lake. In winter, darkness fell very early, and Valerie could see little of the surrounding countryside. Sprinkled thinly along the road were immaculate white farmhouses, lights from the windows glimmering on the frosty grass. At the dairy farms, the chore lights were on in the barns.

"It must be evening milking time," Valerie noted.

"Probably. Remember, at home we milked at five-thirty. Five-thirty in the evening, and five-thirty in the morning, seven days a week, every week, every month, every year. Regular as clockwork."

She leaned back in her seat. "And you hated every minute of it," she finished softly.

"No, I didn't," he said unexpectedly. "I thought I did, but I didn't. Some of the cows were so gentle, and they liked to be taken care of, brushed and milked. I used to think about all sorts of things, out there in that quiet barn, while I put the milking machine on their udders, in precisely the same order. You helped me with the milking sometimes, so you must remember."

Valerie didn't say anything. She understood perfectly how much he'd needed some stability in his life.

His father's bouts with alcohol had always been unpredictable. Sober, Sam Westcott was a quiet, intense, intellectual man. But when he'd been drinking, he changed completely. Sometimes he didn't come home for days, and his drinking had gotten worse over the years. By the time Jay was fourteen, he'd been in charge of the rundown dairy. Even after he went to Ohio State, he was home on weekends, milking cows and scraping manure from the barn floor. He hadn't really gotten away from it until he'd gone to Yale.

And now it was all gone. His father was gone, and the cows had been sold. Jay's mother had died a year ago. It was funny, she thought. Jay had gone to Chicago and left it all behind. And now, when everything but the farm was gone, Jay had come home. She leaned her head against the glass and looked out the window, feeling a familiar sad ache seep into her body. She stayed that way for several minutes.

"Hey, Valerie, are you asleep?" Jay asked softly, in a voice that didn't sound depressed. She looked at him quickly. Despite the half smile, visible in profile, his heavy jaw looked tense.

"No, just thinking."

"Don't. Don't think," he commanded in a low voice. "It's over, Valerie, and I want this to be a happy night. I want every night to be happy." Quickly, he put on the dim overhead light and reached under his seat. "Here," he said, handing her a small leather case. "Why don't you pick out a disc? I'd like some music."

Valerie took her time going through the discs. There was a very eclectic mix, but a preponderance of folk music. She chose some old Simon and Garfunkel music and handed it to him. He put it in the compact disc player and in a minute the small space filled with the sounds of a folk guitar and soft harmonies. Jay sang along as he drove, not at all self-conscious. He had a nice voice, husky but mellow. Valerie realized with a start that she had never heard him sing before. She closed her eyes and let the music float over her.

"You'll need to give me directions from here on," Jay finally told her, breaking into her drifting consciousness.

She directed him to an old farmhouse, a huge, red brick Victorian. "This is Angelo's. It caters mostly to the summer people, but the food's good enough to keep it open year-round."

Inside, the space had been remodeled into one large room, with stucco and wood and lots of stained glass. When they were seated, Jay asked, "Wine or beer?"

"Wine, please," she said, resigning herself to the fact that this was not going to be a quick dinner. Jay obviously wanted company.

He ordered a bottle of Chianti. "Dry, heavy and red, just the thing to go with pizza. That is what we're having, isn't it?"

She couldn't help smiling. "Of course. We came twenty-five miles for it, didn't we?"

"What do you want on it? Extra cheese and pepperoni and mushrooms, and—"

"And everything else," she finished. "But no anchovies, of course."

"We'd like a large pizza with everything on it, but put the anchovies on half only, please," he told the waitress.

Valerie cocked her eyebrow. "Anchovies? For you?"

"Leftover city tastes."

They talked for a long time, sipping slowly to make the Chianti last. The conversation was impersonal but pleasant. They discussed some books they'd read, and Jay told her about a foreign film he'd seen in Chicago that was getting rave reviews. Then they talked about Amsden politics, Valerie's work on the county library board and on the governor's task force.

"I've been thinking about taking some classes, or something, maybe joining a sports club," Jay told her when she finished. "Do you have any suggestions?"

"You really intend to get back into the thick of things, don't you?" she observed with some surprise.

"Of course. I live here now, Valerie." He looked her over. "Did you think I was only passing through?"

The question seemed to confuse her, Jay thought. Once she had understood him perfectly, sometimes knowing what he was going to say even before he said it. Now she'd have to get to know the new Jay, he thought. Just as he'd have to learn about her. It was a pleasant thought.

He sipped his wine, watching her. Valerie was cutting her slice of pizza carefully with the side of her fork. He was enjoying her company, just as he always had. She was bright and articulate, and she had a knack for making friends. In school, she'd been very popular, and he supposed it was natural that the combination of intelligence and social skills had led her to politics.

But for all her ambitions, she had a genuine empathetic quality. In earlier years, he'd felt it often, and it had been apparent again in the car tonight. Valerie was lovely, with shiny hair a shade or two darker than honey, those wide eyes and a mouth that was soft and full. She wasn't a beautiful woman, but she was... lovely. He watched her closely, taking pleasure in getting to know her all over again. In a way, it was as exciting as meeting someone new. But it was more like recognizing an old, favorite song than listening to a brand-new one.

She looked up and caught him watching her. "What?" she asked.

"Nothing," he assured her quickly. She gave him a quizzical stare.

"It's just that you're the only person I've ever known who eats pizza with a fork, even when you get near the crust," he made up hastily.

A blush stained her cheeks. So that hasn't changed, he thought. For some reason, it pleased him that she still colored so easily.

"You drag me out here on a night I wanted to relax with a good book, and now you're commenting on

my table manners?'' she scolded him in mock sever-
ity.

"Sorry,'' he said, grinning at her. "The next time
we come out here for pizza, I promise I won't say a
word.''

Suddenly, she felt a flash of irritation for the third
time tonight. He's taking too much for granted, Valerie thought. His first day on the job, and he'd already
figured there would be a next time.

"You've got to drive me all the way back to town
and then turn around and head for your farm, and
tomorrow's a workday,'' she said suddenly. "We
need to get going.''

She said little all the way home. Instead, she sat
next to him, and struggled with her anger that she
knew was totally out of proportion to anything he'd
said. So he'd made a light remark and some mistaken
assumptions that things were going to be the way
they'd been before.

But these weren't the old days. She leaned back
and sighed as soon as she realized what was really
irritating her. Despite her resolve to keep their relationship purely professional, she'd gone to dinner
with him on his very first day at the office. And the
worst part was she'd had a good time.

"MR. WESTCOTT, could you find the Stein case, and
be snappy about it? It might not be next on *your* list,
but it's certainly next on *mine*.'' Judge Haskins glared
over the bench at Jay. "I want to do the Stein case
now, and last time I looked, I was still the judge.''

Jay sifted through his stack of files, trying to find
the right case. He ignored the sarcasm. Thursdays
were the worst, since the judge tried to cram in the
arraignments and traffic cases he didn't want to do on

Fridays. He and the judge were nearly finished working through the stack. It hadn't been a pleasant morning. Some of the defense attorneys had been late, infuriating the judge. Jay himself disliked the traffic docket, but unlike Judge Haskins, he didn't have the luxury of showing it.

"Mr. Westcott? Are you ready to proceed?"

He couldn't find the case. "Your Honor, I don't seem to have it—"

"Five-minute recess," the judge ordered abruptly. "And Mr. Westcott, let's see if the state of Ohio can come back prepared for business."

At the other counsel table, the defense attorney, Bob Vanette, shot him a look, rolling his eyes. Jay winked at him, pleased with the camaraderie. He tried not to take the judge's comments personally, but it was hard not to. He'd volunteered to do the morning traffic docket every day and although Meg and Valerie were reluctant, they'd compromised, allowing him to do it for three weeks. It gave them a break, and Jay felt it would be a good way to get his feet wet in a new office.

But it had been a mistake. For some reason, the judge was irritated with him all the time, making scornful comments at every turn. Jay frowned. It couldn't be any problem with his legal skills. This was easy stuff. And it was a small-town docket, so he didn't see the need for all this haste. They might have more to do on some days than others but they never had trouble finishing the day's cases in a morning. He was puzzled.

"Excuse me," said a soft voice, and he looked up to find the judge's bailiff, Roberta, standing next to him. "Maybe I can help."

Her small hands quickly sorted through the files,

and she found the Stein case almost immediately. "Here, Mr. Westcott. It was in with the cases you've already done."

"Thank you," he said, smiling at her. "Roberta, I've known you nearly a month now. When are you going to stop calling me Mr. Westcott and move on to Jay?"

"Right now," she replied, suddenly smiling back at him, and he thought how pretty she was when she smiled. It eased some of the tension from her small, freckled face.

"Jay, you're the only person he treats worse than me. You could use a cup of coffee, couldn't you? Go get one, and I'll stall the judge if he takes the bench before you return."

Directing a look of thanks her way, Jay quickly left the courtroom and went over to the reception area. He poured himself a cup of coffee and drank it immediately, trying to hurry. It had been a sorry three weeks, and he appreciated Roberta's kindness.

It wasn't only the judge, or the boring morning docket. He'd obviously done something to upset Valerie, too. Since the night they'd gone for pizza, she had paid him little attention. He raked his fingers through his hair, belatedly realizing his doing so would make it look messier than ever.

It wasn't that Valerie was unpleasant to him, just distant. She'd go to lunch with him if Meg was around, but he hadn't been able to maneuver her into any after-hours conversation, much less a repeat of dinner. Meg had told him Valerie worked long hours, but for the last three weeks she'd left the office at five o'clock on the dot.

He hurried back into the courtroom and saw that

the judge had not yet taken the bench. He gave Roberta a smiling thumbs-up sign, and took his seat.

Valerie. Unwittingly, he was back to thinking about her. Lovely Valerie, with her understanding smile and her softly lush body. Until they'd made love, he'd never even touched her. But once he'd thought about it so much, he'd had her figure imprinted on his brain. And in twelve years, there hadn't been that much change, although now she wore conservative suits and high heels. But she was the same woman, now all grown-up....

"All rise," Roberta intoned, and the judge strode into the room.

The recess hadn't helped Judge Haskins's temper. If anything, it was worse. He seemed to delight in tormenting Jay, dropping comments laced with withering sarcasm at every opportunity. Courtroom etiquette forced Jay to be respectful, although by the time the docket was finished, he would have taken great pleasure in snarling in return.

This was ridiculous, he decided. He was used to temperamental judges; they had power, and some of them liked using it. But this treatment was worse than anything he'd had to put up with before. He needed to find out what he'd done to antagonize the judge, before it interfered with his work.

The last defendant was filing out of the courtroom, and the judge was preparing to leave for his chambers. "Your Honor, may I approach the bench?"

The judge gave him a curt nod, and Jay strode over to the raised platform, and looked up over the high bench. He forced himself to keep his tone even. "Judge, it's obvious I've upset you. I've only been here a month, and I'm sure I have a lot to learn. I'd appreciate your telling me exactly how you'd like me to conduct my business, when I appear in your court-room."

Judge Haskins glared down at him. "Jay, I don't have the time or the inclination to coddle new law-yers. I have to insist that when you come into my courtroom, you have your cases ready."

Jay considered the comment. He did have his files prepared, and today was the first time he'd been un-able to locate a case. He couldn't be doing that poor a job; the judge's attitude made no sense at all.

"Look, Judge," he said bluntly. "I know how to do my cases. But if you're dissatisfied, perhaps it would be best if Valerie and I sat down with you and discussed—"

The judge held up his hand for silence, and there was a small pause. "You don't need to involve Val-erie. It's just this boring traffic-and-arraignments docket," he said, his voice softening. "You aren't doing anything wrong, Jay. I get a little edgy some-times. Eventually, you'll get used to it. All the other lawyers around here already have."

Somehow, after the last three hours of verbal abuse, the judge's words rang false. "Well, if you're sure it isn't anything I've been doing," Jay began, but stopped midsentence as he watched the judge begin to stack his files. The judge's hand shook violently, and Jay watched it, fascinated. Was the man ill? Was that what accounted for his irritability, his quicksilver changes of mood?

Judge Haskins looked up to find Jay staring at him, and his eyes narrowed. "Is there something wrong, Mr. Westcott?" he asked pointedly.

"Of course not," Jay replied quickly.

"Good. Then don't you have somewhere to go? Court is adjourned." The judge swept from the bench, his black robe flowing behind him, and Jay's eyes followed him all the way out the door.

Sighing, he picked up his files. Maybe Meg and Valerie would be free for lunch. He could use a long, friendly lunch, after a morning like the one he'd just endured. As he made his way out of the courtroom, he passed Roberta. She was staring at him, and there was a funny look in her eyes.

"What is it, Roberta?"

She sucked in a breath. "You're not afraid of him."

"Of course not. When we're on the record, I need to be respectful. But when we're in recess, I don't have to put up with anything, and I won't." He stopped, again caught by something in her eyes. "You're not scared of him, are you?"

Roberta, head down, began to doodle over her legal pad. "Valerie says you're from Amsden, but you've been away for a long time, so maybe there are things you don't understand," she said, her hands busy. "In a small town, a county judge is a powerful man. For one thing, if he put out the word, it might be hard for me to get another job."

"You're efficient. Why would you worry about something like that?"

"I've got two boys, no husband and a house on Amsden Lake I can't afford. I need this job." She lifted her chin, finally looking at him, and Jay tried to read her expression. Something was definitely wrong. "Never mind, Jay." Roberta stopped, as if uncertain whether to say more. "I've got to go," she told him hurriedly, gathering the judge's files from where he'd left them and swinging through the door.

"IT'S NOT the kind of thing I'd expect to hear first from Thelma Moore," Valerie's mother said into the telephone, sounding indignant. "You might have told me you're working with Jay Westcott. I had no idea he'd come back, much less that he was in your office."

"I'm sorry, Mom," Valerie replied. "He's been back only a month, and in that time the subject just didn't come up between you and me, I guess. I should have known the gossip mill would be working overtime."

"You are being nice to him, aren't you?"

"What's that supposed to mean?"

"Only that I didn't like your tone just now, dear. After all, you and Jay used to be close, and I'm sure he could use some friends. After all he's been through—"

"It was years ago," Valerie responded quickly. "Jay doesn't want to talk about the past all the time. Anyway, I am being nice to him, but in a different way than you think. Our relationship now is purely professional."

There was a slight pause, then an unexpected chuckle. "All right. What I called for is to tell you to bring your 'purely professional' new associate to Sunday dinner."

"Sara will be back in town, with all the kids," Valerie reminded her. "And with both me and Jay there, that will be a bigger crowd than you're used to. Maybe it would be better to bring Jay some other time."

"Don't be silly. Sara will be very glad to see him. We all will. Valerie," she said, her voice soft, "Jay's mother was my friend. She did her best for Jay, but things were not good in that house. And now she's gone and I'm not going to have Jay living in Amsden and spending Sundays alone. He doesn't have anyone now, and he needs his friends.''

Valerie felt guilt wash over her. It was a familiar sensation. Her mother had an unerring instinct for anyone who needed her, and she'd always tried to instill that sense of responsibility in Valerie and Sara. Regardless of their personal feelings, they were supposed to be there for anyone who needed them.

Jay had needed her family. Valerie had a sudden, unbidden memory of him as a boy, sitting at her mother's table, bare feet hooked around the legs of his chair, munching cookies. Between bites, he would talk. The subject matter hadn't ever made any difference to Jay, but when he was with her mother, he usually discussed her garden or the weather. Her mother would come to the table periodically and smoothed his wayward hair with a comforting hand, as if he were a little kid. He could never stay for dinner, of course. No matter how good a time he was having, no matter how much her mother wanted him to stay, at five o'clock he needed to start home for the milking.

Valerie crooked the receiver into her shoulder. She knew Jay had come back to Amsden for precisely this: good friends who cared. Surely she could allow herself one dinner at her mother's with him. After all, she couldn't avoid him forever.

"All right," she agreed, sighing. "I'll ask Jay today."

"Ask me what?" Jay inquired as she put the receiver down. She hadn't heard him come in. "Mother wants me to invite you to dinner at her house this Sunday."

He gave her a hard, shuttered look. "Will it bother you if I come?"

"Of course not," she said quickly. "Why would you think such a thing?"

"Maybe because for almost a month you've been avoiding me."

Her gaze wavered. "You're imagining things."

He flopped into the chair across from hers, and in one smooth movement lifted his lean legs onto the low table in front of it. He looked relaxed, but she could feel tension in him. "Valerie, we haven't seen each other for years, but I can still read some of your moods. You've been avoiding me. Want to tell me why?"

His directness disconcerted her. She was so aware of him, of his presence. Even in a suit, she could make out the muscles in his thighs, and her eyes were drawn inexorably upward, past his large, flat chest to his shoulders. It was a body that had known hard work, a farmer's body, but now it fit well into a dark suit. Finally, she got to his face. Her gaze swept over his strong jawline, his well-formed lips and those pale blue eyes, so in contrast with his dark, tousled hair. Eyes that shade of blue should have been icy, but his were warm and inviting. She roused herself. She was staring.

"It's awkward, Jay," she finally told him.

"I don't see why. Tell me why this is so awkward for you, Valerie."

Because I used to love you, and you never loved me in return. Because you left, and you never came back. Because even now, your face and your body stir me. Her thoughts took her by complete surprise. She had fallen out of love with him long ago, hadn't she? And she had certainly thought that she had gotten beyond his power to move her physically. She looked at him nervously. "Well, it's only that I never expected you to come home," she told him truthfully.

"And now I have. Have I done something you don't like?"

"Of course not. It's just taking me some time to get used to the idea of your being back, that's all."

He nodded slowly. "Well," he said quietly, "I think I'll take your mother up on her invitation. When should I pick you up?"

"My house isn't on your way. I thought I'd meet you there." She kept her tone carefully casual.

"Don't be silly. I'll pick you up and drive you. It's the least I can do."

"All right," she told him, hearing in her own words a sigh of resignation. "Why don't you come by for me about one o'clock?"

"Fine. I'm looking forward to it." He leaned his head back and closed his eyes. "It's been a hell of a week."

She nodded in sympathy. "The traffic docket got to you already?"

"And the judge. He's chewed me out about six times for nothing, and that's just today. It's quite an initiation."

She prickled at the criticism of Judge Haskins. "You came back because you thought it would be easy, Jay, but we aren't all a bunch of hicks here, you know." She realized she was chiding him, but she couldn't seem to help it. "We have a lot of problems in town now, and there's plenty of hard work that goes on in that courtroom. It's not all easy and laidback, even in a town like Amsden."

At her words, he sat up straight, and his blue eyes blazed. "You think I came back here because it would be easy, Valerie? That's what you think?"

She stopped for a second, trying to govern her tone. Jay had made her nervous again. "Well, that's what you said in your job interview, wasn't it? That you wanted small-town life again?"

"But I never said I thought it would be easy."

"I know you're not lazy, Jay." She hurried to placate him. "It's just what I thought you said. You told me once you were tired of eighty-hour weeks, remember?"

Unexpectedly, he grinned the new self-mocking grin he'd displayed since he'd returned to Amsden. "Is that what I said? I don't remember that. Well, yes, I didn't like eighty-hour weeks, mostly because I didn't like what I was doing. But that's not why I came back."

"Why did you come back, Jay? The real story." Her voice was very quiet.

He hesitated. Finally, he said, "Part of the reason is what I've already told you. I wanted to see if there were still the same things I remembered in Amsden. Good friends, mostly. There's another reason, too, but I think that's a discussion for another day."

There was silence that neither made any attempt to fill. Then he began to speak.

"But it's been harder than I imagined it would be. People say they're glad to have me back, but in the time I've been away, they've gone on with their lives. I don't know why, but I just assumed time would stand still here. Instead, the hardware store is gone, and in its place is a hat boutique, of all things." He shrugged. "It was naive of me, I guess, to believe that people would stay the same."

"I'm sorry, Jay."

"Don't start with that again," he said sharply, leaning forward. "I came back hoping we could be friends, Valerie, but I don't want your pity. I never did, you know. I never could stand it that you felt sorry for me, not then and not now." Swiftly, he got to his feet, and then he was looming over her, the little lines around his eyes and mouth harsh.

"Jay—"

He lifted his hand. "Wait," he commanded. "I don't want to have to say this again. I need to make sure you understand. I'm a man, Valerie. A man doesn't want pity from a woman he...." His voice trailed off.

She felt the hottest of blushes flood her cheeks. It was one of the few times he'd ever come close to acknowledging he might feel an awareness of her as a female. His eyes were charged with electricity as they held her gaze. She wanted to look away, but she couldn't.

Her mouth went suddenly dry. She'd seen Jay in many moods in the time she'd known him, talkative, sad, frustrated. Since his return, he'd been mostly laid-back and light, laughing and easy. Today, there was a new Jay—passionate and self-assertive—revealing a masculinity that left her breathless.

"Valerie, you were due in court at one-thirty. Did you forget?" Brenda's voice cut through the room.

She scrambled to her feet. "I've got to go, Jay."

His hand was on her arm. "Wait a minute. Did you understand what I told you?"

She shook him off. "You don't want me to feel sorry for you. Fine. I won't." She hesitated, then just said it. "It doesn't leave much between us, though, does it?"

One corner of his mouth turned up. "Except friendship."

"Friendship seems to be my specialty," she said,

trying to make her tone light, and only half succeeding. "Of course, you'll always have that."

She turned on her heel and hurried from the room, and he stood and followed her. "I've got to go," she repeated. "I had a sentencing scheduled at one-thirty."

"I'm coming with you. I don't have anything pressing, so I'll watch. The judge has been driving me up the wall, and maybe I can get some clues from you on how to handle him."

If she couldn't get rid of him, she ought to at least be glad the conversation had shifted to business, Valerie thought. "He's not that bad. In the morning, he can be a little irritable, that's all. I'm not sure he feels well, Jay. I'm used to it, and you'll get used to it, too." Her heels made a clattering sound as they hit the marble steps. "You ought to try to see his good side." Jay didn't answer, but kept pace beside her as she strode hurriedly into the courtroom.

"He's been waiting," Roberta told her as they entered. "Luckily, he came back from lunch in a better mood." She smiled a little. "I'm sure Jay told you he was in rare form this morning."

Bob Vanette was at the other counsel table. "I'm surprised to see you back here, Jay. You must have an iron hide."

Judge Haskins came into the room. "Hi, Valerie." He looked from her to Jay to Bob. "Oh, good, my favorite crew. What's on for this afternoon?"

"I'm doing the Gorham sentencing. The robbery and assault case."

He nodded. "Fine. Roberta, let's get Mr. Gorham in here and get this done."

Jay sat back to watch. Valerie stood, and, taking her time, summarized the elements of the crime, gesturing with her finger to emphasize each point. She was theatrical, exactly as if a jury were present. But there was only the judge, and he listened carefully, popping a mint into his mouth at regular intervals. Valerie raised her voice dramatically.

"Through his attorney, Mr. Gorham will tell you about his troubled childhood, and how he wants to change. A troubled childhood is regrettable, but no excuse for committing a crime, and talk about change is easy. The defendant is a repeat offender, and if Your Honor will check the sentencing report, you will see that each time he commits a crime, the violence escalates. If Mr. Gorham had had a gun, something besides his fists to use on the victim..."

She paused and shuddered delicately. Everyone in the courtroom was still, listening to her. "Can we take the chance that next time he won't have a weapon? Because I assure you, Your Honor, there will be a next time, and our only protection is to make sure Mr. Gorham is in jail for a long time. On behalf of this small community, the state of Ohio asks this court to give the defendant the maximum, consecutive sentence."

There was a long pause and then the judge leaned over the bench. "Mr. Vanette? Anything you'd like to say on behalf of the defendant?"

"Thank you, Your Honor." Bob Vanette stood. "As Ms. Brettinger has pointed out, the defendant's problems began in childhood...."

Valerie was good, Jay thought, really good. She'd anticipated what Bob Vanette would say and stolen his advantage. Vanette was cautious, thorough and boring. The attorney's voice was so soft and even, it was hard to concentrate on what he was saying.

He shifted his attention to the judge. Judge Haskins

was obviously as bored as Jay was, but at least he
was quiet about it, in complete contrast to his behavior this morning. His face was flushed and unhealthy-
looking. Jay wasn't close enough to see, but he imagined the judge's hands quivering, as he'd noticed
them doing earlier. Jay watched as, peeling some
waxed paper from his tube of mints, the judge put
another in his mouth.

Suddenly, Jay sat up straight, feeling a shock wave
hit his gut as awareness swept over him. He couldn't
believe it, couldn't believe he hadn't figured this out
before. After all, he of all people should have recognized what was wrong with Judge Haskins.

Swallowing heavily, Jay quickly asked himself if
he could be wrong. No. He thought back on the clues,
and they all added up to one thing. The swift changes
of mood, the nasty temper, especially in the mornings,
shifting to affability after lunch. The red, flushed face
and the trembling hands. Hell, even the mints made
sense.

Judge Haskins wasn't ill, not in the conventional
sense, anyway. He drank. Too much.

This morning, the judge had obviously needed a
drink. His irritability and his trembling hands were
signs that his body demanded the alcohol. Over lunch,
he'd probably had a drink or two, and his body had
gotten the substance it craved. So now he was affable,
falsely friendly. But he was probably nervous about
his drinking, didn't want to take a chance that anyone
could smell too much alcohol on his breath. That explained the mints. Jay had seen it before, all too in-
timately, although the judge was a lot better at hiding
it than Jay's father had been.

Jay glanced toward Valerie. She was alternately
taking notes and watching Bob Vanette, who was still

droning on. Did she know? He didn't think so. He'd noticed that she was touchy on the subject of the judge, wouldn't allow any criticism of him, but he didn't think she was protecting him.

Jay wondered if anyone knew. Some alcoholics were so good at concealing their problem, it was years before any of their colleagues suspected. He despised alcoholics, even though all the books he'd read on the subject emphasized that alcoholism was a disease over which the drinker had no control. Jay had long ago recognized he wasn't rational about the problem. He'd been through too much.

He tried to think. Had it affected the judge's work? Jay hadn't been around Amsden long enough to know for sure, but he didn't think so. He hadn't seen the judge make any actual decisions that were irrational. And that was the key. If the man was doing his job, his personal life was his own business.

Someday, it would begin to affect his decisions, Jay knew. Alcohol destroyed brain cells, and it was only a matter of time before its effects on Judge Haskins became apparent. Until that time, though, Jay would tell no one. He would watch and wait.

CHAPTER THREE

"JAY, IT'S BEEN SO LONG," Valerie's mother said with feeling, kissing him on the cheek.

"Too long, Ginny," Jay told her, giving her an enthusiastic hug. He looked beyond her. "Sara's here! Great. You look wonderful, Sara." He held out his arms and Sara came into them.

She was laughing. "Did my little sister tell you what I've been up to? Jonathan and I live in Pittsburgh and we have three boys now. Come on into the family room and meet them. Dad's here, too."

"I've got to check on the roast beef," Valerie's mother interjected, moving ahead of them through the kitchen door.

Valerie trailed along behind Sara and Jay. Her father, Don, greeted Jay with a vigorous handshake and a thump on the back, his eyes moist. If Jay was embarrassed at all the attention, he wasn't showing it. In fact, he seemed to be basking in it.

The only ones who seemed indifferent to him were Sara's three sons. Bobby and Mark, the two oldest, barely looked up from their toy dinosaurs when Sara introduced Jay.

"And here's Cory." Sara held him out proudly. "He was two months old yesterday, and this is the first time Mom and Dad have seen him."

Jay tickled the baby under the chin and was rewarded with a yawn. "I think he's sleepy," he told

Sara with a grin. ''He doesn't seem susceptible to my overwhelming charm, anyway.''

''Well, you know how it is. Right now, it's mostly sleep, eat and spit up. But once in a while, he smiles at me, and I see Jonathan's expression, and it just melts me. Isn't he the cutest thing you ever saw?''

''As beautiful as you are,'' Jay said gallantly.

There was a second's pause. ''Oh, my,'' Sara said softly. ''What's with these sweeping compliments? Is this a new Jay?''

''Well, maybe. The saying-it part is, I guess. But the Brettinger girls have always been beautiful. I just didn't get as much chance to tell them before.''

She burst into laughter. ''For the last few months, I've felt like a beached whale, and I still don't have my figure back. I guess I'll take my compliments where I find them, exaggerated or not.'' Her giggles trailed down the hall as she left with the baby.

There was silence. Valerie's father was engrossed in a football game on television, and all of a sudden, Valerie couldn't think of a thing to say. Jay cocked an eyebrow at her and she looked away. He walked over to the two little boys and sank easily onto the floor beside them.

''What kind of dinosaur is this?'' he asked, picking up one of the plastic toys.

''A tyrannosaurus rex,'' four-year-old Mark said solemnly.

''Oh yes, I remember him. He's a meat-eating dinosaur, isn't he?''

''Right. He's my favorite meat eater.'' Mark picked up a long-necked dinosaur. ''This is brontosaurus. He's my favorite plant eater. He lived in the swamps and ate water plants.''

"And tyrannosaurus rex ate him!" Bobby exclaimed.

"But not this brontosaurus," Mark told Jay calmly. "This brontosaurus is tyrannosaurus rex's friend. Tyrannosaurus has to get his meat somewhere else."

Jay rolled onto his stomach, fingering the two dinosaurs. "Maybe he has to get his meat in a grocery store."

"Naw!" Bobby put six years' worth of disgust in the one word. "There have to be people to build a grocery store. There weren't any people when the dinosaurs were alive. Everybody knows that."

"Well, I didn't know it," Jay said. "When I was a little boy, I used to like dinosaurs, myself, so I must have known then. But maybe I forgot. Why don't you two tell me about them? We could line them up, make a parade, or something."

Valerie picked up a magazine and pretended to read as she watched Jay become engrossed in the children's play, asking questions that elicited eager responses from the boys. Mark, who had developed quite a passion for dinosaurs, in the way of many small boys, gave Jay slightly skewed information about the different species and their feeding habits. Although much of what he said was funny, Jay didn't laugh. Valerie found she couldn't take her eyes off him. His interest in the children touched her.

And she couldn't seem to stop looking at his body. Since his return, she hadn't seen Jay in anything but elegant, dark suits, and he looked great in them. But she thought he looked even better in the coarsely woven navy blue sweater and the soft, well-broken-in corduroy pants he wore today. The pants fit well, she thought, involuntarily running her eyes up the backs of his lean thighs and stopping at his waistband. Hurriedly, she forced her gaze back to her magazine. This was ridiculous. She shook her head to clear the image she had—a sensation, really—of what it might be like to run her hands over the soft corduroy and feel the hard thigh muscles beneath.

It scared her. She wasn't supposed to be feeling this way. Of course, she'd been a little lonely. Most of the men her age in Amsden she'd known since grade school. Many of them were nice, and a lot of them were friends. That was the trouble, of course. They were just friends. None of them made her feel like this, all trembling inside. The feeling was exciting, but the problem was that it was connected with Jay, and that part didn't feel right at all.

"I'll help Mom with dinner," she announced abruptly. She snapped her magazine down on the coffee table and moved quickly to the kitchen door.

"Can I help?" Jay asked.

At that moment, the kitchen door opened, and Valerie's mother appeared. "Valerie, if you'll fill the glasses with ice water, I'm about to make the gravy."

"Yes, I was just coming to see if I could do something for you."

Jay started to get to his feet. "Let me help."

"No, Jay. Stay here and play with the kids," Valerie told him. "Mom and I will get dinner on the table. Go ahead and enjoy being a guest."

He grinned. "Okay, but only until dinner. Afterward, I can help clean up. I'm pretty good with dishes."

"I might just take you up on that offer," Ginny said as she and Valerie went into the kitchen.

There was a little commotion when Valerie called them all to the table. Sara had to get the boys seated, and they were rambunctious. Valerie found herself sitting across from Jay.

"Hope you still like roast beef, Jay," her father said as he began to carve. "Ginny makes a great one, you know."

"There's nothing like good midwestern cooking," Jay noted as he took a bite. "Mmm, wonderful, Ginny. Just what I've been missing all these years."

She smiled. "I'm glad you like it. I don't suppose your mother ever let you cook, she was so good at it."

He nodded, smiling back. "She was, wasn't she? When I went to Chicago, I finally taught myself, but it wasn't stuff like this. No such thing as a roast for one." He was quiet for a second. "Thanks for having me today. It's always felt so…I don't know… so right at your house."

"You're welcome, dear. I know your mom would be glad you're here."

"It is good here, isn't it?" Sara asked. "Things weren't always so pleasant. Valerie and I used to argue all the time, remember, Mom? But now that we're grown-up, we get along really well."

Mother and daughter smiled at each other, and Jay thought how much he'd missed this family, so very different from his own.

Valerie hadn't said a word. "You're awfully quiet today, Valerie," her father observed. "No gossip to tell us all?"

"Nothing new." Valerie paid a great deal of attention to her plate.

"I watched Valerie do a sentencing the other day. She was really great, had the defense attorney on the run. You would have enjoyed watching her in action."

She blushed. "It was just Bob Vanette. He tries, but really, he isn't a trial lawyer. The sentencing was no big deal."

Her father laughed, gazing at her fondly. "I know she's good, even without your telling me, Jay. Valerie has had a tongue on her all these years. If I'd known that someday it would pay her bills, I might have been a little more tolerant all those times she argued with me. You know, women's issues, politics, there was something all the time with Valerie. We never agreed on anything, but just when I'd think she was really going to blow her top, she'd tell me she 'understood my point of view.' Imagine, something like that coming out of the mouth of a teenager. Anyway, that self-control will come in handy if she ever does run for office."

"Valerie used to tell me about some of your discussions, and then we'd end up arguing about the same things," Jay said. "I don't remember her telling me she understood my points. Her cheeks would always get red, though." Jay cracked a smile and looked across the table at Valerie. "Do you remember, Valerie, all those times at my house, when you'd help with the milking, and we'd make the cows wait while we talked? Remember cow number seventeen? She used to stamp her feet in that funny rhythm when she thought we were making her wait too long."

Valerie had forgotten, but now she remembered. "We called her Clogging Bess," she told the others.

"We never did agree on anything, either, did we?" Jay asked.

"Not too often." She couldn't help smiling. "But it was fun, too, wasn't it?"

"I loved it," he said very quietly, and his eyes had a faraway look. "No one could make me think, not like you could. And it wasn't just politics. When we'd get done with the chores and walk to the hill, I would tell you everything, things I couldn't tell anyone else. There wasn't anything we couldn't talk about.''

The room had grown suddenly quiet, and Valerie's fork had stopped halfway to her mouth. Oh, yes, she thought grimly, there was a lot we couldn't talk about. Jay had told her his dreams, but he'd never let her tell him hers. A couple of times she'd tried to let him know what he meant to her, even though it was hard. And he'd cut her off; he hadn't wanted to hear it. He'd never felt the same way about her, even after they'd made love.

She had lain in his embrace and felt his warm breath close against her neck and thought that finally he would let her love him. But afterward, he had rolled away without a word, his back to her. In the dark, she'd reached out an uncertain hand and touched his shoulder. It was quivering, and then she was sure he was crying, but that couldn't be so because Jay Westcott never, ever cried.

Jay was selectively recalling all the good times, but Valerie knew that the real story about what had happened twelve years ago, had occurred the last time they'd walked on the hill.

As the memory faded, she realized that no one was speaking yet. Sara was looking at her with a funny expression on her face. Slowly, Valerie put her fork down and took a sip of water.

The boys were quarreling. As if from a long way off, Valerie heard Sara's voice, trying unsuccessfully to make the children settle down. ''You boys aren't hungry, that's the problem,'' Sara said in an exasperated voice. ''Grandma let you eat too much sweet stuff today.''

"Grandma's privilege," Ginny said in a dry voice.

"Yes, well, go ahead and play, you two." Delighted, the boys jumped up from the table. "I suppose I should make them eat something healthy, but in less than a week we'll be back in Pittsburgh, and their daddy and I can work on nutrition then. They always behave better for Jonathan. It's too bad he couldn't come this time. You'd like him, Jay."

"I'm sure I would. They're great boys, Sara," Jay told her. His voice was light, his blue eyes happy. "Mark knows everything about dinosaurs."

"Well, he thinks he does, anyway."

The family talked quietly about the boys, and Valerie was relieved. The conversation shifted to Jay, and her mom asked him about his work and his impressions of Amsden.

Finally, Valerie's father pushed back his plate. "That was the best roast we've ever had, Ginny."

"You always say that."

"Well, it's always true." He smiled at her.

"I'll get the coffee," Valerie offered, starting to pick up the plates.

"I'll help," Jay said quickly, standing.

"I've got pie, but everybody's probably too full to enjoy it now," Ginny said. "Why don't we wait, and have our pie and coffee in the family room in a little while?"

"Good idea." Her father began stacking plates. "I'll just help get these dirty dishes in the dishwasher and we won't have so much cleanup later."

Sara smiled conspiratorially at Jay. "Dad, I think we already have volunteers for kitchen duty."

"Yes," Ginny agreed readily. "I remember before dinner Jay offered to clean up. And Valerie will help him, won't you, dear?"

What was this? Her mother and Sara were deliberately throwing her and Jay together, making sure
she spent time alone with him. She couldn't believe
it. They didn't know how she felt about Jay now. She
was furious with herself because right this minute she
could feel the telltale blush wending its way from her
neck to her cheeks.

Jay was smiling at her red face. Of course, *he*
wasn't embarrassed. He'd been the one to bring up—
right in front of her family—those long-ago conversations they'd had in the milking parlor of his farm.
He'd been the one to look at her with that soft, nos-
talgic expression that the other two women had
clearly misread....

"I don't think Jay ought to have to help out his
first day back in our home," her father was saying,
oblivious to the fact that he was supposed to make a
graceful exit, and despite herself, Valerie almost
laughed. "I'll help Valerie and Sara—"

"No, you won't." Ginny took her husband's hand
and practically hauled him away from the table and
out the door.

"There are an awful lot of dishes here, Jay," Sara
remarked innocently. "It won't surprise me if it takes
you and Valerie a long time to get them done. You
might be at it most of the afternoon."

A pleased smile lit Jay's face. "We'll take our time
and make sure the kitchen's really clean."

Abruptly, Valerie began stacking plates. "If you
two spend any more time carrying on, we'll never get
them done." She stepped into the kitchen immediately.

Shrugging at Sara, Jay picked up a couple of water
glasses and followed her.

"Relax, Valerie," he told her softly as he came through the door. "They were teasing."

"It isn't funny."

He sighed. "Your reaction sure isn't."

"Oh? Just what is my reaction supposed to be? Are we going to swap more stories about long ago? Are you planning to think up some other way to embarrass me in front of the family, give them the wrong impression about how things are between us?"

He looked directly at her, the water goblets still in his hands. He spoke in a deliberate tone. "How exactly are things between us?"

"That's the point. There's nothing between us." She slammed the plates down on the counter, hard enough to make them jump. Fortunately, she hadn't broken them, she thought, trying to govern her unusual flash of temper. She waited until she was a shade calmer before she spoke.

"I don't want to talk about the old days," she said in a firm voice. That much, at least, was true.

He came up behind her. Her back was rigid, rejecting. His eyes followed the feathery layers of her honey-colored hair to where it lay against her smooth neck. Even from the back, he felt her presence, the force of her personality. He wanted to turn her around and touch her, feel her cheek, outline her jaw and chin with his fingers, put his mouth against hers and test her reaction. Since he'd come back, he'd been almost overwhelmed by his feelings for her. Part of it was remembering how close they'd been long ago, but there was more, he realized. He liked her. He liked the woman she'd become even more than the girl she'd been, although he didn't understand her as well as he used to. She seemed determined to resist him, to prevent him from getting too close.

Valerie felt his breath on her neck. In slow motion, she turned on the water and began rinsing the dishes carefully. "Okay. Why don't we talk about now?" he whispered, his lips practically next to her ear.

She stepped away quickly, heading for the dining room. "What about now?" she asked sharply.

He didn't answer, and she went into the dining room. She picked up the empty platter and a few utensils. She was thoroughly unsettled, and stood still with the platter in her hand, quivering.

His large, solid body filled the doorway. He was watching her. She tried not to look directly at him, but even without doing so, she was as aware of his masculine presence as she'd been the other day in the office. Her composure was crumbling.

"Now?" His voice came to her as she kept her head down, fixed on the empty platter. "Now I find I'm attracted to you."

Finally, Valerie looked at him. "Why are you doing this?"

"Doing what?"

"Talking like this. You're lonely, but that doesn't explain why—"

Unexpectedly, he chuckled. "You can't believe I'm attracted to you? Why not? Have you ever looked in the mirror?"

She had to get by him. "Excuse me," she said, putting as much frostiness as she could muster into her words.

Jay stepped out of the way, allowing her to come into the kitchen. Valerie put down the platter and went back to the dining room. He followed her, and methodically they brought in the dirty plates and stacked them on the kitchen counter.

He was pushing too hard, moving too fast for her,

he thought. He sighed. He could be patient, maybe more than most people, but where Valerie was concerned, he didn't feel like being patient. Ever since that first night when he'd managed to maneuver her into going out for dinner, he'd been thinking about her. It had only been a month, and he needed to give her time.

But it wouldn't be easy. He was ready now. After all, time and again during those years in Chicago he'd thought about her, wished he could talk to her, share things with her. Now, those twelve-year-old feelings were blending with new ones, feelings that clutched him physically, teased him mentally. He was afraid of where those feelings would lead, but he knew he had to take the chance. It might be his last one, his last chance to feel really connected to another human being.

He was a lawyer, he reminded himself. He'd used his legal skills to move lots of stalled negotiations forward. Strategy was one of the things he was best at, but here he was too personally involved. This wasn't litigation, but... Yes, he thought, he knew what the trouble was. He needed to take a step back here, size up his opponent. Did she like him? He couldn't tell, exactly, but why was she avoiding him? What was stopping her, making her keep her distance? When he figured that out, he'd be able to think of some way to break down all those defenses.

"Valerie, it's okay, you know. We can talk about something else if you'd rather."

She took a deep breath. "I can't banish you from the kitchen until these dishes are done, or I'll have to think of something to say to Sara. Do you think you can behave yourself, at least until we've got the dishwasher loaded?"

"Sure."

She stood at the sink and rinsed the dishes, and handed them to him to put them in the dishwasher. Once, while taking a plate from her, his hand accidently closed over hers and she jerked away. It was as clear a signal as could be that he'd expected too much from her today.

"Your mom's dinner was good," he told her, trying to fill the tense silence.

"Yes, it was. I suppose you weren't kidding when you said you missed this sort of thing."

"It was great, just like old times. The good part of the old times, that is."

She was suddenly intensely curious. "Didn't you have any good times in Chicago?"

Jay pulled damp fingers through his mop of dark hair, and Valerie resisted a sudden urge to reach up and smooth it. He took an audible breath. "I guess so, especially at first. But the last few years were so miserable that I don't really think much about the good times. Anyway, I didn't want any of it, and it was hard when I realized that I'd spent so much time pursuing goals that meant nothing to me."

"Your divorce soured you on things, I suppose."

"That was part of it, of course. But it wasn't Allison's fault. It was my fault for marrying her in the first place. Did you know we were married for over four years and I can hardly remember anything about them?"

"No," Valerie said softly. She didn't want to pry, so she asked no more questions. But, just like in the old days, once Jay started to tell her something, he couldn't seem to stop.

"Can I tell you about it?" At her nod, he took another deep breath, trying to find the words. He had wanted to tell her about it so many times before. "To get a feel for what it was really like, you need to know that I was already changing inside, growing up, I guess. You know when I left Amsden, I had no intention of ever looking back. When I got out of Yale, I got that great job at Rossen, Sebastian and Bowles. I figured if I made partner, I'd be set for life. Those guys have condos in the city, houses in the country, the works, and real power, which they don't hesitate to use.

"It was a long way from milking cows, and that's what I thought was so great about working for the firm. There were a hundred of us associates, and we all hoped to make partner eventually, but of course, only five or so of us ever would." His lips turned up, but the smile never made it to his eyes. "I know you think I'm egotistical, and I guess you're right. I knew I'd make partner at that firm. Sometimes I haven't felt so sure of myself as a human being, but I've got a lot of confidence in my professional skills. I figured I was smart, and I'd work hard, and I knew how to play the game." He stopped. "I'm giving you the long version of this story. Are you sure you want to hear all this?"

Valerie had stopped rinsing dishes as he started telling her about his time in Chicago. She wanted to hear it, definitely. The long version. "Go on, Jay. I'm listening."

This time, the smile did light his eyes. "You always do, Valerie. Well, I did everything right, it seemed, and I got promoted on the fast track to senior associate. It didn't mean I ever got to do anything interesting, but I was making more money, and hanging around with some of the partners. It's a real old boys' network there, and I figured the socializing would get me ahead quicker than being a whiz at law, although I tried to be that, too.

"The senior partners take their special clients to Mexico for Christmas. Only three senior associates get to go, and when I got asked, I felt on top of the world. So I went, of course. The first night there, I met Allison. She was really elegant, and she kept looking at me from across the room. One of the guys told me she was Senator Metcalf's daughter. When he retired from the Senate, Metcalf went into business running several corporations, and he was one of the firm's biggest clients. I couldn't believe Allison was interested in me. But everyone kidded me about how she was looking at me, so I got up the nerve to ask her to dance." Jay raked his hand through his hair again, making it stand on end. "I told you this was the long version."

He spoke lightly, but Valerie knew it hurt to tell her. "Let's give up on the dishes for a few minutes, Jay. I'll make some coffee." She led him to the kitchen table and got the coffeemaker running. He didn't say anything until she brought him a cup.

"Anyway, she was everything I left home for, so I married her," he said, using his cup to warm his hands. "We weren't willing to wait until her dad could have the society bash he wanted, but the Chicago papers did it up, regardless. We were doing everything right, going out, entertaining constantly, and all that was really good for my career.

"But one night I was going home, exhausted from one of those eighteen-hour days at the office, really beat. I remember thinking if I kept it up I would be dead before I could enjoy the perks of partnership. I was so strung-out that all I wanted to do was go home, put on something comfortable and have someone hold me tight, and I realized...well, that I was going home to a stranger. I was married to someone I hardly knew." He stared intently into his cup, speaking softly. "It was...terrifying, to think I was living like that."

Impulsively, Valerie reached over and took his hand in hers. "I know you don't want me to feel sorry for you, Jay, but I can't help it. I can hear the hurt in your voice."

He gave her a lopsided grin. "It's okay once in a while, I guess."

"So," she said quietly, thinking she understood perfectly, "you ended it with Allison."

Jay looked startled. "No, of course not. I was *married* to her, Valerie. I'd intended to spend my life with her."

"But when things got hard..." She let her voice trail away, realizing she'd been about to say that when things got tough for Jay, he simply got out as fast as he could. Hadn't she been one of the first to figure that out? But he didn't need that kind of remark; he needed understanding. Reaching out, she lightly touched his hand.

He was continuing to talk, as though he'd held the words inside too long. "I decided I needed to get to know her. My own wife," he said, as if still marveling at that fact. "I was changing, myself, realizing that Chicago, and especially the firm, wasn't for me. So I tried to tell her about it, and find out what she wanted, too. Things like whether we wanted a family, what we were like inside. Not what we usually talked about—like what kind of sofa to buy, or which partner was holding an open house.

"So, one day I told her I wanted to leave the firm. I and another associate—one who'd gotten turned down for partner—were going to open a small office. We figured some of the clients who liked our work would follow us, and we'd do okay. Then Allison finally told me what she wanted. She told me she liked things exactly as they were, that she'd married me because she knew where I was going. It was the only really frank discussion we ever had." He looked directly at her for the first time. "Two days later, I was offered a full partnership in the firm."

"Wow, what weird timing that was," Valerie said softly.

"Not so weird," Jay replied in a tight voice. "Don't you remember who Allison is? Senator Metcalf's daughter. Do you really think it was a coincidence that I got offered a partnership two days after I told Senator Metcalf's daughter that I wanted to leave the firm?"

"And you turned it down."

Restlessly, Jay got up and strode to the window. "I had to, Valerie. I couldn't imagine myself working for the firm the rest of my life. Allison must have heard what I'd done because when I got back home, she wasn't there." His voice was so low, she could hardly hear it. "One thing about being a lawyer, Valerie. When you need one yourself, you know which to hire. Mine was very efficient. The only time I ever saw Allison again was at the final hearing for our divorce."

"I'm sorry," she said simply.

"Yeah." Jay studied the backyard as if it were in full bloom instead of frosty gray. "Do you know anything about the children of alcoholics, Valerie?"

"Well, I know you." She tried to put as much empathy as possible into her voice. "And you're a fine man, so I guess I know something about the children of alcoholics.'' He didn't say anything to that, so she added, ''But as a concept, no, I don't.''

''Well, you think when you grow up, you can have it all your own way, and that everything will be perfect, if you can just get out. But the behavior of adult children of alcoholics is so predictable that books are written about us. We're emotionally damaged, to one degree or another. I've been reading about it a lot, and I think I fit the profile pretty well. Most children of alcoholics have trouble with real intimacy. They're too…scarred inside.''

Nobody she'd ever known had had as much trouble trusting people as Jay had. Their long, intense friendship had been as close as he'd ever come to trust, she suddenly realized. And she knew now it had meant a lot to him, more than she'd understood at the time. Yet, even that had been cast aside, along with everything else connected with Amsden and his childhood. He would always shy away from true closeness with another human being. How lonely that must be for him, and what a warning it was for her.

But he seemed to think he'd changed quite a bit, and in the little things, he had. ''Since you've come back, you've been so different, Jay. So…I don't know, so light, and you sing. Are you avoiding things here, too?''

''No, just the opposite. It's hard, but this time I'm really trying.'' Again, his voice was low, and Valerie had trouble hearing it. ''Valerie, do you believe a person is responsible for his own happiness?''

She thought about his question for a minute. She thought of herself. She had created a meaningful life, and she was proud of that. ''I guess so.''

''Valerie, come here.'' Jay's voice was soft, but commanding. She went over and stood with him by the window, and he slipped his arm around her waist. It wasn't a romantic gesture, but a brotherly one. "What I'm trying to say is that I think a person can decide to be happy or sad. And, frankly, I've decided to be happy. I'm doing what I really want, now. I wanted to come home, and I did. I wanted to do trial work, and I am. And I wanted your friendship again. I think I have it." He flashed her a grin that deeply creased his face, and he seemed so genuinely contented that for a second she almost melted into his arms. "I'm trying to learn to trust other people, and most of all, to trust myself. If the time ever comes again when I'm not happy doing what I'm doing, I won't hesitate to change my life again."

"Hey, this is a warning." Sara's voice came unexpectedly from the kitchen door. "I'm coming in."

"A warning?" Valerie said.

"In case you two were smooching in here, or something."

She ought to be used to her own blushes by now, Valerie thought about herself impatiently, feeling yet another one sweep her cheeks. "No need for warnings," she said briefly.

"Oh, too bad." Sara flashed a quick look at Jay. "Well, Dad wants his pie."

"Let's have pie, too, Valerie," Jay suggested. "You already have the coffee made, anyway."

THERE WERE warm goodbyes and invitations to come again before Valerie and Jay were settled into his car.

"I should have driven myself over," Valerie told him. "This way, you have to take me to town and then drive twenty miles home."

"It's no bother. Actually, I was thinking it's still

early enough to do a little sight-seeing. We could watch the lights come on over Amsden Lake.''

"Okay.'' Valerie settled comfortably into the leather seat. Jay's story had made her see the past a little differently. She could better understand the need he'd felt to get out of Amsden, and she ached to think of his bitter years in Chicago, when she had assumed he'd had everything he ever wanted. When Jay had left, she'd made it very clear to her family that she didn't want to hear anything about his new life. Now she felt a touch of guilt. He valued her friendship, that was plain, and she also knew she valued his. The past was over. She didn't need anything from him, but she could easily be his friend again.

She reached toward him, and out of the corner of his eye, he caught the movement. He dropped his hand to the seat, and for a brief, companionable instant, Valerie twined her fingers in his. "How about some music?'' she suggested.

He handed her the case, letting her choose, and in a moment he was singing softly with the disc.

Jay threaded through the secondary roads that wound around the low hills. From the top of one higher ridge, Valerie looked down over the bare bones of the land to see a fine gray mist settling over the valley.

"It's going to be dark soon,'' she said. "If you want to see the lights come on over the lake, we'd better head there now.''

Jay nodded, not missing a beat of the music, but he turned the car toward the lake. In a few minutes, he'd started down one of the narrow access roads, and pulled off into a parking lot that served the boat launch. Together, they gazed at the slate-gray, roughly tossed surface of the lake. The twilight sun was hidden under the clouds, and there was no glimmer on the water. It looked cold and barren, so different from the interior of the small, warm car. No lights were on yet in the huge cedar-and-glass houses that ringed the lake.

They were silent for a few minutes, enjoying the stark scenery. Finally, a light came on in one of the faraway windows across the lake, and Jay slipped his hand into hers.

"I love the water," he said quietly. "On a still summer afternoon, I like seeing pieces of the hills reflected in the lake. But mostly, I like how warm the light from the windows looks on a gray day like this, especially when it shines on the peaks of the waves."

"Would you ever want to live out here?"

"No, but I like the houses. I like all that glass. The farmhouse is so dark." He was quiet for a second. "I wouldn't want as many neighbors as there always are around a lake. But I wish I had my view from the hill on my back forty, with Amsden Lake tucked in, all to myself."

"What a modest little wish."

He smiled. "It's because I'm such a modest guy."

Valerie smiled with him. This was the new, lighter Jay, and she liked it fine, she decided. "You know, my house is very Victorian. I always thought I loved it, but you're right, I like the light coming in, too. I wouldn't mind all those big windows, myself."

They stayed by the lake, talking quietly, until it was completely dark. "Would you like to go somewhere else?" Jay asked. "Is there anywhere we could go for some live music?"

"This is Amsden. Surely you remember nothing is open on a Sunday night." She, too, was reluctant to end the day. "I guess you might as well take me home. Next week is a rough one for me, three speeches, and I ought to make it an early night.''

They headed back to Amsden, not talking much on the way, but the silence was comfortable, as it used to be in the old days. Valerie felt a quiet contentment.

That contentment ended abruptly a few minutes later on her big, old-fashioned porch. ''Thanks for having me to dinner, Valerie,'' Jay whispered as she was getting ready to slip her key in her door.

''My mom had you,'' she reminded him.

''I think you know what I mean.''

She thought for a second. ''Yes, I think I do.''

''Good.'' She saw him take in a breath. ''Then maybe you'll understand about this, too,'' he muttered, and very quickly, his mouth came down on hers.

His lips were dry and warm, and also hard and demanding as they touched hers, immediately exploring. Whatever Jay was demanding with his mouth, it wasn't her friendship, Valerie thought weakly. In the chill air, his warm breath came strongly against her face, and his eyes were closed, thick black lashes against his cheeks. For a moment, less than a second, really, Valerie thought she ought to pull away. It wasn't right to give him the impression that she wanted him to kiss her.

But she did, she thought shakily. She wanted him to kiss her almost more than anything she'd ever wanted before. It scared her to realize just how badly she wanted it. She felt her own eyes closing, her head dropping back in invitation. She felt his hand behind her neck, pulling her against him. It was a good thing, too, because all of a sudden, under the sheer weight of his kiss, Valerie's legs felt too weak to hold her.

When her lips parted, Jay's tongue slipped inside

her mouth. And, all at once, she felt as if something was flicking along her limbs, firing little paths of nerves. It was…it was not nearly enough.

There was a little sound and Valerie realized with a start that the moan had come from her own throat, and that she was clinging to him. One hand came up, her fingers twining in all his coarsely wavy hair, holding his mouth tightly to hers.

Jay shifted, spreading his legs slightly apart, and his arms slid down along her hips, pulling her solidly against his body. Suddenly, she was flooded with hot, shivering desire, intensely, unmistakably sexual. She shook with the force of it. Through the worn corduroy of his pants, she could feel his arousal, and he positioned her, lifting her a little so that he seemed to fit between her own thighs. For a moment, that was satisfying; his hardness cradled against her. But almost immediately, she experienced the same sensation she'd felt just a moment before: it wasn't enough.

Jay's mouth was leaving hers, but not to break off the kiss. Instead, his lips roamed, taking in her forehead, her eyelids, the tip of her nose, her cheek, her chin, the knot in the front of her throat. Impatiently pushing away the high flap of her knitted jacket, he bent to the sensitive hollow where her neck met her collarbone, nipping lightly, over and over. Between breaths, he whispered her name, once, twice. Hearing her own name spoken that way by him practically undid her. This was Jay, she thought shakily. Jay. Jay wanting her. Jay's arms squeezing her so tightly. Jay's thighs pressed hard against hers. Jay's voice whispering her name with open desire.

Another small moan escaped her then, and her head fell onto his shoulder. Her cheek lay against the cold buttery smoothness of his jacket, and her nostrils filled with the mellow sharpness of leather.

His mouth moved up again, this time to pull strands of her hair between his lips, and finally his mouth was against her ear. "Valerie," he whispered hoarsely, "I want you, and you're feeling it, too." His words held passion, but they also held wonder, and it was the wonder that squeezed her heart.

But this wasn't supposed to happen. Not now, not after all this time. Not after she'd put her own life in order. Not when he was vulnerable and reaching out and mistaking loneliness for something more.

"Jay." She was foggily surprised at the effort it took to say his name. "This is crazy."

"Oh, yes," he murmured, hot breath warming her ear. "Marvelous climb-the-walls crazy..."

"No," she said shakily, trying to make her mouth form sensible words. "Crazy, as in I just can't do this. Not now. Not again."

Pressed against hers, his whole body stiffened. There was a heavy, awkward pause before he spoke slowly. "I thought you wanted—"

"It's okay," she interrupted hastily. Her trembling voice didn't sound like her own, but her sensible, understanding words were pure Valerie. "It's not anyone's fault. We shared our thoughts again today, Jay, something we've both missed doing, and I don't blame you for mistaking that exchange for something else."

With painful slowness, he drew back on the dark porch, dropping his arms to his sides. "I see." He turned his head away from her, so she couldn't read his eyes.

"It isn't right," she tried to explain.

"I see," he repeated. Then he put his hands gently on her shoulders, kissed her lightly on the forehead and was gone, sprinting down the dark walk to his car.

CHAPTER FOUR

IT WASN'T EASY to face Jay at work Monday morning, but it got easier as the days wore on. Once, he tried to talk about what had happened on her porch, but she'd managed to cut him off. He hadn't tried again.

It wasn't as if her emotions were complicated. She wanted to be his friend, nothing more. Jay wanted her friendship, too, but there had been this interfering kiss, and her frightening, overwhelming physical response. Had he planned that kiss? She'd never have the nerve to ask him.

Valerie's courtroom boldness didn't extend to her private life—particularly where her relationships with men were concerned. Her body's response, which he couldn't have helped feeling as he'd held her against him, was positively embarrassing. Business, she reminded herself. Keep it just business for a while, and let the other stuff fade. And then she could let him close enough to be friends again.

On Wednesday afternoon, he was sitting with her and Meg at the small conference table, as they were allocating the cases. Meg and Jay were sharing the joking camaraderie that Valerie hoped she could comfortably join in again someday. Sighing, she flipped the folder on the last file and set it on the stack.

"Well, that's next month's work, nicely parceled out."

"Hey, how about a cup of coffee, you two," Meg

invited. "They always have a fresh pot going at Kaiser's, and I'm a little hungry, too." She rolled her eyes and tossed her red hair. "That egg salad I had at lunch didn't seem to do the trick today."

"Valerie?" Jay questioned her.

"I'm busy. Why don't the two of you go, though?"

He looked hesitant. "I've got a jury trial coming up I want to go over with you."

"Okay," Valerie said. "Meg, why don't you go on to the restaurant, and Jay can come as soon as he's done here."

"No, wait for me," Jay told Meg as she rose from her chair and began to leave the office. "I'll only be a minute." He turned to Valerie. "You know that jury trial I've got coming up, the chop shop case?"

"The Robinson's Garage case, yes, of course, I do."

"It's been a big deal in the newspaper, and I know you don't want to lose it, Valerie."

"I never want to lose a case," she said quietly. She saw his grinning face. "All right, all right, I don't want to lose a case *especially* if it's in the newspaper. You've caught me acting like a politician. Satisfied?"

"Very," he told her, still grinning, and for a second, the light comfortable mood was between them again. It gave her hope. "Valerie, I've got a bad feeling about this. Not Robinson, of course. He owns the place, and we've got him cold. But building a case against his silent partner, Jeff Michaels, is a lot tougher. There's no direct evidence leading us to believe he knew anything about stolen cars coming into the place."

"But he did it."

"For sure," Jay said impatiently. "He's so smooth, though, and he's pretty popular around town. He's hired Bob Vanette, and while Bob isn't the greatest at trials, he does a lot of digging and probing. He'll give me fits over every piece of evidence I try to introduce. It'll be tedious just establishing that the car parts the police found are really from stolen vehicles.

"Our best evidence against Michaels—our only direct evidence, really—comes from Lindy Cowles, his former girlfriend. Frankly, she's got me worried. She's willing to testify that she heard him talking about the fact that two vehicles were stolen. That's why Michaels is charged on two counts."

Valerie nodded. "That testimony ought to do it. Still, a former girlfriend, that could be tricky."

"That's what I think, too. I've tried to prepare her. I've asked her how it feels to be testifying against her former lover, and she insists she wants to put the whole thing behind her, that she has no bad feelings toward him. But I wonder if the jury will buy that. Juries are so funny sometimes. They could end up sympathizing with a guy who's hung by his girlfriend."

Valerie nodded again. "What do you think we should do, Jay?"

"I thought you might have some ideas."

"What have you offered Bob to settle the case?"

"Not much. I want to put Michaels away for a long time, and I can't do that if I drop the charges too far. I offered to dismiss one count if he'd plead guilty to the other." Jay leaned forward in his chair. "He turned me down cold. That worried me more. He knows something."

"Even if he does, maybe he won't know how to play his hand at the trial."

"Maybe."

She sighed. "You know how I feel about this kind

of thing, Jay. I'd like to win this one, sure, but what's the right thing to do?''

He laughed shortly. ''Only you worry about that so much. Well, I don't want to offer him more, so I'm going to take the chance and go to trial. Is that okay with you?''

''Absolutely,'' she said, genuinely surprised. ''I trust your judgment. And your trial skills.''

He cracked a smile. ''Finally, a little compliment for my ego,'' he teased. ''I really thought after Sunday night, you'd freeze me out permanently.''

She licked her lips, suddenly nervous again. She was not going to talk about that kiss, ever. ''I'm not going to discuss Sunday night, Jay, so you might as well stop bringing up the topic.''

''Okay.'' For a second, he looked a little embarrassed, but his next words made her decide he was shameless, after all.

''What's your mother cooking *next* Sunday?''

''Lasagna. And I'm bringing pecan pie. Don't look at me that way,'' she commanded, almost laughing, in spite of herself, at the exaggerated way he leaned forward and angled for an invitation. ''Okay, she wants you there. In fact, she told me you have a standing invitation.'' Valerie paused a moment, looking directly into his eyes. ''But next Sunday, and every one after that, I'm driving myself over. I'll meet you there.''

''Okay, okay,'' he told her, and he couldn't help grinning as he headed toward his own office. Until this afternoon, he'd been afraid he'd blown it, that he had pushed her too fast. He'd certainly meant to kiss her, but not that hard. Not that hot, with his whole body molded to hers. But how could he have helped it, when she'd clutched him herself, when she'd put those cool fingers on the back of his neck and then twisted them in his hair, holding him to her with an unmistakable signal of need?

Oh, right. Definitely unmistakable, he thought mock-ingly, but without the sternness he'd used to talk to himself on the way home from her place. He'd made a mistake, that was all, and now it didn't seem irrevocable. She liked him, but not as much as he liked her. It was as simple as that.

Not that he was giving up, of course. He hadn't been sure what he'd find when he came back to Amsden. Would the town be the same, and, more important, would Valerie open up and let him be her friend again? Would she be the same woman he'd remembered? It was almost unbelievable luck that she was still here, still unattached. Jay didn't believe in fate, but he thought that after all this time, he deserved his share of luck. Now he'd need to be very careful.

But their becoming close again seemed possible. The thought made him feel cheerful, so cheerful that he started to whistle to himself as he reached for his topcoat. Meg was right; it felt like a long time since lunch, and a bacon cheeseburger would taste wonderful. With fries.

Out of the corner of his eye, he caught a movement in the open doorway. "I'm coming," he started to say, when he realized it wasn't bouncy Meg. This figure was still, and white as a snowfall. It was Roberta.

"Roberta," he said in surprise. "What's wrong? Was I due in court?"

Her small face was pinched, and the freckles stood out clearly. "I've got to talk to you," she told him in a rush.

"Sit down," he invited, indicating one of the two

chairs that faced his desk. He took the other one, and waited, watching her.

For a moment, she didn't say anything at all. Roberta often seemed scared and nervous to Jay, but today those words seemed inadequate.

Finally, she looked away, and still he waited. "Jay," she said slowly, facing the wall, "there's something you don't know about Judge Haskins."

She didn't say anything more. He wondered if she needed help getting the words out, so he said them for her. "He's an alcoholic."

She whirled to face him, swiveling in the chair. "How do you know that?" she asked, clearly astonished. There was a second's pause. "He's so good at hiding it. Everyone knows he has a social drink or two, but I didn't think anyone knew his drinking was a problem."

He couldn't help the bitterness in his voice. "Let's just say, I've had more than my share of experience with mean drunks, and frankly, I think he qualifies."

Her eyes widened. "I knew I was right to come to you. I knew you'd at least listen. He's not always nice, but he covers his bad behavior with everybody else by slapping them on the back later, doing them little favors. He doesn't do that with you."

Jay knew that. "He doesn't like me." He shrugged. "Maybe he's figured out I know about his drinking."

"But you don't know the rest of it." Roberta looked at him, and her eyes were bright with unshed tears. Her lip trembled.

"Tell me. You can talk to me, Roberta," he said encouragingly.

Jay saw her gulp for air, as if she couldn't take in enough. When she spoke, she rushed the words. "He talks to me about...well, he pressures me about...having sex with him. I can't stand it anymore.''

Silence followed her incredible statement, and although Jay knew she was waiting for him to fill it, for a moment he couldn't find any words. Of all the things Roberta might have said, this was the last thing he'd expected. He tried not to let her see how astonished he was. Jay could tell it had cost her to tell him, knew he should reach out to her, say...what? What on earth could he say to her? The tears she hadn't shed were flowing now, streaking down her cheeks, but she wasn't sobbing, just sitting there in silence.

He saw himself hand her his handkerchief, saw himself go to the door and shut it, heard himself on the intercom asking Brenda to hold his calls, to please bring a couple of cups of coffee and to tell Meg he wouldn't be able to join her at Kaiser's. The small chores gave him time to think. He was a lawyer—once, he'd been a corporate lawyer, and he'd frequently lectured his company clients on how to avoid sexual harassment claims. But as little respect as he had for Judge Haskins, he'd never have guessed that this was what was troubling Roberta.

Brenda brought the coffee, and he handed a cup to Roberta. When he saw her put it aside, he did the same with his own cup, although he needed its scalding warmth badly. A cold anger was growing steadily in the pit of his stomach.

"Roberta," he said softly, trying to find the right words, "you're going to have to tell somebody a little more about this, go into more detail. Maybe you'd feel better telling a woman. I could go get Valerie or Meg, or anyone you want."

"Not Valerie," she said quickly. "Jay, I don't

think I want to tell Meg, either. I think I want to tell you.''

And she did. He took no notes, but sat back, watching her in silence, taking in her words, her demeanor, her story.

''It started when I'd been here a month. I was telling the judge I had a child-support hearing coming up the next day with my ex-husband, that I needed money. He said he knew I needed this job, that's why he'd hired me. I used to wonder why he had. After all, all I've got is my high school equivalency certificate, although I can type pretty fast. This was a good job, better than anything I'd had before. So, anyway, he told me I was small and cute and that I was his type.'' Roberta stared down at his handkerchief as if fascinated by it. ''And then he told me he especially liked my…breasts, only that's not the word he used, Jay, and he told me what he thought I'd look like without my clothes on, in a whole lot of detail. I just stood there and listened to it, all those ugly words.''

She took a deep, shuddering breath. ''You were right to tell someone,'' Jay told her quietly. ''Is that all of it?''

''Is that all of it?'' she echoed, her voice rising by several decibels. ''Oh, my God, no, that's not all of it. Do you think I'd come to you if that was it?''

''It's enough,'' he said softly, trying to calm her. ''But there's more, I take it.''

There was, and she told him in graphic detail just how much more. He felt sick. It hurt him to know that something like this had been going on right under his nose and he'd never spotted it.

''So, now it goes on almost all the time, and every time I get 'restless,' as he calls it, he tells me if I don't like it here, I should get another job. Then he always adds, 'If you can.' I'm scared to death that he might fire me. He knows everybody in town. It might give him some kind of thrill to make sure no one else hires me. And I've heard him tell other people I'm no good at my job, which is just not true.''

There was a long silence after she finished her story. All of a sudden, Jay remembered his first day at work over a month ago and being introduced to Judge Haskins. The judge had made some negative comment about Roberta's work that day, a comment that seemed in flat contradiction to what Jay later observed. And when Valerie had offered to talk to Roberta, the judge had discouraged her. Jay remembered it vividly because it was his first impression of the judge and it had made him vaguely uneasy. He put his chin in his hand, thinking. It all fit. It definitely did.

"Roberta, I'm sorry, but I have to ask you a question or two. Is that okay?"

She nodded, and he tried to sound reassuring. "He's been saying all these things to you. But I need to know, has he ever touched you?"

She nodded miserably. "Do I have to tell you about it?"

"No, but it's really important."

"Okay." She pulled herself up, and again she couldn't seem to look at him. "Once, he…licked my ear. And once, he…" Her voice dropped, and Jay had to lean forward to hear her. "Once, he pinched my breast, so hard I had a bruise." Shakily, she picked up her cup and downed the now-cold coffee in a couple of swallows.

"I'm sorry I had to ask," Jay told her calmly, "but I'll tell you why I needed to know. His talking to you that way is bad enough, but when he touched you, Roberta, he committed a serious crime.''

"A crime," she whispered. "Oh, yes, a crime, all right."

"And now, we need to decide what we should do."

She gave him a look that was so trusting, for a moment he couldn't breathe. Lots of people had needed Jay's legal skills, but no one had ever looked at him with that kind of trust. It was scary as hell. Right then and there, he made himself a promise. Roberta could count on him.

"Jay, what should I do?"

"The next step is for us both to talk to Valerie."

"No! She won't believe me, Jay. You know how she is about the judge. No one can say anything bad about him. She'll tell him and they'll gang up on me."

He couldn't help the sternness in his voice. "Do you think I'd let that happen to you?"

Roberta just stared at him, and Jay forced himself to speak more gently. "Roberta, I know you understand the seriousness of what you're telling me. Judge Haskins is the county judge, and Valerie is the prosecutor. She needs to make the decisions." Roberta still looked unconvinced. Jay took a different tack. "Valerie and I are old friends. No matter what you think, I can tell you that she believes in fairness." He stopped for a second. "She's a kind, understanding person, and right now you'll need to trust me about that."

He hoped he was right. He thought he knew Valerie. She had been kind to him; she was understanding with everyone. And she always talked about doing the right thing. But she was so touchy about the judge, so protective. Undoubtedly, she was used to complaints about his treatment of the lawyers, and she'd made it clear she wouldn't tolerate criticism of her old friend and mentor. But she couldn't refuse to act on these allegations, could she?

Of course she couldn't, he thought as he herded the reluctant Roberta toward Valerie's office. But he felt a stab in his gut as a thought struck him. He knew it was selfish to be thinking about himself and Valerie while Roberta was in such pain, but there it was. Their budding relationship was so fragile. When he told her the truth about Judge Haskins, how would she feel about the messenger?

HE HAD TO HAND IT to Valerie, Jay thought. She was the consummate professional. She sat through it all, listening intently, saying little. If she believed or disbelieved Roberta, she didn't let on. It was unfortunate, though, that Roberta didn't seem able to tell Valerie things the way she'd told him. Even with his prompting, she left out many of the details, and told her story in a wooden manner. Mostly, she worried his wet handkerchief, knotting it and unknotting it, twisting it, pleating it accordion-style, over and over. Finally, she was finished.

Valerie looked from her to Jay. "Well, Roberta, while this is being looked into, you'll want to be reassigned, of course. Tomorrow, we'll call Auto Title. They can always use someone temporarily."

Valerie's careful neutrality bothered him, and Jay wished he could read the expression on her face.

"We'll just tell the judge the broad outline of your allegations, so he knows why you won't be working for him for a while," she said.

Roberta looked terrified. "He'll fire me."

Jay looked at the woman sympathetically. "He

can't, not in retaliation for this." He looked at Valerie, challenge in his eyes. "Can he, Valerie?"

"No. It's against the law to do that, so you don't need to worry about your job."

Roberta bit her lip. "Can't I just take vacation time for a couple of weeks, think this over, maybe get used to the idea before you tell him?"

Jay took over. "Roberta, the point of telling is to get it to stop."

"Just a week or two," she pleaded.

"Okay," Valerie said. "But we'll still need to get to the bottom of this, Roberta. An allegation of sexual harassment can't just hang out there."

Roberta swallowed. "I know that."

Suddenly, Jay couldn't stand it anymore. "Roberta, you need to go home and try to get some rest. Is there someone to drive you, or do you want me to take you?"

"No, Jay, I can call my sister." Shakily, she got up and started blindly for the door. At the doorway, Roberta turned and her gaze took them both in. "I just want to say thanks." Then she was gone.

For several minutes afterward, Valerie made notes on a legal pad, and Jay watched her with growing concern. When she had covered several pages, she looked up at him and asked a few clarifying questions about Roberta's allegations. Her voice was again that calm, neutral one that was really starting to bug him. He knew she was simply being a good lawyer. Sexual harassment was a very touchy subject, but one he'd always handled with the kind of professional detachment Valerie was showing. But this wasn't an anonymous Chicago client. This was Amsden, and the county's only judge had just been accused by his bailiff of sexually harassing and assaulting her.

Valerie was speaking again. "Well, Jay, you're the corporate lawyer here. You know the law in this area, don't you?" He nodded. "And Roberta chose to come to you, although she hardly knows you. That's a little puzzling, but hardly the main issue, is it?"

He shook his head. He couldn't speak.

"What should be the next step?" she asked.

He still couldn't read her expression. "Valerie, what do you think? You believe her, don't you?"

"It doesn't matter whether I believe her, or not. She's made the allegations, and now someone needs to investigate them. It's the only fair way to go about this, as I see it."

It matters to me whether you believe her, he wanted to say. Instead, he asked in as careful a tone as she was using, "Whom did you have in mind?"

She bit her lip, the first sign he'd seen that this was anything more than a routine matter for her. "I suppose it's my responsibility."

"I'm not sure that's a good idea. Not that you wouldn't proceed objectively," he added hastily. "It's just that everyone knows you're close to him, and I don't think you'd want people saying it was an unfair investigation."

Valerie nodded slowly, deep in thought. "You're right, of course. We'll keep it as quiet as we can, but this is a small town, and the lawyers will find out sooner or later. I don't want there to be any question of the judge's innocence. It wouldn't be right to drag Meg into this, and that leaves you. Where this case should be, I guess, since Roberta came to you."

"We could call the police. You heard Roberta—she says he touched her. That makes it a crime, Valerie." Her expression made him impatient. "Get the book and look it up. It's called sexual imposition, and it's defined as sexual contact with a person when the offender knows that contact is offensive—''

''Don't lecture me, Jay!'' she suddenly snapped. ''I know what it means, and I can do my job.''

With effort, he tamped down a sharp retort. ''Sorry, I know that.''

She nodded, then said, ''I think for the judge's sake we shouldn't call in the police until we have done some investigation of our own, at least until I'm convinced a crime really has been committed.''

''You don't believe her.'' It was a statement, not a question, and he wasn't surprised when she shook her head. ''If she'd only explained it to you like she did to me, you wouldn't have any doubt about it, Valerie.''

''I know the judge, Jay.'' Looking very pale and very serious, she picked up her pen and studied her notes, but he had the feeling she wasn't really reading. ''He's crusty, but he'd never do a thing like this.''

''And I know something about this area of the law. I can tell you there's no profile for the kind of person who does this. They don't wear a sign on their foreheads proclaiming it, and they can be very highly placed people.''

She sighed, but at least she had dropped the pose of disinterest. ''These are easy allegations to make, and hard to defend against.''

''I don't think these charges were very easy for Roberta to make, Valerie, and what other explanation could there be for how upset she is?''

''I don't know.'' She looked him fully in the eyes. ''But you do believe her.''

''Yes.''

''I see. Then you aren't any more objective than I am. So I can't let you lead this investigation, either.''

They were being so formal, he thought. Cold and distant. If she would only let him be her friend as well as her colleague. He was afraid to approach her, so he continued the same careful, tiptoeing conversation. "What are we going to do?"

She didn't hesitate. "You believe her, and I don't. That ought to make for an objective investigation, if we work together."

Together. It was really the only word he heard. Thank you, he said to his newfound luck, not realizing until he let it out that he'd been holding his breath. They'd had an honest disagreement over something important to her, and he'd trusted her to understand his own opinion, knowing she wouldn't like it. It hadn't been a perfect understanding. It had been tense and hard. But just now it was enough that she was at least still speaking to him.

"Jay," she said in a small voice, and he looked up to see unexpected tears coming down her cheeks. He was on his feet and going to her immediately. Her mouth quivered. "I think I need you to hold my hand for a minute. This is a really terrible thing we have to do."

THEY WERE CAREFUL not to discuss Roberta's allegations at Valerie's parents' house on Sunday. Thursday and Friday had been a difficult two days, and Valerie was glad they couldn't talk about it with anybody else present. It guaranteed that Sunday, at least, would be tolerable.

Valerie didn't believe Roberta's allegations, but she hadn't slept well since she'd heard the whole ugly, impossible story. She had spent several hours each night going over the facts as she knew them and thinking about the characters and possible motives of the key people involved.

There were many conceivable reasons for Roberta to have manufactured those allegations, ranging from personal problems of her own, to the money she might collect in a lawsuit, to spite for real or imagined criticism of her job performance. She had always been a little—what had the judge said?—flighty. Yes, she had been that. The judge had not been happy with his bailiff's work for some time, Valerie knew, and with his temper, he might not have been too gentle about telling her so.

Certainly it was preposterous, incredible, to think that the elderly judge would harass his bailiff sexually. That wasn't at all like the man she knew. He had been married for thirty-odd years, had children and grandchildren, for heaven's sake. And he had so much at stake: political power, a lengthy career and the respect that went with his judicial office.

Not going straight to Judge Haskins to hear his side went against the grain. At first, she'd wanted to say anything to Roberta to keep things under control, and had willingly agreed when Roberta had asked for two weeks off. But after that, Valerie was going to insist that they tell the judge.

She had let Jay map out the investigation. He'd done similar work in Chicago, and she couldn't help being impressed with his grasp of the issues. First, he was having Roberta write everything down in as much detail as possible, trying to zero in on dates when the events allegedly took place. Then he said he'd check the personnel records to make sure she was actually on the job on those days. It wasn't perfect, but it would be a good place to start checking her story.

Then he'd suggested calls to her former employers, to see what kind of employee she'd been and whether she had a history of making similar allegations. Jay told Valerie that in the end, the victim's credibility often came down to her reputation and character. When he'd said that, he'd acted as if he was saying something distasteful, but Valerie didn't see anything wrong with it. After all, Judge Haskins's character was being called into question, too.

As awful as the claims were, she felt good working so closely with Jay. He knew she was touchy about the issues, and he was being very careful with her. But even with that, a sexual harassment case was an interesting challenge for a lawyer. She forced herself to think about the situation that way. After all, she wouldn't be a very good lawyer if she couldn't approach a problem with professional detachment. And no matter what, the process was going to be fair to everyone. Of that, she would make sure, and she knew that for all his sympathy for Roberta, Jay would do the same.

She looked across the table at him. He didn't seem as unsettled as she was. He was joking with her dad, and it struck her again how much Jay valued this time with her family. He was so relaxed, even the tension around his mouth was less noticeable. His eyes were crinkling with good humor, and as she watched, he threw back his head and laughed out loud. In the old days, Jay had smiled, but he'd seldom laughed. He looked wonderful when he laughed.

"Penny for your thoughts," Valerie's father said to her.

"I'm sorry, I was just thinking about work."

"Not today," Jay warned quickly. "No shoptalk

on Sunday, unless it's another one of your war stories."

Valerie could relax up to a point, but recounting amusing courtroom stories was beyond her today. "I can't think of one."

"Well," her mother said briskly, "how about some of the people, then. I haven't heard you mention Meg in a while, Valerie. How is she doing?"

"Okay at work. Actually, Jay and I are working on a big project together, and I'm sure she's curious, but you know Meg. She just figures she'll worm it out of me soon enough." Valerie took a sip of wine. "On the personal front, actually, I'm worried about her, Mom. You know she sees that police officer, Dave Grau. But he always has her so unhappy."

"Yes, that's what she's been saying at lunch, too," Jay remembered. "What's wrong with him?"

"I don't know. When I first met him, he was nice, I thought, and he seemed to dote on Meg. You know how bouncy she is, and they'd have a great time together. But lately, he's been real moody. The last time I was with them, we went to a pub where you can sing along. They used to like to go there, but this last time, he stared into a glass of whiskey all night like it held the secrets of the ages. By the time we got out of there, I thought Meg was going to cry."

"Poor thing," Ginny said.

"Yes, Mom. I hope he either snaps out of it or Meg sees the light." Valerie sighed, feeling sorry for Meg. It wasn't at all hard to feel sad today.

After the meal was over, she found herself in the kitchen, alone with Jay, doing the dishes again. This could get to be a habit, she thought as she rinsed the dishes and handed them to him to put into the dishwasher.

"I know you're feeling bad today, but it'll all work out," he finally said. "Don't worry about Meg, Valerie. She's sensible, and she can take care of herself."

"I know. It's not just Meg, it's how bad the...the other makes me feel."

"Not today," he warned her again. "We're going to be looking into Roberta's charges for quite a while, and if you stay in a blue funk over them the whole time, you'll drive yourself crazy." Unexpectedly, his eyes twinkled. "I must not be very good company if I can't keep your mind off the office. I could try kissing you again and see if that helps."

She was suddenly exasperated. Was he trying to take advantage of her by bringing up a kiss that she most emphatically had no intention of ever repeating? "Jay, I told you we're not going to talk about that kiss."

"I'm not talking about *that* kiss. I'm talking about the *next* kiss."

She threw up her hands in a gesture of frustration, splashing him with warm water, but she couldn't help smiling a little. This new teasing side of him kept her off center, and the sensation was both irritating and—darn him—rather exciting. She tried to match his banter. "How about this? I won't talk about the office if you won't talk about kissing me. Deal?"

"Deal," he confirmed gravely. "Nice doing business with you, Counselor. Glad we could work it out."

Her mouth was open to say something sarcastic, but all of a sudden she couldn't remember what it was. Instead, she stood there grinning at him, a helpless dopey grin that she supposed looked like the one that spread over his face.

"Oh, for heaven's sake," she said, her smile taking

the bite out of her words. "Let's find something else to talk about."

He was quiet for a second. "Okay, how about something serious? How about how sorry I am that Sara and the boys went back to Pennsylvania yesterday. I'd have liked to see them again."

"You liked the kids, didn't you?"

"Yes. I like big, boisterous families, and those boys were so cute."

She sighed. "I wish they lived closer. I don't get too much chance to be a real aunt to them."

When she handed him a plate, he took it, but didn't load it into the dishwasher. That meant she had to turn off the water and stop rinsing the next one.

"Valerie, have you ever thought about having children of your own?"

"I think I ought to concentrate on having a husband first," she said, trying to sound light. Instead, she sounded defensive, she thought. She tried again. "When I was engaged to Ellis, he used to say I should have a whole pack of kids, to give me someone besides him to mother."

"What did you want?"

Automatically, she turned on the water again and reached for a plate. "I guess he was right. I always wanted to have kids, but not...not with Ellis, as it turned out." The blush she felt across her cheeks was totally unexpected. "He's a nice man, though, Jay. I don't want to give you the wrong impression. I just liked him more than loved him, I guess." It was her old problem, she thought. Every man she'd ever cared about had ended up being just her friend.

Jay reached up and touched her cheek lightly, and the barest touch of his skin to hers sent electricity singing along her limbs. This would not do at all.

Hurriedly, she rinsed a plate. "Come on," she said, practically jabbing it into his ribs. "We've got to finish up here."

He took it from her, and Valerie was sure he knew the effect he was having on her.

They finished the dishes in silence. Whenever she looked up, she caught Jay watching her with a frank sensual interest that was downright unnerving. That he didn't try to hide it bothered her more. As soon as they were done, she told him she had to go home.

"Not on my account, I hope."

"Don't flatter yourself," she told him tensely, embarrassed at the glint of amusement in his eyes. "I've got to go because I'm tired and I have work to do at home."

"Of course," he agreed, guiding her into the family room.

Ginny wouldn't hear of her going. "It's only four o'clock," she protested. "I thought you'd want to visit for a while."

When Valerie hesitated, Ginny turned to Jay. "You don't have to go, do you, Jay? Couldn't you stay for a while?"

"I'd like that, of course, if Valerie can stay. How about it, Valerie?" His eyes were full of amused challenge.

"Oh, all right," Valerie capitulated, appalled at her lack of graciousness.

"You know what I'd like to do?" Ginny said. "Why don't we play something. Cards, maybe, or how about Scrabble?"

"Scrabble?" Valerie echoed.

"Scrabble," Jay confirmed. "A well-known board game based on a crossword puzzle, where you get points for making words."

"Of course I know what it is. I just haven't played in so long. Maybe years."

Valerie's mother brought out the game from a high closet shelf. "We used to have a good time with this when Valerie and Sara were both home," her father told Jay. "Before the girls thought being around their parents was a fate worse than death, we used to spend just about every Saturday night with pizza, popcorn, and Monopoly or Scrabble."

"Sounds like fun."

"It'll be fun again," Ginny said, eagerly turning all the wooden tiles upside down.

It was. All of them were good with words, and they laughed and teased when someone reached for an obscure one, sometimes sending the player to the dictionary to confirm that it was a legitimate word. Suddenly, after a run of excellent luck, Jay began to lose badly, not being able to form anything for a while. Then he came up with a six-letter word. He had spelled "kisses."

"That's a triple-pointer," he chortled, looking under the tiles for the score.

The game went on, with Valerie and her parents doing much better than Jay, although he scrutinized the letters on his tray intently. Once, he flashed Valerie a glance full of mischief. It surprised her. Knowing how competitive Jay was in court, she hadn't expected the lighthearted amusement in his demeanor. Finally, he got another word, this time "love." Gleefully, he picked new letters from the pile. "I think I'm on a roll."

"Pass," Valerie said after looking at her own letters.

Valerie's mother and father played, each forming a short word. When it was his turn again, Jay didn't hesitate. Building on "love" he managed "beloved."

"Get my points down, Valerie."

Then, Valerie had a good turn, putting her ahead. Her mother followed and formed "car," and after looking at his letters carefully, her dad passed.

"You did me a favor, Ginny," Jay told her happily. He used her word, "car," to form "caress."

Valerie shot him a quick, disgusted look, feeling like an idiot. She was supposed to be smart, but it had taken her four turns to figure out his moves. "Jay—"

"Boy, I sure had plenty of *s*'s," Jay interpreted innocently. "Those always help. Did you get my score, Valerie?"

"I think I've got your score, Jay," she said dryly. "And your strategy."

He flashed her an exaggerated wink that told her he was laughing at her. Looking around, she saw her mother and father exchanging knowing glances, and her predictable blush made her cheeks hot. Feeling it, she was overtaken by a distinct flash of irritation. "You may think you're so funny, but you're not going to win that way, you know. I intend to pound you."

And she did. Her mind was suddenly sharp, using every strategy to maximize her scores, coming up with odd words seemingly out of nowhere. Now Jay matched her intensity, scowling at his letters and coming up with good words, too. But his earlier goofing-off cost him the game. Valerie was unstoppable.

After it was over, Jay shook her hand gravely. "Good game, Valerie. You're a worthy opponent."

"Glad you noticed. It helps if you aren't distracted."

"I'll have to remember that."

Valerie had almost forgotten they weren't alone, until her mother cleared her throat noisily. "Well," Ginny said softly, looking from one to the other, "maybe next time we'll play Monopoly."

There was a moment's pause. "Does that mean I can come back, even with my bad manners?" Jay asked teasingly.

"I told Valerie you were to come every Sunday." She was serious. "Didn't she tell you?" She shot a glance at Valerie.

"Of course I did," Valerie said impatiently.

"She did," Jay confirmed. "I just don't want to wear out my welcome. I know this family time is important to all of you."

"You're always welcome here, Jay, you know that," Valerie's father said gruffly.

Valerie glanced pointedly at her watch. "Yes, well, now I really do have to get going. It's really late."

Her mother walked them to the door. "This was a lot of fun, you two. See you next Sunday."

"Thank you again, Ginny," Jay called as she shut the door.

Valerie headed immediately to her car. "You'll have to move your car first, so I can pull out."

He came close to her. "In a minute."

The day was beginning to wear on her. Truth be told, Jay was beginning to wear on her. "Look, I'm tired and it's freezing. I suppose you thought you were funny in there, but now I've got to go."

"I was funny."

"That depends on whether you like the game. Frankly, I don't."

He loomed closer. "I've been wondering about that, Valerie," he whispered. "Shall we see?"

This time Valerie knew he was going to kiss her.

She started to turn her head away, but he reached out quickly, capturing her chin with his hand. If he had kissed her with the hot, open desire he'd displayed the last time, she would have found the strength to resist him. Instead, he put his mouth gently on hers, as if genuinely interested in her reaction. She felt the warmth there and couldn't help it; her eyes closed. His lips were tender, soft, liquid on her own. They brushed hers, over and over.

Valerie heard her breath start to quicken. He must have heard it, too, because she felt the tip of his tongue come out to lazily trace her lips where his mouth had just been, coaxing and inviting. For a moment, she was caught in time, lost in that simple caress. Then she felt his mouth again, harder and hungrier against hers.

Quickly, she pulled her face away, forcing her eyes open. She had expected Jay's own eyes to be closed, in preparation for the passion he was beginning to arouse. Instead, she caught him watching her with a blue-eyed seriousness that startled her. She didn't like the thought that during their kiss, he'd been looking at her. She took a gulp of air, feeling ridiculous and suddenly very unsettled.

"This is my parents' driveway. Do you know how many neighbors could be watching us?" She gestured to the bright streetlight overhead.

He pressed her gently against her car. When he bent to snuggle his face into the open collar of her jacket, Valerie felt the cold tip of his nose make contact with her warm neck, felt the ends of his crisp hair brush her cheek. "Yes, I guess you're right." His voice was muffled. "I bet the whole neighborhood has been sitting up until midnight on a Sunday night to watch us kiss like teenagers in your parents' driveway. We ought to make it worth the wait.'' His chuckle was heavy on her neck, sounding as much erotic as amused.

He was making her crazy. She didn't understand the new Jay, but it didn't make any difference, because understanding the old Jay hadn't gotten her what she wanted. Even knowing why he'd gone away didn't make his having gone any less painful. Now she needed to defend herself against this assault on her senses, defend herself against his teasing and the sexual desire that simmered just below her skin whenever he started it. She had intended to speak lightly, matching his banter, but what came out had a completely unplanned edge to it.

"I don't know what you're playing at, Jay, but I think maybe the problem is that you haven't met many women since you came back."

He lifted his face from her neck. In the harsh light of the streetlight, she could make out every feature. There was no more sexy amusement in his expression. His hands gripped her shoulders. It hurt a little.

He shook his head slowly. "You think that's what this is all about? That I've gone too long without a woman? Like I have some kind of uncontrollable masculine drive that makes me devour any woman that's handy?"

"Well, not exactly." His words jarred and she tried to soften them. "I know lots of women must find you attractive. After all, you're nice-looking." Lord, that was an understatement, she thought, suddenly teetering on the edge of self-control. Her voice shook a little. "I suppose in a big city like Chicago, things are different."

"Different, how?" His eyes had a dangerous glint.

"Never mind." She started to look away, but he grasped her chin and pulled her face back to his.

"No, Valerie. You started this. I'd like to hear what's on your mind."

She was genuinely angry. She wasn't sure exactly where that anger had come from, but it was unmistakably there, inside her somewhere, like a long-buried seed that had been watered and had come to life. It made her bold. "Different, like lots of women will take whatever you're willing to give. *All* you're ever willing to give. They don't care that what you offer is only a fling."

He looked at her as if he couldn't believe what she was saying. "Maybe you're right, but I wouldn't know," he replied in a tight voice. "I'm not interested in having a fling, as you call it, in Chicago or in Amsden. Don't you know at least that much about me?"

"What other explanation can there be? You don't have to hide it from me. I know how men are."

"Good, very good. You can just lump me in with half the human race, draw some stereotyped conclusion and tell me all about what I'm feeling, can't you? What the hell makes you so defensive with me?" He was staring at her, as if, despite his rising frustration, he was genuinely puzzled. "You know me, Valerie. We go back twelve years."

She could stand anything from him, anything at all…except mention of the amount of time he'd spent moving out of her life. That thought pushed her over the edge, and she discovered that she wanted to hurt him, hurt him because he'd left, hurt him because despite what they'd shared he had never come back to her, and most of all, hurt him because of the certain knowledge that he would never be able to give her what she needed.

Her voice rose. "Every chance you get, you kiss me, and when you aren't kissing me, you're talking about it. You obviously like it when I...when I kiss you back. So I know you want to have sex with me." A defensive hardness crept into her voice. "Did you want to pretend it was romantic? Does it bother you that I call it what it really is?"

His hands on her shoulders gripped harder, and furiously, she tried to shake them off.

"Valerie, stop it."

"That's all it is, isn't it? Just sex. After all, aren't you the one who has so much trouble with real intimacy?" As soon as the words were out of her mouth, she was shocked at her capacity for cruelty. "Oh, my God," she whispered, shamed by both her words and the stricken look on his face. "That was a terrible thing to say. I'm so sorry."

"Good night, Valerie." He spat the words, jerking away from her. "I get your point, and I think you're right. It's time I took my uncontrollable masculine urges somewhere else."

CHAPTER FIVE

SHE WAS ASHAMED. All her life, she had been taught to respect other people's feelings. Her mother had taken in everything from stray puppies to foreign exchange students, saying that a good meal and comfortable talk were all that anyone, human or animal, really needed. She had grown up that way, and being thought of as understanding and empathetic was a big part of her self-image. For her to have thrown Jay's own words back in his face was unforgivable. All he'd done was tease her, a little unmercifully, sure, but not enough to rouse that huge wash of anger that had suddenly swept over her in her parents' driveway.

The anger frightened her. She sometimes allowed herself to be angry in court. But it was just that—she allowed it, in a calculated attempt to sway a jury to her way of thinking. She rarely felt anger coming unbidden. It was hideous, this uncontrolled churning that made her say horrible things and left her feeling weak and troubled.

It was Jay. He managed to get to her on every level. He had hurt her, more than once, and badly enough so that she had to defend herself against him. But she respected his intelligence and understood his complex moods. She wanted to help him with his troubled side. The teasing that was part of him now was more difficult for her to accept, but as long as it didn't come too close to her raw emotions, she enjoyed that, too.

It was good to laugh, to hear him laugh with her. The sexual desire was there and familiar by now. But the anger? That was something new. And it wasn't right.

She waited until ten o'clock on Monday morning and took him a cup of coffee as a peace offering.

"Here." She held out the little disposable cup. "It's good. Brenda just made a fresh pot."

Pen in hand, Jay was making bold black slashing marks through parts of the typewritten pages on his desk. He didn't look up. "Thanks. Just set it on the edge of the desk. I'll drink it later."

"Jay, I'm sorry. I was sorry as soon as I said what I did last night."

He looked up finally. He didn't look angry, but there was a tightness to his mouth. "Apology accepted."

She recognized the tightness; it was in her own throat. "Jay, please. I don't like to make people angry, especially not on purpose. I can't take back what I said, but I want you to know how sorry I am."

His voice was even and there was an unmistakable distance about him. "You're pretty careful about that, aren't you, Valerie? About letting yourself go, letting people see you upset. You're supposed to be there for other people when they're hurting, but they aren't supposed to see you break a sweat." He sighed a little, faintly. "Don't worry about it. As I just said, I accept your apology. Actually, I'm glad in a way about what happened last night. Not about everything you said, but about some of it."

She raised her eyebrows in surprise as he continued. "It's good to know where I stand. I know you've been saying things to me like, don't kiss you, don't come too near, but sometimes I thought... Well, never mind what I thought. I may not know what you want, but now I know what you don't. That's helpful."

"Well, okay," she said uncertainly.

He cracked a smile that had no warmth. "Believe me, you don't have to worry about my kissing you anymore. Now, you'll have to excuse me, Valerie. I've got the Michaels trial to get ready."

OVER THE NEXT FEW DAYS, Jay didn't seem to be deliberately trying to avoid her, but all of a sudden he had a lot of research to do, descending into the dungeonlike basement of the courthouse to spend hours in the law library. Twice she returned to her office after a day in court to find he'd left several books and articles on her desk about the law of sexual harassment. They had notes attached that said things like, "You need to look at this" or "Check chapter on evidence of harassment."

She didn't expect a note to contain a personal message, of course, and there was no need for him to use her name in greeting or even sign the notes. She'd got what she'd wanted—he was constructing a relationship with her that was purely professional—but she hated that she'd had to wound him in the process.

She neglected other work to read what he gave her. What an eye-opener. For one thing, the sheer number of articles on the subject was staggering. In looking through the articles on what constituted a proper investigation, she confirmed what she had already been told by Jay; ultimately, the bottom line was whether or not you believed what the victim was saying. Unfortunately, the best investigations seemed to be the ones in which the allegations became known. Once news circulated, if the allegation was true, other victims seemed to come forward.

But Valerie knew she couldn't allow this investigation to be openly discussed. The lawyers and courthouse personnel in Amsden were close, and the town loved gossip. The judge was an elected official, and his guilt or innocence wouldn't matter. The allegations alone would be enough to ruin a lengthy career, ruin an innocent man.

On Thursday, she returned to her desk at five o'clock to find Jay waiting for her.

"Oh, finally up from the bowels of the law library, I see," she started with what she hoped was the right touch of cheeriness.

He smiled at her. "Not exactly. Today, I went to the public library, and I brought you some reading material." He held up a forbidding-looking textbook. "This one has some psychological profiles on people who commit sex crimes." He saw her wince. "I'm sorry, Valerie, I'm having trouble not calling this by the words that seem to fit. But I'll try harder." He picked up a smaller book with a colorful jacket. "This is sort of pop psychology, the kind of stuff you see on talk shows, but it contains some interesting case studies. I think you'll find it helpful. I'll leave it and the rest of these books with you."

"Thanks. It'll be my weekend reading." She was relieved to note that he didn't seem in any particular hurry to leave her office. At least on some level, he must have forgiven her. "You haven't asked me what my mother's making for dinner this Sunday."

He shrugged. "It hardly matters, does it?"

She took a deep breath, feeling ashamed all over again. "Does that mean you're going to let our argument keep you home? You don't need to stay away, you know. My mom always wants you."

He smiled at her in a way that she could only interpret as gentle. "I want to come. I just thought it would be easier for you if I didn't."

She was touched. "Jay, it's not just my mom who wants you. I'd feel terrible if you were still so angry with me that you wouldn't come for Sunday dinner anymore."

He hesitated. "Okay."

"Okay, as in okay you'll come?"

Unexpectedly, his eyes twinkled. "Yes, I'll come. But only if we play Monopoly."

My, she thought, it felt good to laugh.

VALERIE FELT an overwhelming sense of relief at finally letting Judge Haskins know about Roberta's allegations. She had asked Jay to do it, and he spoke quietly and carefully.

"Basically, she alleges that on twenty-two separate occasions over the last six months, you made comments to her of a sexual nature, and that listening to you without complaint is a condition of her continued employment."

Valerie watched the judge's face carefully as he listened. He had a red face generally, and she couldn't tell if there was any new color there. But she had worked closely with her friend, and the look of shock on his face was unmistakable. His mouth tightened perceptibly and his head came up straighter. Finally, he spoke.

"This is a very serious charge."

"I'm sorry, Judge, about everything," Valerie replied.

"Yes, well. When do I get to say that it is all absolutely false?"

She held up her hand. "Please, Judge. Let Jay finish."

Judge Haskins spoke in a firm voice. "I didn't know there was more. Please, Jay, of course, continue."

Jay wet his lips, trying not to betray his nervousness. "Roberta further alleges that you touched her in a sexual fashion twice, one time injuring her breast."

"*What?*" This time his voice rose.

"She says you touched her twice—"

"I heard you, Jay! My God, I knew Roberta was a troubled woman, but this is too much."

"Judge." Valerie put her hand out, touching his lightly. It trembled violently under hers. "I knew this would be upsetting, but Jay and I are looking into the charges, and believe me, you'll be treated fairly."

He nodded, staring at her intently. "Valerie, that's all I ask. I trust you, you know." His gaze swept belatedly to Jay. "And I trust you, of course, Jay."

Jay nodded slightly.

The judge sat for a moment in silence. "Well, what's the next step? Will you be calling in the police?"

"Jay and I are going to do a preliminary investigation, if that's all right with you. Unless we think a crime has been committed, it won't ever go any further. In the meantime, I've sent Roberta over to Auto Title as a temporary employee."

The relief on Judge Haskins's face was plain. "Valerie, I'm sure you know that if this false accusation gets out in Amsden, it won't matter a damn when you discredit her story." Again, his voice rose. "I've been a lawyer for almost thirty years, a judge for twenty. It's so damned unfair that now I can be accused of something like this and my career ruined."

"I know, Judge." Again, Valerie's hand came out

to soothe him. "But Jay and I will do our best to see that the truth comes out, with as much discretion as possible."

"I know that, my dear. And I'll do anything I can to cooperate with your investigation."

"Thanks," Jay said briefly. The judge seemed to have forgotten him, but now the older man looked him over thoughtfully.

Jay spoke again. "You might want to think of getting your own lawyer, Your Honor."

Judge Haskins was quiet for a minute. "I've got Valerie to look into this, and you, too, of course, Jay. I think, for now, that's enough lawyers. If I need one, I'll get one."

"Right now, we're still waiting for the full details from Roberta," Valerie said. "Jay conducted some of these investigations for corporate clients in Chicago, and he knows what needs to be done. That's one of the reasons he's doing the investigation with me. He warned me this might not be over very soon, so I suppose I ought to warn you about that, too, Judge."

He nodded, looking suddenly older. "Keep me posted."

"We will, Judge, I promise."

As she and Jay prepared to leave the room, the judge sat still, lost in thought.

Jay had already started to open the door, when Judge Haskins spoke again.

"Jay."

He waited, his hand on the knob.

"I've given you a hard time since you got here. You're not going to hold that against an old man, are you?"

"Of course not. We're lawyers, Judge. We're all going to put our personal feelings aside on this one."

The judge visibly took in a heavy breath. "I appreciate that. You know, I've always liked you, Jay. Sometimes I get temperamental, but it doesn't mean anything. Remember that."

Jay felt his gut tightening, but forced back a sharp reply. "Well, if there's nothing else—"

"I'm going to make it up to you, for the way I've treated you."

Without waiting to hear more, Jay threw open the door and strode through it, and with a backward glance at the judge, Valerie followed.

"Jay, don't be angry," she whispered. "Couldn't you tell how scared he was?"

"I don't appreciate that kind of manipulation."

"It was blatant, I know, but couldn't you see it was pathetic, too? The man's career might be over, all depending on what we do."

Jay sighed as he felt the disgust suddenly leave him. He'd recognized the look in the judge's eyes, too. The man felt trapped, and no one understood that feeling better than Jay. "I know, Valerie. I won't hold it against him, I promise."

THE FRONT of the courtroom was crowded with auto parts, some up on the large table but most arrayed on the floor. An automobile door was the crowning touch, its dangling tag identifying it as evidence. Jay had had the part hauled in, even though he could have had it photographed, instead. He wanted the jury to see actual pieces of what had once been other people's vehicles. Of course, he'd had pictures taken, too. There were over a hundred of them, eight-by-ten color glossies.

The expert was going through them now, one by one.

Jay could feel his tension mounting. This wasn't just any case. It was his first big case, one of the critical steps to his building a career in Amsden. And most important of all, Valerie trusted him to pull off a guilty verdict. He knew he'd disappointed her one too many times in the past, but he had resolved that he was done disappointing her, in the little things as well as the big ones.

"Now, Mr. Callahan, I would like you to look at state's exhibit ninety-one, and I'll ask if you can identify the object in the picture."

"Yes, it's part of a dashboard from a Corvette."

Jay gave the photo to the jury foreman, and the jurors began handing it off, one by one. He focused his attention on the witness again.

"You've reviewed the service records of the last eighteen months of Robinson's Garage. Do those records reflect that, at any time, the garage was supposed to do bodywork on a Corvette?"

"No. Bodywork on Corvettes is very specialized, not something your average body shop does."

Jay glanced at the jury to make sure they'd heard. They were wearing the slightly glazed looks that told him they were fast losing their ability to concentrate. It was part of his strategy to bring in all this stuff, to overwhelm the jury with the physical evidence, but their eventual boredom was the price he paid. Strategically, it wasn't good for juries to be too bored, and he'd need to wrap up his questioning soon.

He asked a few more questions, then swiftly sat down.

"Your witness," Judge Haskins said from the bench.

Bob Vanette rose. "No questions, Your Honor."

That was amazing, Jay thought. He had spent a

good part of the morning slogging through evidence in a grinding, thorough manner because he thought Bob would question the prosecution's witnesses relentlessly. Had he done that good a job, or did Bob realize that Jay's evidence was solid? There was no real reason to take a bored jury back over all the evidence, but he'd expected Bob to do so because it was the way he always operated.

The judge was speaking. "Let's take a twenty-minute recess."

After the jury filed out, he and Bob took care of a couple of procedural matters with the judge, and then everybody else left. Jay looked around the empty courtroom for a second, before closing his eyes and leaning back in his chair. Being in front of a jury was exhausting. You had to be careful of everything you did, the way you dressed, the way you sat; heck, he thought, you couldn't even blow your nose. And Jay loved every minute of it, the game, the competition, the strategy.

He lifted his long legs and draped them over the arm of the seat next to him. The chairs were comfortable, but sitting at a table all day made him long to stretch.

His next witness was the key to his case. Lindy Cowles was his star witness, and he was worried about her. He'd gone over every question he intended to ask her, to make sure he knew what she planned to say. The sin of sins was asking your witness a question without knowing the answer. He'd even told her what to wear: dark suit, not too expensive, white blouse, no jewelry. But he couldn't help feeling that her detached attitude was all wrong.

At twenty minutes on the dot, the judge was back. When the defendant and the lawyers were in place,

Judge Haskins signaled for the jury to be brought in. It was time for Lindy Cowles.

Jay got through the preliminaries without a hitch.

"How do you know Jeff Michaels?"

"I was his girlfriend."

That was good, Jay thought. Better than "lover"; some of the jurors were elderly, and probably wouldn't think much of a young woman saying it so boldly.

"You're no longer his girlfriend?"

"No."

"Why is that?"

"Because I knew what he was doing in the garage. He and his partner were stealing cars for their parts, and he was stealing cars so they could be used to run drugs to Detroit."

Bob was on his feet. "Objection. Lack of foundation."

"Sustained."

Jay backed up and took Lindy Cowles through her story in elaborate detail. That she knew the garage well, that she had been there with Michaels many times. That Michaels knew exactly what Robinson was doing. She was answering again.

"Yes, I remember the day because I'd bought a new dress and I'd stopped at the garage to show it to Jeff. He and Mr. Robinson were talking, crowing about how a small town was the perfect place for their operation, that no one from the big law enforcement agencies ever came to Amsden. They said Blazers were fetching a better price whole because right now the drug dealers liked them for taking drugs into Canada. But they were going to cut up the Corvette for parts." Her big eyes filled with tears. "Jeff asked me what I brought, and I showed him my dress. He said it was pretty, and that if I stuck with him, he'd buy me a closetful.''

"What happened then?"

"Then, I knew I couldn't stand it anymore. I knew what Robinson was up to, but up until that moment, I didn't want to think Jeff was involved. I knew that even though I loved him, I'd have to tell somebody about what he was doing.'' The tears spilled over. "No matter what else happened, I wanted him to get help. He…he won't believe me, but I had to tell because I loved him.''

Great, Jay thought. It had gone just great. The jury was rapt. "No further questions.''

"Mr. Vanette?"

Bob got up slowly and approached the witness.

"Miss Cowles, how do you feel about Jeff Michaels now?"

"How do I feel?"

"Yes. Look over at him. He's sitting next to me. Do you feel sorry for him? Wish him well, wish him ill? What?"

Jay's mouth was open to object that the question was irrelevant. But the jury would want to hear this.

"I want him to get help. He has problems.'' Her eyes filled again.

"You care about him?"

"I care for him, deeply. I want what's best for him.''

Good old Bob, Jay thought. He was going over old ground, playing right into Jay's strategy. The jury would see her as a good, honest person. Lindy Cowles had gotten mixed up with a bad crowd, but she was doing the right thing now by telling the truth. He could almost hear the foreman reading the guilty verdict.

Bob pulled a small piece of paper out of his pocket and scrutinized it.

"Miss Cowles, do you know a woman by the name of Karen Markham?"

The change in Lindy Cowles was instantaneous. Gone was her ingenuous expression, and she looked suddenly older. Not just older, cheap, somehow, Jay thought. He sat up very straight.

"Miss Cowles? Answer the question," Judge Haskins told her.

She wet her lips. "Yes, I know Karen Markham."

"Who is Karen Markham?"

In the instant before she spoke, Jay knew he'd committed a grave error. He'd underestimated Bob Vanette.

Her eyes swept the courtroom without pausing to look at Jay. Instead, she shot a glance full of undisguised venom at Jeff Michaels.

"Karen Markham," she said, slowly and deliberately, "is the woman Jeff Michaels was sleeping with all the time we were together."

There was noise in the spectators' gallery, and as if from a long way off, Jay heard the judge banging his gavel for quiet. Finally, the crowd calmed down.

Bob put the paper back into his pocket. "Thank you, Miss Cowles. No further questions."

"Mr. Westcott? Does the state of Ohio have any further questions?"

There was, of course, no point in any more questions. "No redirect, Your Honor. The state rests its case."

It was a long afternoon, Jay thought, one of his longest ever. Bob put on his expert witnesses, but they didn't really contradict the testimony Jay had worked so hard on this morning. But he cursed himself for a fool. He'd suspected Lindy Cowles was too good to be true. If only he hadn't made so much of her charitable motives. If he hadn't, her woman-scorned performance might not have had the impact it did. He sighed, knowing he hadn't had a choice. The jury would have mistrusted her too much otherwise. His other evidence was only circumstantial, and the guilty verdict that had seemed in the bag only this morning was a lot less likely now.

The trial wasn't over until well after seven o'clock. The judge decided to give the jury an hour for dinner, and then have them deliberate for a while before going home.

"I'm not trying to rush you," Judge Haskins told them. "If you can't decide tonight, you can come back tomorrow."

Jay could see that didn't sit too well with some of the jurors. They obviously weren't looking forward to coming back. Well, neither was he. He headed for the men's room, almost stumbling with tiredness. It had been a long day, and it was probably going to be a long night. He couldn't go home while the jury was deliberating.

He looked in the mirror. With his heavy, dark beard, he already looked as if he could use a shave. He had hollows under his eyes.

His thoughts turned to Valerie. It had been two weeks since that scene in her mother's driveway, and she was right back to that understanding, kid-sister routine. If that had satisfied him once, it didn't now. And lately, he'd been wondering if that was all he'd wanted from Valerie, even then.

Her rejection hurt. But he wasn't running away from it, walling it off the way he used to when things hurt too badly. He let it hurt, and in a way he was glad for the pain. If he could hurt, he could feel.

He'd been too lost in thought to hear the door opening. "Jay? Are you still speaking to me?" Bob Vanette's voice was tentative. Jay looked in the mirror again and met his colleague's wide-open, freckled and boyishly genial face. Bob's straight brown hair was carefully parted, his warm eyes concerned.

"Sure. That was quite a dramatic stunt you pulled," Jay returned, admiration in his voice.

Bob flushed. "Thanks for the compliment, and thanks for not sounding surprised I could do it."

Of course, that was exactly what Jay had been thinking. He had to look down so Bob wouldn't see the truth on his face, and there was an awkward silence.

"You know, we've got an hour or so to kill. Are you hungry? Kaiser's is pretty fast."

Jay suddenly felt a little better. "Thanks, I am. Let's go."

Over cheeseburgers and French fries, they talked easily. Jay liked Bob, but it was the first time they had spent any time together outside of court.

"Are you interested in sports? As a participant, I mean?" Bob asked.

"Well, I played baseball in high school, and it got me a scholarship to Ohio State. I run a few times a week. How about you?"

"Basketball." Bob smiled happily. "Some of us get together every Wednesday night at the high school." He mentioned a few of the other players, and Jay recognized the names as attorneys who primarily did defense work. "It's as friendly a game as it can be with a bunch of lawyers playing."

Jay laughed and took a long pull at his coffee, finally beginning to relax.

"The thing is," Bob continued, "we could use another player, and I wondered if you might like to join us. Only if you have time, of course."

The offer sounded great. "Well, if you don't think the other guys would mind. They're all defense lawyers."

"They suggested I ask you."

Jay felt a warmth seep through him that had nothing to do with the hot coffee he was drinking. "I'd really like to."

"Good." Bob swallowed a bite of his cheeseburger before changing the subject. "Well, what do you think about the trial? What will the verdict be?"

"I think you won this one."

"Jeff Michaels is guilty as hell. You know it and I know it."

Jay nodded, looking Bob right in the eye. "But has the jury figured it out?"

Bob looked embarrassed, but he spoke, anyway. "I know we're supposed to be interested in justice, and all that, and I always tell myself it's okay to lose a case if the defendant is guilty, that it means the system is working. But, just this once...just this once, I want to win a big one."

Jay understood. It was hard to keep the competitiveness down, not get caught up in the game, and Bob didn't win very often. But he hadn't seemed the type to care much. For the second time that day, Jay thought he'd been foolish to underestimate him. It was a mistake he'd never make again.

"I'm a decent lawyer, Jay," Bob was saying. "I do great with contracts, real estate, stuff like that. I'm just not a trial lawyer. It doesn't come naturally to me. But I've been learning.''

Jay grinned. "Me, too. All you have to do is watch Valerie.''

"Not Valerie. She's good, but her style, all that feminine intensity, isn't something I can duplicate.'' He looked sheepish. "The person I've been learning from is you.''

Jay was genuinely astonished. "But I haven't been here that long, and I haven't done many trials myself.''

"But you have a great sense of timing,'' Bob said seriously. "I always ask too many questions. When I asked Lindy Cowles about that other woman today, it was all I could do to stop there. A month ago, I would probably have gone on for another half hour with more questions. But I thought about how you would proceed, and I realized I'd made my point, so I should sit down.''

Jay chuckled in spite of himself. "If you win, won't that be ironic?''

"Yeah.''

They were silent for a few minutes, and Jay realized he was no longer as worried about the outcome as he'd been. He'd done his best, and now it was up to the jury.

"Let's forget the trial,'' Jay suggested. "Why don't you tell me about yourself? Have you ever thought you might want to go out on your own, open your own practice?''

"I've thought about it,'' Bob confessed. "Every lawyer does, I guess. I think I'd like it. But I've got a personal reason for wanting to stick with what I've been doing for another year or so.''

Personal, Jay thought. That meant he didn't want

to talk about it. Or perhaps he simply didn't want to talk to Jay about it. Jay recalled the admiration for Valerie he'd seen on Bob's face and a sudden thought struck him.

"Personal usually means a woman," he said carefully, and knew he'd been right when Bob colored a little. "You don't have to talk about it if you don't want to. Valerie's very pretty, and she's so smart—"

"It's not Valerie, Jay."

A light went on in his head. "Meg."

For a moment, Bob looked panicked. "For God's sake, don't tell her," he entreated. "She hardly knows I'm alive, and she's seeing Dave Grau."

"What have you been doing about it?"

"What have I been doing?" Bob echoed, sounding perplexed.

"Have you asked her out?"

"No way. She's seeing someone."

"So you've just been hanging around, hoping someday she'll figure out you're there." Jay winced to himself. That had come out sounding more critical than he'd intended. But Bob was one nice guy, just the perfect, solid foil for an effervescent woman like Meg. It was obvious, though, that he had no idea how to go about interesting her.

"Dave Grau is not the man for her, and I think Meg knows that. She just needs a push to help her see it."

"Maybe." Bob sounded doubtful, and he dropped his gaze shyly. "You know, it's kind of awkward, talking like this. Could we talk about law again?"

Jay looked at his watch. He'd come to a decision. It was a very quick one, but it felt right, and he'd finally learned to trust his instincts when it came to things like this. "Actually, I'd like to talk about law, but we need to get back, and I want to show you something first.''

He insisted on picking up the check, and they went out into the cold street. ''Come on,'' Jay said, striding purposefully down the sidewalk toward the court-house.

A block before the courthouse square, he turned abruptly down a side street. Just two storefronts from Main Street, he stopped. He gestured to an old, two-story brick building, a little old-fashioned but still solid.

''What do you think of this building, Bob? It was for sale when I came to Amsden. I thought it was a great location for a law office. Close to the business district, close to the courthouse. The bottom floor could be rented out to a retailer, and the top could be divided into offices.''

''I've thought the same thing, but it's so expensive. The prices have shot up in town over the last few years.''

''I think the investment is worth it,'' Jay said confidently. ''There isn't an empty storefront on Main, and new businesses are coming in all the time. Amsden is booming. And out by the lake, nearer where my farm is, real estate prices are skyrocketing. When I think about that dairy, how we barely held on some years, how many nights I sweated with my mom over bills we couldn't pay, when my old man was out in some bar somewhere, I just—'' He stopped, thoroughly embarrassed at how much he'd almost said to another man about his feelings.

''It's okay,'' Bob said softly.

''You know about it, then?''

Bob nodded. Jay tried not to be irritated that even

the newcomers knew about his background. Gossip was just an inevitable part of small-town life.

"Anyway," he told Bob quickly, "I thought this building was worth it, and I had some spare cash from that outrageous salary they paid me in Chicago, so I bought it."

"You bought it?"

"Right." Jay stopped and let the news sink in. "And I'm looking for a partner. Someone who likes the paperwork, leaving me free to do the trials. How about it?"

Bob stood still for a moment. "Let me get this straight. You're opening up your own practice, and you want me to come in with you."

"Yes, but not right away. I need to become more well known in town, and of course, I need to give my assistant prosecutor job a year. I figured I'd go ahead and get the remodeling done, rent out the bottom floor, and by the time everything comes together, my year will be up and I won't feel bad about leaving the prosecutor's office." He paused. "I think it's a good opportunity, Bob. Why don't you think about my offer?"

Bob stuck out his hand. "I don't need to think about it. It's a great opportunity, and even I can see that. I'm learning to go with the flow, remember?"

Jay chuckled as they headed back to the courthouse. "Just keep our plans under your shirt for a while, okay? We've got a lot of details to work out between us, and I don't want everybody in town speculating about this. Their talk would make it hard for us to do our jobs."

He wasn't sure what he was going to tell Valerie, or when. He had no idea how she'd react, even though he'd certainly never promised more than the year's commitment that was standard with most legal positions.

At first, taking the job with Valerie had seemed a good way to learn the ropes of trial law and readjust to life in a small town before setting up his own practice. After Rossen, Sebastian and Bowles, he had been looking for a way to slow down, find some new values in his life, and he had hoped his childhood friend would hire him and give him a chance to come home to Amsden. At the time of his interview, he had been certain that was his motivation.

Of course, he hadn't been completely honest with himself about why he wanted to come home, even then, even after Allison and his miserable years in Chicago. He'd been lying to himself even after he'd resolved to tear down the wall he'd carefully constructed to keep him from having to make any emotional commitment. But he knew now that applying for this job had had much less to do with his wanting to learn new trial skills or coming home to Amsden than it had with needing to connect again in some way with Valerie.

But he had no choice about leaving the assistant prosecutor position eventually. It was entry-level, designed for someone just out of law school. He'd need to move on to private practice if he was ever going to earn a good living and support a family.

"We'll have to hurry," Bob said as they reached the steps of the courthouse. The hallway light was on, but they had to wait for the custodian to unlock the door and let them in.

"We're late," Bob said through clenched teeth as he watched the elderly custodian open the door, scraping the key in the lock with painful slowness.

"So what?" Jay felt suddenly careless.

"So, the judge is always looking to bite your head off. Why give him any more ammunition?"

Jay gave him a lopsided grin. "I think you're about to see another side of Judge Haskins."

Bob didn't get a chance to reply because the door was finally open and he was taking the stairs two at a time. They arrived in the courtroom to find the judge already on the bench.

"Where were you guys?"

"Out to dinner," Jay said briefly. "We tried to watch the time, but we couldn't get served and back here exactly on time."

"Sorry, Judge," Bob added quickly.

"Fine, fine," the judge said pleasantly, waving the apology away. Bob looked at Jay in open astonishment, mouthing 'what gives?,' and Jay couldn't help smiling.

Judge Haskins leaned forward. "After you two left, the jury asked for dinner to be sent in. They wanted to get started with deliberations instead of taking a break, and I decided to let them. They've been waiting with a verdict for twenty minutes." The judge's words wiped the smile off Jay's face. That had been awfully fast.

"Maybe we'll get a conviction on one count, a not-guilty on the other," Jay whispered to Bob, hoping inanely that they could both win.

"Come on, you're a better lawyer than that." Bob got into position at the defense table as Michaels was being led into the courtroom. "They bought your case, or they didn't," Bob told him. "The verdict will be all or nothing."

Jay knew Bob was right, and he settled in to wait for the bailiff to bring the jury in. He was nervous again. No one ever knew what a jury would do.

Finally, everyone was in place. There was always an air of drama in the announcing of a verdict, one of the few remaining great legal rituals. Judge Haskins was asking if the jury had reached a verdict, and the foreman was assuring the court that it had. The judge instructed the defendant to stand, and over at the defense table, Bob stood also. The foreman handed the paper **with** the verdict to Judge Haskins, who shot Jay an **odd** look. Oh, no, he thought. In spite of the fact that the outcome was out of his hands, it was damned hard to lose this case.

The foreman pulled himself up importantly before he spoke. ''On count one of the indictment, we the jury find the defendant guilty as charged. On count two, guilty as charged.''

The courtroom buzzed as the judge ordered Michaels taken into custody. Bob was asking for a poll of each juror, and the judge was obliging, but it was all over. Jay had to wait until the jury was excused, and he was dying to leave. There was only one person he wanted to share this victory with.

CHAPTER SIX

VALERIE OPENED the door cautiously. "Jay, you should have called first. I'm not dressed."

He could see that. Well, she was dressed, of course, but in a shapeless, pink chenille bathrobe that sported so many loose threads, it looked like a cat had clawed it. Valerie wore no makeup and her hair was mussed and she had never looked so good.

"I'm sorry," he said, his eyes shining. "I couldn't wait to tell you. The jury just came back on the Michaels case. We won."

She was pleased with the verdict, of course, and happy for him. "We didn't win, *you* won," she corrected. "Congratulations."

"Thank you."

Valerie hesitated. She couldn't just leave him out on the porch, not with him so excited about his victory. She should ask him in for coffee. After he'd told her his war story about his day in court, they could talk about the news she'd gotten on Roberta's case, the news that had simmered in her head all through this long evening. No, she thought hurriedly, it would be better to wait with that until morning. Jay was positively aglow with triumph, and it wasn't fair to tell him now that she had evidence Roberta was lying.

"Come in," she invited. "I've got coffee in the kit-chen, and I'll find you something to eat."

He followed her bare feet across the polished floor

of her foyer into the kitchen. He tried not to look too curious about the rest of the house, although he managed a quick peek into her living room. It looked cozy and restful.

When she invited him to sit down, he sat exactly the same way he always had, with his legs splayed a little, feet hooked around the chair legs. She had an irrepressible vision of him at her mother's table, in the old days. She pulled her thick robe more snugly around her.

"How about a sandwich? I bet you didn't get any dinner."

"Thanks, but I ate with Bob."

"You ate with Bob?"

"Yeah. I had a great time, too. He's a good lawyer, Valerie, and a super guy."

She must have looked surprised because he laughed softly. "You're right, I didn't realize it before, but I do now," he said.

Valerie poured him a cup of coffee and brought it to him, taking the seat opposite him at the kitchen table.

"So, I'm all ears. Tell me how you pulled it off."

She let him talk on and on. She recognized his need to come down off his self-induced trial high. She felt it herself when she won a big case; most lawyers did. He drank three cups of coffee, and she was glad it was decaf. If he didn't sleep tonight, at least she wouldn't be responsible.

"Well, you'll get your name in the paper," she said at last.

"Yep." His eyes sparkled with good humor. "So, boss. Time for a compliment. Did I do good, or did I do good?"

"You did good," she confirmed, and he laughed

out loud. He started to reach for her and visibly caught himself. Valerie wondered what she would have done if he hadn't.

What she had on underneath her robe was so transparently lacy as to be almost nonexistent, and in a brief flash of fantasy, she had him opening the thick robe to find the skimpy garment, had him thinking she was beautiful, had him pulling the thin straps from her shoulders.... With a wallop of self-realization, she knew that if he made one move toward her, it would be hard, maybe too hard, to keep herself from opening that one tie at her waist.

She gave him a shaky smile. "It's time for you to go home and get some sleep. You're running on nothing but nerves."

He pushed his cup away. "I guess you're right. But I wish I could win a big one every day. It makes the other stuff a lot easier to take."

"I know what you mean," she said cryptically.

"What's happened?" he asked quickly.

He was so in tune with her sometimes, she thought. He'd read something in her voice. "We can talk about it in the morning." She wanted him out, right now.

"Has something happened with Roberta's case?"

At the mention of Roberta's name, all the simmering desire went out of her, leaving her limp. Roberta, Judge Haskins, the investigation. She opened her mouth to tell him the news could wait, but she couldn't stop herself from filling him in on what she'd learned.

"This isn't the right time to tell you this, Jay," she began slowly. "But I got the personnel records from the county today, finally. I went over them while you were tied up with the trial." She put her hand out and touched his arm lightly. "I know you want to believe

Roberta. After all, she came to you with this. But on five of the twenty-two occasions she alleges that the judge harassed her, she wasn't even at work.''

She read the shock on his face, and she could think of nothing to do but make another pot of coffee. She wanted to take care of him. ''Are you sure you don't want something to eat?'' she asked uncertainly.

He gave her a grim smile. ''No thanks, but I'll take another cup of coffee. I'll just float home tonight, I guess.'' He studied his cup, thinking. ''It doesn't necessarily mean anything, Valerie.''

''How can you say that?''

''She might have gotten her dates mixed up. I'm sure she didn't keep a calendar and note when he made these offensive comments.'' He took a long pull at the hot coffee, wincing a little as the liquid burned its way down his throat. ''She was relating the incidents to other things, like when certain trials were scheduled, when he was going out of town, things like that. Under these circumstances, she could have unwittingly screwed up the dates.''

Valerie got up quickly and took her own cup to the sink. Putting a drop of detergent in it, she swirled the cup around, rinsing it carefully and putting it into the rack. ''Doesn't five times seem like a lot?''

''Yes, it does,'' he admitted.

''Doesn't this prove she's lying?''

''No, Valerie,'' he said quickly. ''I admit, it doesn't help her. But she could have made a mistake. We'll have to talk to her and the judge.''

She turned from the sink. ''I was hoping this would be the end of it.''

''I'm sorry, but it's only the beginning.''

She wished she could recapture the easy intimacy they'd shared before the subject of Roberta had come up. Nothing was worse than these tense, tiptoeing conversations they always seemed to fall into when they started discussing the sexual harassment investigation.

"Jay, I hate this," she heard herself saying. "I hate it that we can't talk to each other about Roberta's case without it being so...awkward."

He stood. "Me, too, Valerie." They looked at each other from across the room for a long moment. "Come here," Jay invited in a husky voice, holding out his arms.

Valerie came into them without hesitation and he folded them around her. She leaned her head on his chest and felt his hands press comfortingly along her spine. "We'll have to try harder," he whispered. "We've always been able to talk to each other."

"Always," she agreed, tears coming unbidden to her eyes.

She didn't know how he could know she was crying, but he did. He pulled her face from his chest and used his thumbs to gently wipe the corners of her eyes. "No tears, Valerie. Please."

"No tears," she repeated, trying to smile.

He smiled at her, his hands going to her upper arms. Almost unconsciously, he stroked her, and his smile turned slowly to a grin. "Hey, where did you get this lovely thing?" he teased her, his voice soft and low. "Did you raid a fire sale?"

She felt her lips moving in a tentative smile of her own. "It's my favorite robe," she confessed. "There's nothing like washing something lots of times to make it soft."

"Make me a promise, Valerie. No matter what, promise we won't let the judge and Roberta ruin our friendship."

Her voice was unsteady. "I'll try."

"Promise me."

It would be such an easy promise to make, here in his arms. Easy, but very dishonest. "I can't, Jay. I want to, but I can't. I don't know how I'll feel if...if things don't go right with the investigation."

His hands stopped stroking her, and they came to rest, one on each elbow. "I work for you, remember?" he reminded her gruffly. "You call the shots on this. In the end, you'll make the finding."

She felt a sharp stab of some emotion go through her, apprehension, and something she couldn't put a name to. "What will you do if you don't agree with my decision?"

His eyes darkened as he shook his head thoughtfully. "I don't know. Maybe I'll have some decisions of my own to make."

His voice was quiet, but she couldn't miss the implication of what he'd said. "Jay," she began quickly, "I don't have a choice. I have a responsibility to the county, and I have to make the decision, just like you said."

His hands gripped her harder, as if through them he willed her to understand. "I know that, Valerie. What I'm trying to say is I've made some promises. Not promises to Roberta, but to myself. Promises I have to keep, no matter what."

He was telling her he would leave if he didn't get his way with the investigation, she thought. After all, he would probably have to go if he insisted on pushing so hard on behalf of Roberta, in the face of evidence that undermined her credibility. When the judge was exonerated, it would be very hard for Jay to practice law in a town that had one courtroom; there was no way he'd stick it out if things got that uncomfortable. Jay's insistence on believing Roberta seemed like some kind of test he'd set himself. Why did he have to pick this as the one thing in his life he was determined to fight for?

Suddenly, she realized what was happening. The issues were all mixed up. The fierceness in Jay's voice told her eloquently that there was far more at stake than the judge and Roberta. And for her, too, there was so much more.

Now he was sticking by Roberta. But he had never stuck by Valerie.

"You always leave," she accused as she took a half step away from him. She hadn't meant to say it, and her own words took her by surprise.

His mouth had opened in preparation for more argument about Roberta. Instead, he shut it, looking completely nonplussed. "I always leave? What's that supposed to mean?"

"Jay, you should be able to figure it out." There was a quaver in her voice. "You always leave."

He started to reach for her again, but she took another step away and evaded him. Her own hand gripped the back of the kitchen chair.

He shook his head a little. "I don't know what you're talking about. I don't always leave."

"For starters, you left twelve years ago."

"Twelve years ago?" He was trying to think. "Twelve years ago, I went to Yale for law school."

"And you didn't come back!"

For a moment, her words hung in the air between them. "Valerie." His eyes were beseeching, his voice soft, but his whole body was taut as he faced her. "You of all people knew why I had to go. You knew I wasn't coming back. I *couldn't* come back, not to Amsden." He swallowed heavily. "There was nothing for me here then, nothing but shame and rage and pain.''

And love, she thought. *And commitment.* The kind of thing Jay Westcott could never handle. Hadn't he sat at her mother's kitchen table and told her that, not so very long ago?

She understood him; after all, she always had. He meant to do the right thing, but he would always leave, if not over disagreements about Roberta, then because of some other problem he would not be able to face, or some strong emotion he couldn't handle.

And the frightening truth was that in the face of all reason, she still wished she could go back into those warm arms and kiss that rough cheek, and feel all happy and excited. She wished she could promise they'd work everything out and—most impossible wish of all—that he could make enough of a commitment to give her the confidence that they could.

"THAT CAN'T BE IT," Roberta said through her tears. "I got the dates mixed up. Valerie, I made a mistake.''

"Five mistakes," Valerie reminded her gently. "I'm sorry, Roberta, but that's quite a few.''

She shook her head. "I wasn't exactly writing this stuff down in my diary. Can you remember what you were doing four months and two days ago?''

Valerie shot a glance at Jay, hoping for help. He looked away.

"These are unusual investigations, Roberta. There isn't a lot of physical evidence, and it isn't easy to figure out who's telling the truth—''

"You're right, Valerie," Roberta interrupted. I should have come to you and shown you the bruise I had on my breast. The one your precious judge put there. Would you have believed me then? Or maybe I should have taken him up on his offer, let him have sex with me, and then the boys in the lab could find the evidence you need.''

Valerie hoped her voice was level. ''Calm down, Roberta.''

''Calm down, Roberta,'' she mocked. ''Calm down? After what I've gone through? You're a woman, Valerie, and you ought to know how hard this is. What's the matter with you?'' Her voice rose. ''Of course, you're above all this. You'd just handle it if this happened to you, wouldn't you? You'd just tell him to stop, and that would be that, wouldn't it?'' The tears started down her cheeks again. ''Only, what if you couldn't stop it? You're strong, you're in control. What if someone took that from you? How would you feel if your boss told you he wanted to—''

''Roberta.'' This time it was Jay, and she looked at him uncertainly. ''This isn't helping, you know.''

She sat down, immediately deflated. ''I know.''

''I want you to think this over. Try to remember again what was happening when these comments were made. See if you can come up with something more solid.''

''I don't think I can.''

''You need to try,'' he said encouragingly.

''Roberta, I think we need to broaden this a little,'' Valerie started, looking at Jay again, this time for confirmation. At his slight nod, she went on. ''Is there anyone you confided in? Someone who could confirm some of what you say?''

''I told my sister.''

''Would she be willing to give us a statement?''

''I think she would, but what would be the use?

The judge would only say she's lying. After all, she's my sister.''

"We need to talk to anyone who knows something," Jay told her. "Can you arrange for her to talk to us?" He saw her nod. "Good. Now, how about employees, people who have reason to be in the courthouse?"

"I never told anybody, Jay, except my sister and you."

"I don't mean that. I mean, did you ever hear any rumors about Judge Haskins and anybody else? Ever hear any of the other women say they were avoiding him, anything like that?"

"They all said they didn't like him."

"Of course," Jay said impatiently. "Nobody really likes him." He smiled thinly at Valerie. "Except you, Valerie, so save your comments."

She tried to tamp down her irritation at his mocking tone. "Jay, I'm not sure how public we want to go with this right now. Maybe we should talk privately some more about how we want to conduct the rest of this investigation."

"I'm not going public," he told her, then turned to Roberta. "What I meant to ask you is whether anyone else ever seemed to be afraid of him, tried to avoid him."

She thought for a minute. "Brenda," she said at last.

Valerie was incredulous. "Brenda? Our secretary Brenda?"

"Well, I'm not saying he did anything to her, but she always seemed to stay away from him. When you'd send her down with something for the judge, she'd leave it with me instead of taking it to him."

"We'll talk to her," Valerie promised.

"Thanks." Roberta stood to go, but paused uncertainly. "Valerie, I'm sorry I got so upset. It hurts that you don't believe me, that's all."

Valerie got up from behind her desk and walked to the window, staring out without seeing anything. Sometimes, it was hard not to believe Roberta, and even harder not to respond to a woman who was so obviously in pain. When Roberta had been so angry at her, she had been almost convinced the woman was telling the truth.

"Valerie?" Jay prompted softly.

She knew she was supposed to say something to Roberta, tell her she accepted her apology. But at the moment, she couldn't turn away from the thought that had just struck her. Could Roberta be telling the truth? Jay believed her. But the certainty that the judge wouldn't do something as horrible as Roberta charged was firmly implanted deep inside Valerie. It was a gut feeling. No, she thought, it was more than a gut feeling. Roberta's allegations, for now, anyway, hadn't survived the first test. They weren't consistent with her days at work.

Behind her, she heard the door opening, and when she turned, she realized Roberta had let herself out. Jay was staring at her, disappointment in his expression. Well, so be it, she thought. She wouldn't always be able to please him. She lifted her gaze defiantly to his and caught a movement in the doorway.

"This isn't a good time?" Meg asked, sounding tentative.

"Come on in," she said, forcing a smile.

"You two aren't arguing, are you?"

"Not really." Jay sat down with a sigh. "Valerie, we have to talk to Brenda. Doesn't it seem unfair not to let Meg in on what's going on?"

Valerie couldn't miss the eagerness in Meg's expression. She addressed herself to Jay. "We promised the judge we would keep information about this situation on a need-to-know basis."

"Telling Meg is not spreading the news all over town, and she might know something that could help our investigation." He wanted her to tell Meg. Meg was her best friend, and if anyone could shake some sense into Valerie, it would be Meg.

"All right," Valerie capitulated. "Go on, tell her."

Jay outlined the allegations for Meg. She sat as silently as Valerie first had, taking it in, various emotions playing across her expressive face. She waited until he seemed finished before she spoke.

"Wow," she said, her voice barely above a whisper. "I knew you two were working on something big, but I had no idea *how* big."

Valerie realized she was glad Meg knew. It would help to hear the thoughts of a woman she trusted. "Well, do you think he's guilty?"

Slowly, Meg shook her head. "I don't dislike the judge as much as some of the lawyers, but I don't trust him the way you do, Valerie. I think he's too smart to get mixed up in something like this, though."

Jay's voice was sharp. "Smart doesn't have anything to do with it."

"It was a bad choice of words, Jay, but you don't have to bite my head off."

When he didn't apologize, Meg looked at Valerie in surprise.

"Don't mind him, Meg," Valerie said in a tight voice. "Jay's not very rational about this. Sometimes, not very adult, either." She shot a look at Jay, who got up and began to pace.

Meg leaned toward Valerie. "You're so close to Judge Haskins, Valerie. Has he ever made these kinds of suggestions?"

"Of course not. Do you think I'd let something like that go on?"

"No, I don't. He's never said or done anything to me, either, at least nothing any more abusive than he's said to half the town's lawyers. If Roberta's charges were true, would the judge have behaved this way only with Roberta? Does that make sense?"

"*I* don't think so," Valerie replied. She inclined her head toward the bookshelves, where Jay was prowling, restlessly scanning the titles. "It's Jay. He thinks it happened, and he keeps telling me I don't understand sexual harassment."

From across the room, Jay folded his arms over his chest, regarding them both with a scowl. "Think for a minute. If I stole something from Valerie, that would make me a thief, wouldn't it? Now, let's say she's the only person I stole from. You could bring in a hundred witnesses, all to say Jay didn't steal from any of us, and that wouldn't make me any less of a thief, would it?"

"I guess not," Meg agreed slowly. "I hadn't looked at it like that."

Actually, neither had Valerie, but she pushed the thought aside, to be considered later. "So, Meg, you see why things have been so strange around here the last few weeks."

"Oh, yes, but in a way I'm glad you're just upset about work. I thought maybe you and Jay weren't getting along."

Jay snorted, and Valerie blushed. Meg looked from one to the other. "Is there something else going on I'm not privy to?"

"No," they both said at once.

"Yes, well, I guess I ought to get out of here and leave you to whatever you were doing." She made no move to go.

"Did you want something when you came in?" Valerie asked her belatedly.

"It can wait."

"No, go ahead," Jay urged. "Do you want me to leave?"

"Actually, no," Meg said, smiling a little. "What I wanted to talk about has to do with both of you. Dave asked me to go with him to Sandy's on Saturday night, and I thought you two might want to come along."

"Sandy's is a fancy pub over near the lake," Valerie explained to Jay. "They have sing-alongs on Saturdays." In spite of everything, she cracked a smile. "That sounds like something you'd go for, Jay."

He looked uncertain, and Valerie realized he was still a little angry. "Meg, don't you and Dave want to be alone?"

Meg shook her head. "Dave and I can't be alone these days without our getting embroiled in an argument. I thought with both of you along, he might behave."

"Oh, Meg," Valerie said, impulsively taking her friend's hand. "Isn't it time to give up on him?"

Meg's lip wobbled. "I don't know. It's just...I'm in love with him."

VALERIE REGARDED the clothes spread over her bed with exasperation. No matter what she dragged out, nothing seemed right, and she had only a half hour before Jay picked her up. The problem was that most of her clothing consisted of suits and nice white blouses, things that were in excruciatingly good taste but much too conservative for a sophisticated, trendy night spot like Sandy's.

It was even more irritating to realize she cared what she was wearing. Obviously, she was out of practise when it came to dating. Not that this was a date, she hastened to assure herself. She had no intention of dating Jay, even if he asked her, and of course he hadn't. She and Jay were along to chaperon Meg and Dave. They were friends doing a favor for another friend. Sighing, she picked up a black mohair sweater from the bed. Maybe if she wore her paisley scarf with it...

Then she remembered the blouse. It was buried in the back of her closet where she'd stashed it six months ago, embarrassed that she had spent an outrageous amount of money on an item of clothing so totally unsuited to her life-style.

Pulling the blouse out, she looked at it again, wondering what had ever possessed her to buy such a thing. The price tag was still hanging from the collar, and she winced anew. But she slipped on the top.

Made of shiny, champagne-colored satin, lighter than her hair, the garment fit her like a second skin. Cut in a western style, with a high neck and a deep yoke edged with glittering gold fringe, the yoke itself was sewn with bits of leather and swirling gold braid and sprinkled with gold studs and blatantly fake gems. Funky chic—not Valerie at all. She never wore anything so obviously designed to attract attention, and the way the fringe exactly outlined the curve of her breasts made its clingy lines seem even more provocative.

Valerie turned a little, noting how the thick fringe moved with her and caught the light. She knew the blouse looked really good, but did she have the nerve to wear it?

And if she did, what would she wear it with? The darned thing screamed for a pair of tight leather pants, but of course she didn't have any.

She pawed through the closet. Ah, she thought, her jean skirt, her favorite until it had become faded and snug from too many launderings. It buttoned up the side, and Valerie had always been careful to keep every last button closed. Now she opened the bottom two, showing an inch of thigh when she walked. It wasn't enough to carry off the blouse, so holding her breath, she opened a few more. One more for good measure, and she was going to have to be very careful when she sat down.

She needed a belt. She pulled a sparkling gold one from a good dinner dress and buckled it around her waist. Now, if only she had a pair of cowboy boots, the fancy-dress kind with sky-high heels. Cowboy boots? Dear heaven, she thought, what had gotten into her? She slipped on a pair of suede pumps and made it downstairs before she could change her mind.

When the doorbell rang, it was all she could do to keep her fingers from buttoning her skirt again. Instead, she threw the door open, feeling nervous and a bit reckless.

Jay stood there, his smile of greeting frozen as he took her in. It was Valerie, but not a Valerie he'd ever met. She looked glittery and flashy and brazenly sexy.

She caught his expression before he could mask it and took a step back. "I knew I shouldn't have worn this," she began, her hand going to her throat, blushing to the roots of her hair. "The outfit isn't me at all, and if you'll wait a minute, I'll go change."

He stepped into her foyer and caught her wrist, bringing it down in front of her, causing the fringe to move with a shimmer. "It's not a you I've ever seen before," he admitted, his voice husky. "But please don't change. You look great, Valerie."

"Well, thanks," she said hurriedly, not able to let go of his eyes before noticing they had changed to a smoky blue. "I'll shut off the kitchen lights, and we can go. Hang on a minute." Trying to keep her dignity as she felt his eyes on her back, she headed toward the rear of the house.

Jay couldn't stop looking at her soft bottom, cupped snugly in that threadbare little skirt. When she came toward him again, he saw that it was more than half-unbuttoned, and he caught a good glimpse of thigh, thinly covered by a silk stocking. She didn't want him to touch her, he reminded himself, and he'd vowed not to try again until he was more sure of her feelings. Tonight, he didn't know if it was a promise he could keep.

But he took her coat and held it for her while she put it on, and he made inane conversation when he got her seated in his Porsche.

They weren't two miles outside of town, when he seemed to run out of things to say. That was a first, Valerie thought. She reached under her coat to yank on her skirt, overly conscious of his hand on the stick shift right next to her leg. She was suddenly glad she'd chosen this outfit and that it had such an effect on Jay. It was hard to admit that she wanted to be attractive to Jay, but there it was. She wanted to go somewhere like Sandy's with him, wanted it to be a real date, wanted him to be so turned on by her that he'd pull her into one of those soul-melting kisses by the time the evening was over.

Her mouth went dry at the thought. She'd accused him of wanting an affair with her, but what was it she wanted? Right now, she wanted him badly enough to peel those dress jeans he was wearing right off his thighs. Her thoughts were so boldly carnal they scared her thoroughly.

Quickly, she turned her head to the window, looking out at nothing as they passed through the rural areas outside of Amsden. Wearing the blouse did make her feel different, even inside; it had made her want to be daring.

But she knew an affair with Jay would never be enough. It would leave her hurting even more than before. She wanted it all, and all was something she could never have. Hadn't she learned that long ago? Hadn't she realized it again at her house after the trial? He'd said it himself. He might be changing, but he was the same man who'd left her all those years ago, the man who'd married someone as different from her as possible, the same man who'd admitted he couldn't handle intimacy. But if she didn't want an affair with him, why the deliberately provocative clothing, why the sweet rush of pleasure when he'd said he liked how she looked tonight, why—

"Tell me something about Sandy's." Blessedly, his voice broke her train of thought. "It must be some place, for you to get decked out like that."

"It's an English-style pub, more a city kind of place. A lot of people drive all the way from Columbus, it's gotten so stylish. On Saturdays, they bring in a guy from Cleveland who has a great voice and a lot of stage presence. He gets everyone singing along. They have a little dance floor, too."

"Sounds like fun. How did I miss it before?"

She didn't answer. If she had, she'd have told him

that if he'd stayed in Amsden, he wouldn't have missed anything. Don't start, she told herself.

"How about limbering up your voice?" she asked, instead.

He laughed. "Like this?" He started singing a set of scales, opera-style, so exaggerated that she couldn't help laughing, too.

"Help me with this," he suggested.

"Oh, no. I can't sing at all."

"How are you going to manage a sing-along, then?"

"Well, when everybody else is singing, I can, too, quietly, of course. But not in this little car with just you."

A smile slanted the corner of his mouth. "Afraid of letting down your hair, showing me a less-than-perfect Valerie?"

"Shut up, Jay," she told him, but unexpectedly, she heard her voice caressing the words.

"Nothing much shuts me up. You should know that by now, Valerie." He took his eyes from the road to look at her for a split second. "But it might be…interesting…to see you try. How would you go about it, do you suppose?"

She pressed her knees together to keep them from knocking. "Just drive, Jay. We're almost there."

He didn't say a word, but she could tell he was laughing at her. He knew the effect he was having on her, and he was obviously enjoying it thoroughly. This was going to be a long night, and she almost wished she had worn her black mohair sweater.

Meg and Dave were waiting outside for them when they drove up. Jay had met Dave. The tall, thin, sinewy young man with short, sand-colored hair had testified in court on several occasions. He looked strong and might have been handsome except for the faint pallor of his skin.

Inside, Sandy's was smoky, dark and very crowded. Loud talk and laughter swirled around Valerie as they looked for an empty table. They found one of the last ones, too small for four, but Dave brought over two more chairs and they squeezed around it. Valerie ended up so close to Jay, she was practically on his lap. For the next few minutes, she fingered her drink with one hand and tugged at her skirt ineffectually with the other. "Relax," he finally whispered in her ear. "You look fine." He reached down and squeezed her hand reassuringly, making her feel like a sixteen-year-old.

"I'm Gary. Everyone remember me?" a voice boomed through the microphone. After the patrons shouted greetings, his voice came over loudly again. "Is everyone ready to party?" The crowd shouted, "Yes!"

Valerie looked up to see a middle-aged man sitting on the small stage, experimentally plucking the strings of an electric guitar. "Who wants to sing tonight?"

There were shouts of "we do," "me," and "us." Across the small table, Dave Grau's face lit up. "This guy's great," he told Jay, just before he planted a smacking kiss on Meg's cheek. "Ready to party, honey?"

"Oh, yes," she said, smiling at him.

Fortunately, this seemed to be one of those evenings when Dave was going to have a good time, Valerie thought, relieved. He seemed in high spirits.

Song sheets were being passed from hand to hand and the group was starting to sing as Gary led them from the stage.

"You're breaking my heart for sure," the crowd sang tunelessly, rocking back and forth, and Jay joined in enthusiastically.

Soon they were all singing, joining with a hundred other voices in country and folk lyrics. They moved on to some silly tunes, following the words on the song sheets. Things got more raucous as the night wore on. The waitress came over to their table again and, draining his glass, Dave ordered another round of drinks.

"I'm going to sing you one of my own," Gary finally told them, and the guys at the bar roared their approval. "Now, all you have to do at the end of every line is yell, 'I want to spoon with you.' Can you do that?"

"I want to spoon with you," they shouted back.

"Right, you got it." He smiled and began, "Under the stars, the stars so high..."

"I want to spoon with you!"

"I'll hold you tight and hear you sigh..."

"I want to spoon with you!"

The song went on and on, the lyrics moving from tenderly old-fashioned, to funny, to blatantly suggestive, and even after Jay put his arm around her shoulders, Valerie shouted with the rest.

It was finally over, and people stamped their feet, pounded the tables and roared for an encore. Gary obliged with a soft love song, and as the last notes faded away, Jay leaned close to Valerie's ear. "I want to spoon with you," he sang, his voice sliding over the words, more whisper than song. Dreamily, Valerie started to lean toward the sound.

A hand slapped the table right in front of her. Startled, she looked up to see that it belonged to Dave Grau. His cheeks were unnaturally flushed. "Jay, old man," he called over the noise of the boisterous crowd, "you haven't finished your beer, and I just ordered you another."

"No, thanks, I'm driving," Jay said firmly.

"Oh, come on," Dave began, but Meg quickly shushed him.

On the stage, Gary was taking a break and recorded music was playing. The small dance floor was filling up quickly.

"Let's dance, Valerie," Jay suggested, already on his feet and pulling her to follow him. Valerie shot a quick glance at Meg. She nodded that everything was all right, so Valerie allowed Jay to lead her to the dance floor.

There were so many dancing couples that it was hard to find a few square feet of space for themselves. Valerie put her arms around Jay's neck and, in the crush of people, he had no choice but to hold her close. Not that she minded being held so tightly, she thought, willing herself into the dreamy state she'd been in a few moments ago. It was hot, and none too comfortable, but Valerie hardly noticed. She was conscious only of the music and Jay's arms around her, his cheek on her hair and the scent of the skin of his neck.

The song ended and another began. Jay didn't let her go, but continued to move in time to the music. It was funny, she thought. In all the years she had known him—all the graduation parties and the weddings they'd both attended, she couldn't remember ever seeing him dance. It must be like the singing, she thought, something new he'd picked up.

"You smell good," Jay murmured, his arms tightening around her waist, his hands splayed across the small of her back.

"So do you," she whispered back before she thought. She heard and felt his heavy chuckle rumble in his throat as she buried her blushing face into his shoulder.

"I hope they play these slow records a little longer, instead of the sing-along," Jay murmured a few minutes later.

"I thought you liked the sing-along." But she knew what he meant, even before he said it.

"Believe me, I like this a whole lot better."

She had no idea how long they stood there, thighs lightly touching, swaying together. She lost track of how many songs were played. Only Gary taking the stage again brought her out of her half-conscious state, and she was startled to notice that the music had ended. When Jay stopped, she had to catch herself to keep from stumbling. Smiling at her with heavy-lidded eyes, he caught her around the waist and began to lead her back to the table.

There reality set in fast. One look at Meg's set, white face and Valerie knew with a sinking heart that she and Dave had had another argument. "Meg," she started to say at the same time Dave lurched to his feet.

"I've got to take a piss," he muttered. "Get me another beer while I'm gone."

"You don't need any more, sweetheart," Meg said plaintively, and Dave swore at her viciously.

"Meg, shut up and order me a beer."

He disappeared into the crowd, and as Gary began to sing again, Meg put her head in her hands.

Jay quickly assessed the situation. "I'm going to follow him, Meg. I'll get his car keys, and then I'll call a cab for you both."

"Thanks," she said briefly, her small face pinched with misery.

Jay threaded his way between the tables in the direction Dave had gone. The sing-along had started again, and the throng of revelers had begun to clap and rock back and forth; it wasn't easy to get through.

After Jay had gone, Valerie took the seat next to Meg. She reached out and squeezed her friend's hand lightly. "What happened?"

Meg didn't answer for a moment, staring down at the slick wood of the table as if for inspiration. "I don't know, I really don't," she whispered, and Valerie had to lean forward to hear her. "He's drunk, I guess, only he didn't have that many, not enough to explain how really out of control he is. One minute we were having a good time, and the next he was finding fault with me. He told me I wasn't dressed right, and he asked me why I didn't wear something like you had on."

"I'm sorry," Valerie said quietly.

"Don't be." She managed a thin smile. "You look fabulous, Valerie, and if I didn't feel like crying, your effect on Jay would be really fun to watch. I thought he was going to rip your clothes off before you could leave the dance floor."

Shakily, Valerie took a sip from Jay's untouched beer. "What a night."

Meg agreed, sounding despairing as she continued. "So, anyway, after Dave went on about my appearance, he asked me why I wasn't nice to him anymore. He meant because I haven't let him stay over in a long time." She averted her eyes. "I could have changed the subject, I guess, but instead I told him the truth—that he hadn't been nice enough to me lately for me to feel like being *nice* to him. You can imagine how things went downhill from there.''

Valerie could imagine. She and Meg sat quietly together, half listening to others around them having a great time. Valerie sipped slowly, but she had finished half of Jay's beer before he joined them again.

''Has Dave come back?''

Meg half rose. ''You didn't find him?''

He shook his head, looking grim. ''The men's room is jammed,and I banged on every stall door, making a fool of myself. Then I think I checked every inch of this place.''

''He left me here,'' Meg said, sounding incredulous. ''He's done some cruel things, but...''

''You might be better off.'' Jay spoke firmly, but there was sympathy in his voice. ''He's had too much to drink, and I don't think you'd want to be in a car with him tonight.''

''He shouldn't be driving,'' Meg agreed quickly. ''Don't you think a police officer would know that?''

''Stay here and I'll check the parking lot. With any luck, he'll still be there.''

Meg told him what kind of car Dave drove and Jay was off again. Valerie took Meg's hand once more while they waited.

''This is it, Valerie,'' Meg said at last, looking exhausted but resigned. ''I can't deal with Dave any longer.''

Valerie nodded, trying to hide her relief. ''I'm sorry,'' she said simply, resisting the urge to tell Meg she had made the right decision. They fell into a silence that lasted the short time until Jay returned.

''I think he's gone,'' he told them both, sinking into his chair. ''I hope he manages to get home all right.''

They sat in silence for a few minutes, each lost in thought. Finally, Meg roused herself. "I'll go call a cab."

"Don't be silly. We'll drive you home," Jay told her.

"I'm not up to sitting here, and you are—were," she corrected herself, "having a great time. Don't mind me. I ought to be used to this by now."

Both Valerie and Jay insisted she go with them. Valerie couldn't speak for Jay, but for her, the night was over.

When they got to the parking lot, Jay looked at the inside of his car. "This car is really useless," he said dryly. "You two are going to have to scrunch together in that bucket seat."

Valerie got in first, trying to make herself as small as possible as Meg squeezed in beside her. Jay came around to his side of the car and got in.

"Valerie, can you get a little closer to Meg? I won't be able to work the shift."

She was wedged almost on top of him, but there was nothing romantic about the position. For the thousandth time in her life, she wished she were skinny and petite. Her leg was cramped, and she knew she was showing practically her whole thigh in her ridiculous outfit. Meg didn't complain, but the woman's misery held sway over the three of them. It was a very long ride to Amsden.

"Do you want me to stay with you tonight?" Valerie asked when they got to Meg's house.

"No, I'm okay."

"Are you sure, Meg?" Jay asked. "Maybe Valerie should stay. You don't know what kind of mood he's in, and if he shows up at your place tonight, he could be nasty."

"He's never hurt me, Jay," Meg assured him. "And if I have to, I can call the cops." In spite of herself, she giggled at the irony. "I'll just get one of his buddies out here, I guess."

"You can call Ellis," Valerie suggested. "The chief will take care of you."

"It's okay," she assured them again. "I'm all right." Maneuvering in the tight space, she managed to flip her door handle and very nearly fell out onto the driveway.

Jay insisted on walking her to her door, and Valerie stretched gratefully. She knew it would be impossible to get back into the daring mood she'd been in earlier, and she didn't even try. She watched Jay as he hugged Meg quickly and waited for her to let herself in. In so many ways, he was a good man, she thought, and if Dave hadn't ruined the evening, she could only speculate on what might be happening between them now.

In another minute, he was settled beside her, letting frigid air into the car, radiating coldness from his leather jacket. "Well, that's that, I guess. Do you want to go home, or somewhere else?"

"Home," she said firmly. "I'm sorry, but I'm not up to anything else tonight. I'm too sad and tired."

He let out his breath on a long sigh. "Me, too," he admitted. "This was upsetting as hell. I can't see why Meg puts up with that kind of treatment from anyone. There are a lot of decent men out there." He was thinking of Bob Vanette as he started the car and drove Valerie the few blocks home.

"She says this is the end for the two of them. I hope so, anyway."

He stopped his car in her driveway and followed

her up the porch steps. "Thanks, Valerie." He hesitated for a moment. "You looked beautiful tonight."

"Thanks yourself. Until Dave ruined the evening, I was having a good time. A really good time."

"Me, too." There was another moment's silence. "Does tonight change anything?" He hurried on before she could answer, as if afraid she'd say it didn't. "I mean, for one thing, can I drive you to your mom's tomorrow, instead of you meeting me there?"

"Yes, that sounds good."

"Okay." He stood there a second, looking uncertain, but he made no move to touch her. "Well, good night, Valerie. Sleep well."

"Good night, Jay. Please be careful driving home."

He started back down the walk, then turned to her again. "I'll see you tomorrow."

She felt a strange reluctance to let him leave. The mad, reckless urge to take him upstairs to bed had fled in the aftermath of the scene with Dave and Meg. She considered his question. Does tonight change anything?

As she went upstairs alone, she unbuttoned the rest of her skirt. Then she hung her satin blouse again, all the way in the back of the closet where she kept the things she never wore. *Does tonight change anything?* Valerie hadn't had a chance to find out.

CHAPTER SEVEN

FOR ONCE, Jay seemed in a hurry to leave the Brettinger home. It wasn't long after they had the dishwasher loaded that he said they ought to be going.

"Don't you want cherry pie?" Ginny asked, clearly mystified that he would want to go before she served dessert.

"Thanks, but I'm stuffed, and I'm tired, too. I need to make it an early night."

Valerie was surprised, but she was tired, herself. After Jay had left last night, she hadn't slept well. She'd lain awake thinking about Dave and Meg. Dave's behavior was so strange, so intense. He seemed to feel both his highs and lows more strongly than other people. Last night's temper tantrum was no more vicious than a number of them she had witnessed over the last couple of months, but for him to stagger off and leave Meg was inexcusable. Valerie was glad her friend had finally decided to end the relationship, but she knew Meg would be hurting for a long time.

She'd managed to keep from thinking about Jay, but when she'd finally fallen asleep, Valerie had dreamed about him. They were the same dreams over and over, misty, hot dreams. In all of them, she'd been making love to Jay with wild abandon, the kind of letting go she had never permitted herself with anyone before. She'd awakened several times, gasping and embarrassed at the intensity, but wanting to sleep again so the dreams could replay.

The most disturbing one had occurred just as dawn was breaking. Jay had been with her in the bed, whispering to her, and singing to her. And smiling. Then he stopped smiling and moved over her, and she could feel his heaviness as if his body were really there. He'd enjoyed her body thoroughly. He'd told her so. And she'd liked his, too, liked it with a fervor that had shaken her. Then she'd reached for him again and he wasn't there. He'd made love to her, and he'd left her.

The dream had been so real that when she had first awakened, she'd actually felt the other side of the bed, expecting it to be warm from his presence. She hadn't slept after that.

"Valerie?" Jay was holding the car door for her, and she realized she was standing next to it, probably with a stupid look on her face. She realized that she only dimly remembered kissing her dad goodbye. Funny that last night's dreams could seem more real than what had happened two minutes ago. She shook her head to clear it.

"I hope you didn't want to stay," Jay said a moment later as he turned the corner.

"Not really. I'm tired, too."

Jay shifted, adding more speed as they reached the straight stretch that led into Amsden. "I'm not tired. That was just an excuse. It gets dark so early in the winter, and I want to show you something while we've got plenty of daylight."

A nervous smile played at the corner of his mouth and she was suddenly very curious. "What?"

"You'll see in a minute," he promised, stopping right in the middle of town. Amsden was deserted, the way it always was in the off-season on a Sunday afternoon. He pulled up to the curb and got out, and she scrambled to follow.

"Now, what am I looking at?"

His hand swept up the high rosy brick facade of a large building, its first-floor window boarded up with plywood. It stood in sharp contrast to the colorfully painted Victorian storefronts around it. "I'm showing you a building that's going to get a face-lift. And I'm showing you—" he paused for effect "—the future home of Westcott and Vanette, Attorneys-at-Law."

The news didn't quite register. "The future home of…"

He was smiling, but his eyes looked anxious as he waited for his announcement to sink in. He didn't have to wait long.

"You're opening a law practice with *Bob Vanette?*"

"Yeah, isn't it funny how things turn out?" Now that he'd gotten up the courage to tell her, he wondered why he'd been so nervous. Valerie was practical, and she would surely see this was a great opportunity for him. And for her, if she'd only let him plan a future that included them both. "What do you think?"

"I think it's up to you, of course," she said automatically. But she was stunned, and she let her mouth make words without thinking about them. "I didn't know you and Bob were so close. When did all this happen?"

"The idea to go in with Bob is recent. But I bought the building when I first came back. I figured, with its location, I'd need to move fast."

He bought it when he first came back, her mind repeated, adding an edge to the words that hurt. *Used* was the only word that fit the way she felt, Valerie thought. She'd agonized over hiring Jay, wondering if she could handle him coming home, seeing him down the hall from her all the time. Then she had hired him, and found that she loved working with him every day. She'd thought he liked it, too, thought it meant something that they shared so much, and all along what he'd wanted was any old job so he could come back to open his own practice.

Yes, she felt thoroughly, totally used. Correction. Used one more time. His plans to leave her and open his own office were just one more proof that he was never going to commit to anything for long, not to a job, not to a town, not to a real relationship with a woman. And as usual, he seemed quite willing to hurt even the people he claimed to care about, as long as he got what he wanted.

"Good luck," she managed to say.

Jay reached out to take her hand, but she brushed it aside. At the same time, she moved, putting a few paces between them. He started to explain. "I'm not going to do this right away. You were kind enough to hire me, and I have every intention of giving you your full year in the office, even more time if you need it."

"Kindness had nothing to do with it. You were qualified, so I hired you."

"Just as if I were someone off the street."

"Right. Just as if you were someone I'd never met."

This was going as badly as he had feared, Jay thought. All along, he'd known she wouldn't like his plans without being able to figure out exactly why she'd disapprove. He didn't know what she wanted him to say.

He kept his voice even. "Valerie, you love being the county prosecutor, and you're great at it. It's an important job, to make the kinds of decisions you do. But there's only one county prosecutor, and I don't make those decisions. Did you really think being an assistant would be enough for me, for the long term?"

Thinking back, she realized that she'd known from the beginning it wouldn't. He was too smart, too experienced, too ambitious for the entry-level position. All the time they'd spent together since his return melted away and she was back to day one, wondering why he'd come home and why he wanted to work in her office. Well, now she knew, and anger mingled with the hurt of yet another defection.

"Jay, if this is such a good move for you, you don't need to wait." She held out her hands stiffly in front of her, studying them to keep from having to look at him. "After all, I've never tried to hold you back."

He took a step toward her. "That's not what I meant. I want to stay. Working with you means a lot to me. It's just that the job itself won't always be enough, so I had to plan."

"You don't owe me any explanations."

"Maybe not, but—"

"But nothing, Jay! I'm the one who's supposed to understand you, remember? I know exactly why you're doing this." He would never change. He would always leave. No matter what happened, she needed to remember that. Really, he was right; for her peace of mind, they shouldn't even be working together. It would be better if he were gone. "Go ahead. Leave. Do whatever you think is best for Jay Westcott." Angry at him, angry at herself for every moment of the last few months that she had allowed herself to hope things might someday be different, she swiped quickly at a wayward tear.

He shook his head slowly. "I'm not leaving. Not this way."

"Twelve years ago—"

His own voice rose as he interrupted her. "It was twelve years ago, Valerie! Why do you keep bringing that up like nothing's changed?"

Sobs began to shake her, and seeing the combination of frustration and mystification in his eyes infuriated her. Losing her last vestige of self-control, she stamped her foot, looking directly at him. "Because, damn it, twelve years ago, I loved you!"

He went suddenly still. "Oh, my God," he muttered. His eyes were twin lakes of blue, bottomless, threatening to pull her under. They stood a couple of steps apart, both breathing hard. She tore her eyes from his and turning, started to run.

He took two long steps, caught her and pulled her against him. "I'm sorry, Valerie," he started to say, but had to stop to concentrate on holding her. Panting and squirming, she struggled to get away.

"Let me go!"

"We need to talk."

"Jay, let—me—go." She wormed her fists upward to push ineffectually against his hard chest.

Ignoring her furious protests, he swept her up in his arms and marched to the car. He put her down, somehow got the passenger door open and pushed her inside. He tried to be gentle, but Valerie's flailing arms and legs made that impossible. Shoving her toward the shift, he wedged in beside her and shut the door behind him. Then he held her tightly. When she finally stopped struggling, Valerie ended up mostly on his lap, her feet on the driver's seat.

"Shh," Jay soothed as her protests gave way to great, heaving sobs. The tears that hadn't been shed twelve years ago were overflowing.

"You love me," he whispered finally.

"Loved. Past tense," she managed to say between sobs.

Loved. Past tense, he repeated to himself. That hurt, hurt like hell. "You never told me that."

She looked up at him finally, streaky tears marring her cheeks. "Jay, we made love. How could you not know how I felt?" She sighed miserably. "I never said the words, but you didn't give me the chance. You were always too busy telling me how you couldn't wait to leave Amsden. And do you know what hurt worst of all? Even though I understood why you had to go, what really hurt was that you never came back."

Jay leaned back against the seat and closed his eyes, feeling her soft body pressed against his. Of course, in some place deep inside him, he'd known how she'd felt, but he hadn't been able to deal with the truth. Instead, he'd worked so hard to convince himself that they were just good friends, special friends.

And on the night they'd made love, he remembered how he'd walked her in the dark to her car afterward, then taken her hand and told her in a halting voice how sorry he was it had happened, that he had gotten carried away, that he took full blame, as if what they had done was somehow wrong, a mistake. At the time, he'd known he was hurting her, but he couldn't seem to help himself. Now, for the first time, he faced up to just how much pain he must have caused a vulnerable young girl. He was her first lover, and afterward he had told her how special she was as a *friend.* How could even he have possibly been that callous and selfish?

Because he *was* selfish back then, he thought. Because he was so desperate that there be no ties to keep him in Amsden. As special as she was, at that time, he'd seen Valerie as one more obstacle to overcome in his rush to leave.

The amazing thing was that he'd really convinced himself that the intense coupling on a dark, high hill in the moonless night had resulted from a combination of youth and sympathy, opportunity and longtime friendship. Of course Valerie could never forgive a man who had held her and joined with her, kissed her and cried, and then never seen her again.

And she had loved him.

He'd been so happy when he came back to find her still here, still unattached. And all the time, he hadn't realized he'd blown his chance before he'd even set one foot back again in Amsden, Ohio.

Valerie was still crying, and her choked words of a few moments ago still burned him. *Loved. Past tense.* Pride—hard-earned after the shame of his childhood—kept him from telling her he loved her. Instead, he argued with her. "I don't see how you could have loved me. You were only eighteen."

"Yes, I was young. We both were."

Faintly encouraged by her agreement, he forged ahead. Would she understand? "I wasn't a very lovable person back then, Valerie. I kept all my emotions so far away from me that I didn't even know how screwed up I really was. You might have thought you loved me, but I don't see how you could have."

"I did," she insisted, her voice muffled by his chest. Well, he thought, at least she had stopped crying.

"I don't think I was capable of loving you back, not then. It was for the best that you didn't tell me. If you had, I would still have hurt you, even worse than I did." Be honest, he instructed himself. She deserved his honesty, after all these years. "I've had twelve years to grow up, and believe me, I've needed every one." He stroked her hair, then laid his cheek against the silky waves. "I'm sorry."

She shook her head. "Don't keep saying that. I hate that."

In spite of everything, Jay smiled a little. "I know. I hate it when people feel sorry for me, too."

She sighed against him, finally calmer. "Will you let me out of the car now? I'd like to get some air."

He used his handkerchief to wipe her streaky face, and she endured his ministrations with a grimace. Then he let her out, and went over to the driver's side.

Pulling the frayed edges of her pride back together, she straightened her spine. "My house is close by. I'll just walk home."

"Get in, Valerie," he commanded. "I'm not going to chase you down the street. Haven't I already proven that today?"

After a moment's hesitation, she got in again.

He started the car and pulled away from the curb. "Valerie, I know I shouldn't have grabbed you, but I didn't know what to do." There was a small silence before he finally said, "I just knew I couldn't let you get away from me."

"You were right, I suppose. Your method was...crude, but we needed to talk." If nothing else, they needed to be polite to each other, Valerie thought. For a while longer, they'd still be working together. And after that, it would be better for everyone if they were able to maintain some sort of friendship. Once he went out on his own, and for as long as he stayed in Amsden, they'd probably be on opposite sides of cases every so often. It was a bleak thought, because in spite of everything, she was aware of the powerful tug that kept pulling her toward him. It seemed beyond her control.

She was so lost in thought that she didn't notice their surroundings until they were a mile or so outside Amsden. "Hey, I thought you were going to take me home," she protested.

"I'm going to drive by Amsden Lake first. I think we both need some time to wind down." He shot her a look, daring her to disagree. "We can watch the lights come on again, out over the lake. I mean, the water will probably be frozen over, but we can still watch for the lights."

She turned without a word, staring out the window.

After a few minutes, he took a deep breath. He had to ask. "You used to love me. How do you feel now?"

She turned to look at his profile. He was so incredibly handsome, so appealing, and she felt regret as keenly as if he'd left home yesterday. "I could never feel that way again, if that's what you're asking, so you don't need to worry about it."

"Never?"

"Never." Her breath caught with the painful need to be honest. This time, no matter how hard it might be to say, it had to be all out in the open, resolved, once and for all. "I don't think I could trust that you were always going to be around."

A jolt of pain went through his whole body. Thank God he was looking at the road, he thought. He felt as if he were dying inside at her words, and he didn't think he could bear her seeing that in his face. He struggled for control over the emotions that raged through him. If only he'd had a little more practice, maybe he could handle this better. Instinctively, he sought the anchor of their old relationship. "I see," he said hoarsely. Above all, he needed to be sure of what she wanted this time. "But we are friends, aren't we?"

"Oh, yes. Only real friends could be this truthful with each other." She studied her hands, clenched tightly in her lap.

"I see," he said again. There was a short silence before he spoke again, and when he did, his voice had firmed. "And how do you explain that we can hardly keep our hands off each other?"

Valerie moistened her lips. "There's an easy explanation for that, Jay, and you know it."

"Right," he agreed bitterly.

They were both lost in thought as he swung down the access road to the boat launch. The day was cold, capping several days of frigid weather, and he edged the heater up. He pulled the car over toward the railing so they'd have a good view over the lake.

They waited quietly for the sunset, and after a while Jay felt a little better. The sight of water never failed to calm him. Valerie was still with him, after all. If she'd loved him once, given time and patience, couldn't she love him again? He'd need to give her time. He wasn't going to leave again. Surely he could find some way to prove that to her.

He reached over and covered her clenched hands with a big one of his own. "I thought the lake might be completely iced over by now," Jay said softly into the silence. Here and there, patches of open water glimmered in the late-afternoon sun.

"It's a large lake, and some years, doesn't freeze completely until the end of January. I remember one time it didn't freeze at all. They couldn't even have the ice-fishing tournament in February." Normal conversation, Valerie thought. If he could make normal conversation, so could she.

"What ice there is must be thin, or we'd see lots of the ice-fishing shacks—" Jay stopped, suddenly leaning his head forward. "Look at that, Valerie."

"What?" Valerie said, but even as the word came out of her mouth, she saw it, too. Two tiny figures, walking far out on the ice. "It's not safe yet," she said quickly.

Jay was out of the car, and she hurried to follow him. He ran to the railing that separated the parking lot from the lake and cupped his hands around his mouth. "Come back" he called out over the lake.

The figures stopped. "Come back," Jay shouted, motioning with his arms. The two out on the ice started to move again.

"What kind of crazy people would—" Valerie never finished the sentence. At that instant, one of the bodies went through the ice.

Jay was off in less than a second, scrambling partway down the boat launch and vaulting over its side into the lake. Valerie heard a sickening crack as his feet hit the thin ice. She leaned over the railing and saw him far below. "Jay! You can't!" she called frantically. "The ice won't hold!"

"Go for help, Valerie," he commanded. "Now!" He turned and ran toward the center of the lake, his feet slipping on the ice.

"Wait for help!" she shouted. He paid no attention, and Valerie tried desperately to stay calm. The water was too cold. If Jay fell in, even if he managed to keep from going under the ice, he could last only a few minutes before he'd die in the frigid water.

There were still no lights on in the houses near her, and most would be closed up for the winter, anyway. It was impossible to tell which were inhabited, and she couldn't take the time to knock on doors. She threw herself into the driver's seat of Jay's car. Leaving him on the ice was almost unbearable, but she'd have to drive for help.

She glanced down, seeing the stick shift as if for the first time. She hadn't driven a stick in years, and she had almost forgotten how. The clutch. She had to put it in and then let it out easy or she'd stall. Lurching a little, she made it out of the parking lot and back onto the access road. Involuntarily, she glanced at the lake. Jay was far out now.

Driving as fast as she could, Valerie careened out of the access road. They'd passed a gas station on the main road a few miles down, and she headed for that.

She didn't have to go that far. A car was coming and she managed to flag it down. The man inside would make the call for rescue. Intensely relieved, she watched the other car make a U-turn and then she did the same, back onto the access road.

Then she herself was scurrying down the boat launch, her heart banging in her chest, her breath coming hard. She couldn't jump over the side, so she half ran, half slid to the bottom. The ice looked rotten. Would it hold? She looked out and could see that Jay had reached the two on the lake, and she could hear distant screams and shouts. She saw him drop to his stomach. Then she couldn't look anymore. The rough but slippery ice demanded all her concentration. Fiercely, she willed herself to focus only on the task ahead.

Here and there, sticks and other debris appeared in the ice. She tripped and fell over one big branch imbed-ded in the lake. Skirting a huge patch of open water, Valerie tried to stay on what she thought were the most solid parts. Once in a while, she stepped on what looked like thick ice, only to find a layer of slush under her feet. A little snow had fallen a few days before, covering the ice and making it more difficult to pick out the solid parts. In some places, her shoes made footprints that instantly filled with frigid water.

She knew she was closer because she could pick out Jay's voice, shouting to someone, and a younger-sounding voice yelling, too, but she didn't dare look up. Half sliding, half running, she finally got there, bumping into something solid.

It was a child. He or she was about eight, and hysterical. Valerie gripped the snowsuited shoulders, shaking them a little. "Listen to me!" she shouted, and miraculously, the youngster was quiet for a second. "We're here to help, but you have to go and stand a ways back. Far away, do you hear me?" Desperation pricked her words. "No matter what happens, don't come near here." The face stared at her, tears streaming down red cheeks.

"Do what I say," Valerie commanded again. "Go over there, and stay far away from the edge of any water. Look over at the boat launch." She pointed, and the child's eyes followed the direction of her hand. "Someone's coming to help right away. It's going to be all right." She had to get this child to a position of some safety and help Jay with the other one. With no time to spare on comfort, she gave the little figure a push and was relieved to see it start to move away from her. She tried to keep watch, even as she turned immediately to Jay.

"Jay!" she called. He was lying facedown on the ice. For a second, she was afraid to approach, not knowing if the extra weight of her body would put them both through the ice. Chancing it, she began to inch forward, listening for any sound that might tell her the ice wasn't going to hold. As she came up behind where he lay, Valerie dropped to all fours to spread her weight.

Jay was lying partway in the water, his half-submerged arms holding on to a wet jacket. She could see a head bobbing facedown among small chunks of ice.

"Jay," she called again, fear making her voice quaver over the one syllable, drawing the sound out.

His panting words came over his shoulder in short, despairing sentences. "I can't pull him out. I can't get his head up. I can't hold on to him anymore."

"Help is on the way. Just hold on a minute longer."

"I...can't."

"You can!" she shouted, putting as much command into her voice as she could. But she looked at the numbingly cold water, and knew Jay was right. He could never hold on to the still figure long enough for the rescue team to arrive. And if he let go, the child would slip under the ice, and then they'd never find him in time. She needed to do something.

"Jay, I'm going to grab your feet and drag you away. Don't struggle, just concentrate on holding on to him."

"Do it," he gasped.

Valerie gripped his ankles, one in each hand. She felt him start to move as she pulled as hard as she could, not knowing she was capable of such brute strength. She had to be careful not to jerk and dislodge Jay's tenuous hold on the body in the water. The sheen of water that was over the ice helped her, and she began to make a little progress.

Just as the body reached the edge of the hole, Jay felt pieces of ice loosen. This wasn't going to work, he thought in despair. Each time Valerie dragged him enough to pull the body along, ice from the edge of the hole fell into the water. He hadn't felt his own arms in a long time. Dear God, he was cold, but above all he prayed that his fingers were frozen, locked in a position that still gripped the child's coat. Suddenly, a large chunk of ice gave way under his chest.

Scrabbling with his feet, he managed to squirm back a yard or so onto more solid footing, but now he was soaked from head to toe. The effort seemed to take all his remaining strength. He looked back into the hole in the ice, now considerably larger, terrified of what he would find. But his hands still gripped the lifeless body.

After a few more seconds, he was so frozen, his brain felt heavy and stupid. It would be easy, blessedly easy, to slow down in this cold, slow down enough to die. By sheer force of will, he made himself think coherently. He knew it was no use, and dangerous to them all for Valerie to keep trying to pull him away. "Stop, Valerie. Now."

She stopped right away. "Don't let go, Jay. Help will be here."

He didn't say anything, and Valerie didn't know if he heard her. He must be fading quickly. "Jay, listen. If you can hang on a few more seconds, I'm going to crawl up beside you. My hands are warmer. I can hold him a few minutes."

"No!" He spat the word out, using his last

strength. "The ice…don't know if it will hold with both of us on the edge… I've got to do it.…"

It sickened Valerie to know he was right. "Jay, hold on, hold on to him," she repeated over and over, noting with detached surprise that while her body shook, her voice sounded calm and sure. Out of the corner of her eye, she saw that the other child was sitting on the ice a little distance away, safe for the moment. Instantly, she turned back to Jay. "Jay, you can hold on. Hold on."

After a minute or two, it was the only thing Jay knew, that voice coming from somewhere, telling him what he had to do. *Hold on, Jay, hold on, hold on.* His body was numb, his mind was numb. *Jay, Jay, hold on.*

He had no idea how long it had been. Forever, probably. He closed his eyes, trying to struggle against the bottomless cold, but he was so tired. It would never end, and he would always be here, hanging on to something in the cold, cold water. *Hold on,* the voice said. Hold on. Hold on to what? Hold on to what's in the water. *Hold on.*

Someone was yanking hard at his feet, pulling him away. Stop, he wanted to say. Please, stop. I can't hold on if you jerk like that.

Then he was on his back looking at the sky. Faces filled it. Valerie. Strangers. Strapping him into something. Dragging him bumpily across the ice. He was so…confused.

Finally, they were back at the parking lot where the ambulance waited. Valerie was relieved that one of the paramedics was a man she knew. "Chet, will they be all right?" Valerie anxiously asked.

Chet didn't stop connecting tubes but gave her a quick, measured look.

"Chet, please. Tell me."

His hands were busy over the small boy they'd managed to snag from the water. "I don't know about this little guy, Valerie. I'll talk to you at the hospital, okay?"

"All right," she said helplessly, knowing it wasn't right to interrupt when they were trying to hurry.

"What's the man's name?" Chet's head was inclined toward Jay.

"Jay."

They loaded the little boy into the rescue vehicle. The other child was already inside, sitting up. Now Jay was being pushed inside, too, and Chet bent over him as the door was closing. "Jay, do you hear me? We got him out. Jay, you did real good, pal."

CHAPTER EIGHT

VALERIE WAITED at the hospital for what seemed like ages. On getting there, Jay and the two children had been whisked away immediately, and Chet and the other paramedics were busy with paperwork. She felt helpless in the face of all this efficient bustle. Helpless and scared.

Finally, she saw a kind, familiar face. "Ellis!" she gasped in surprise, coming quickly to her feet.

"Valerie, are you okay?" he asked, folding her into his arms. "You're shivering."

"I'm still a little damp and cold."

"I'll get the doctor."

"No! I'm all right, Ellis. Just worried about the others."

He sat her down next to him with his arm around her. "I was listening to the emergency frequencies and heard the call come in. When I learned one of the people involved was you, I thought you might need a friend."

"Thanks, Ellis," Valerie said, sighing gratefully against him. Sometimes it was hard to remember why she'd ever thought herself in love with Ellis Campbell. But then she remembered his kindness, and she knew. He had never inspired much passion in her, but he was a good and caring man, and right now he was right. More than anything, she needed a friend.

"Ellis, could you try to find out what's going on?

I've asked, but nobody wants to tell me anything. You're the chief of police and I bet they'll talk to you."

"All right. Don't worry, Valerie, I'll get the straight scoop." He gave her a sympathetic grin. "It helps to have friends in high places."

He was gone for a long time. Finally, he was back with Chet in tow. "Okay, here's what's happening," Chet said, squatting in front of her. "I've talked to the doctors, and the kid who was in the water might make it. He's only six years old, and the littlest ones survive this kind of thing best. For some reason, their bodies shut down when they're under the cold water, go into a kind of—I don't know what a layperson would say—a kind of suspended animation, I guess. Do you understand?"

Valerie nodded.

"So the doctors try to bring them out of it gradually, to keep the brain from swelling. If everything goes right, that prevents the worst of the brain damage."

Brain damage. Valerie felt a surge of nausea.

"His sister is fine," Chet went on in a calm voice. "She didn't get wet at all. When we got there, she was just cold and crying."

Ellis made a sound of disgust. "What kind of parent would let their kids go out alone on that half-frozen lake?"

"Not a parent, a baby-sitter. Your officers are still trying to notify the parents," Chet told him.

Valerie braced herself, trying to find the words to ask about Jay.

"The other guy, that Jay, will be all right, too, Valerie."

Valerie didn't know she was crying until she felt

Ellis's hand in hers, passing her a handkerchief. She mopped at her eyes, trying to calm herself.

"Can he go home?" she asked shakily.

She caught Chet exchanging a concerned glance with Ellis.

"Tell me," she said in as calm a voice as she could. She knew that Chet wouldn't tell her anything if he thought she was going to lose control of herself. She drew a deep breath. "Go on, I'm fine."

"Well," Chet said quietly, "he's suffering from hypothermia, of course. That's to be expected, his having been in and out of all that ice water for so long." He hesitated. "It's his extremities. He's lucky, he's sustained a moderate case of frostbite, and he won't lose any fingers. But his hands are real bad."

She bit her lip. "Is he in a lot of pain?"

"The doctor says yes, but that's good, Valerie. It means he has circulation. But he's going to lose quite a bit of skin, and they need to watch for infection. He's pretty shook up, naturally. He'll be here overnight, at least."

Valerie felt the last of her remaining energy leave her. She lay back in the seat and closed her eyes, feeling the tears ooze out from under her eyelids again and start down her cheeks. Impatiently, she swiped at them with the back of her hand. She could feel the two men looking at her. Finally, she sat up.

"Jay Westcott is a good friend of yours, I take it?" Ellis asked.

She nodded miserably. And if Ellis was curious about anything else, he didn't say so.

Chet was speaking again. "Well, that little boy's damned lucky Jay was there. If Jay had let go, I don't think we would ever have found the kid under the ice. Not in time, anyway." He was silent for a moment, and when he spoke again, there was a quiet, respectful hush to his words. "I don't see how the guy managed to hang on so long. The average person couldn't do it, I don't think. What an extraordinary will it would take, to lie out there on that ice and hold on."

"He's a hero," Ellis agreed quietly.

"Ms. Brettinger? You can see Mr. Westcott now," said a new voice, and Valerie was out of her chair without a backward glance.

Jay lay under harsh lights in the hospital bed. His cheeks and nose were bright red under a white cream that had been smeared on them. Other than his eyes, skin and hair, everything was white, it seemed. White cream, white sheets, white hospital gown, a thin layer of white gauze that completely swathed his hands.

"Hi," Valerie said softly, taking a chair by the side of the bed.

"Hi, yourself," Jay whispered.

"How bad are you hurting?"

"Bad enough," he admitted, and she could tell by the hot brightness of his eyes that it hurt a lot. "They gave me a shot, and it's supposed to dope me up pretty soon. I hope so, anyway."

She wanted to take his hand, and instead settled for stroking his hair back from his forehead. "I've been talking to some people out there. They're saying you're a hero."

He snorted a little. "I'm no hero. I was out there before I had time to think about it. You were the one, Valerie. You were out there with me, and I kept hearing you telling me things. It made the difference. Do they know that?"

She smiled, and finally he started to close his eyes. Valerie reached up and snapped off the fluorescent tube over his head, dimming the bright room. Suddenly, he opened his eyes again.

"Valerie, could you do me one favor?" At her nod, he went on, "I want to get out of here tomorrow morning. Could you go to my house and get me some more clothes?"

"Let's see how you feel tomorrow morning," she murmured.

"I want you to go get me some more clothes," he said stubbornly. "Now, tonight."

"Jay, the hospital will dry the clothes you had on—"

"No!" he said sharply, starting to sit up. She put her hand on his chest, restraining him. "You don't understand, Valerie. I can't put on those clothes again, ever. I was so cold in those clothes. Cold enough to die."

His eyes were hot, and he was becoming irrational. Valerie sought to soothe him, and if he wanted some clothes, it was the least she could do. "All right," she agreed.

"Will you get them now?"

"Right now," she promised. "Jay, get some sleep while I'm gone."

FEELING LIKE an intruder, Valerie let herself into Jay's house with his key. He obviously hadn't expected to be out after dark, since he hadn't left a light on. Fumbling, she found a switch that illuminated the front hallway. In the living room, she found a lamp on a cardboard box and turned that on, too.

She was startled when the room was lit. There were a few pieces of furniture in the shabby, once-familiar room, but not much. There was an old sofa, comfortable but leaking a little stuffing. A rocker sat next to the cardboard box bearing the lamp, and on the box was a book. It was an extra-thick spy thriller, opened and turned down, spine up. On the floor were a few issues of *Ohio Lawyer* magazine, with a yellow legal pad scrawled over in Jay's bold black handwriting. There was a compact disc player, with a large stack of discs next to it. Finally, she saw a few opened boxes of books on the floor. And that was it.

Walking through the dining room toward the kitchen, Valerie illuminated rooms as she went. The dining room was completely empty; even the curtains had been stripped from the walls. In the kitchen was the battered table she remembered, with four chairs around it. He was sure taking his time about unpacking, and the emptiness of the rooms was vaguely unsettling. Pushing the feeling aside, she rummaged under the sink for a paper bag to put his clothes in.

She turned off lights as she went back through the rooms to the hall and pulled herself up the stairwell, her uneasiness increasing. It didn't feel right to be alone in his house. At the top of the stairs, she saw that all but two of the doors leading off the upper hall were closed.

She walked into the first open doorway, finding the bathroom. Hurriedly, she gathered shaving gear, some shampoo, a brush and comb and his toothbrush, and put them in the bottom of the sack. Handling something as personal as his toothbrush gave her an odd feeling.

Biting her lip, she went to the other open door. If she was feeling this unsettled by his toothbrush, how was she going to feel rummaging around in his underwear drawer? When Jay said he couldn't wear his clothes again, did he mean he wouldn't wear his old underwear, either? Wouldn't grabbing his jeans and a sweater do?

All of a sudden, she felt utterly giddy, still tightly wound from the incredible stress of the scene on the ice. She had given in to his request, and now she had to fulfill her promise. She tried not to look at his bedroom. Her being here felt like a tremendous invasion of privacy, but she had no choice. The small room was dominated by his bed, parked in the vee of the eaves. Seeing the blanket pulled up neatly to two plump pillows sent an immediate, unwelcome rush of sensation shooting through her. She didn't have to analyze the feeling. It was sexual desire, pure and simple, and she started to tremble. If just the sight of his bed could do this to her...

Get a grip, she told herself sternly. This had been one of the worst days of her life, and she couldn't handle even one more emotion. She made herself pass the desk piled high with huge legal books and go to the dresser. Opening the top drawer, she found a pair of socks and an undershirt, which she put in the bag. Holding his briefs with her fingertips, she added those, as well. She felt a little better about folding his jeans and putting them on the growing pile.

There was a bulky wool turtleneck sweater draped over the back of his desk chair, and she put it on top of the nearly full sack. In the closet she found a bright blue parka, and she hung it over her shoulder. He'd definitely need a jacket. She didn't think the leather one he was wearing this afternoon would survive the soaking it got in Amsden Lake. Feeling intense relief, Valerie was ready to leave.

But she hesitated once more at the doorway to the living room and then turned the light on again to find the paperback he'd been reading. She didn't know if he'd be out of the hospital by morning and he would probably like something to read.

Looking at the neat but barren room one more time gave her the same uneasy feeling she had gotten before. That's when it hit her. These rooms were so empty. Too empty. Valerie thought for a second. He was staying in Amsden; he was opening his own law practice. So why did this room look almost as if no one lived here? It was just too empty for someone who was planning to stay.

VALERIE AWOKE with a start. Jay's eyes were closed in sleep, but he was moaning, tossing his head from side to side. Quickly, she pulled herself out of the chair beside the hospital bed and leaned over to stroke his cheek with her hand. She tried to soothe him without waking him, but it was no use.

"Jay, wake up. You're having a nightmare," she finally whispered sharply.

Waking him was so hard. Perhaps the drug they had given him was responsible, or perhaps his complete exhaustion. By the time he opened his eyes, she was sitting beside him in the bed, cradling his head against her side. His cheek was warm and sticky against her hand.

She felt him shudder deeply and she hugged him, at the same time trying not to touch his arms or hands. Finally, he was still, and she drew back to look at him, expecting his eyes to be closing again. Instead, she was startled to find him looking up at her gravely.

"You had a nightmare," she told him again.

"And how," he breathed.

"Did you think you were back out there on the ice?"

"I don't think so. It wasn't cold, or anything." He

shook his head, trying to clear it. "It was dark, and things were crowding in. I lifted my hands and they were on fire, and then I felt my head burning. Someone was telling me I'd never feel anything inside again."

She felt his forehead. It didn't seem hot, but she'd need to get the nurse to check on him.

He was whispering again. "Valerie, my hands hurt like hell."

She nodded. "I know. I'll go get the nurse."

The light felt too bright when the nurse snapped it on, but the woman's words were reassuring. Jay's temperature was normal, and he was told again it was a good sign that his hands were hurting.

"I know that's not much comfort," the nurse said sympathetically, "but I can get you a pill for the pain, and that should help some."

Minutes later, he was in the dim room again, with Valerie stationed in the chair next to his bed. "Did you get my clothes?"

"Yes, they're in that bag."

He smiled wanly. "I bet you thought I'd lost my mind, but I couldn't bear the thought that I might have to get into my other clothes. It seemed real important at the time, but I'm sorry I made you drag yourself all the way out to the farm."

"It's all right, Jay. Now, let's see if you can get some sleep."

"Okay. What time is it?"

She checked her watch. "A little after three."

He sat up quickly. "Three, as in three a.m.?" At her nod, he stared at her in astonishment. "Valerie, you must be beat. You should have gone home hours ago."

She shrugged, smiling at him. "Forget it. After all,

you're the hero. I'm supposed to bask in your presence now, you know.'' She tried to speak lightly. ''And anyway, who'll wake you if you have another nightmare?''

''I guess I need to say thanks. I seem to be thanking you a lot today.''

He closed his eyes, and Valerie tried to sit very still, hoping he would fall asleep. At last, he said drowsily, ''Valerie, could you sit with me again?''

''I'm right here,'' she assured him.

''No, I mean next to me, like when I woke up.''

Valerie slipped into the bed beside him, gently cuddling him against her as before. As big as he was, as confident as he was, tonight he needed her comfort. She was terribly, achingly glad to be able to give it to him, and a great tenderness washed over her as she watched him fall asleep in her arms.

SHE WAS still there when he awakened the next morning, but she had moved to the chair next to the bed. Once she was sure he was awake and reasonably comfortable, Valerie left the hospital. At home, she showered and changed, called the office, then paced. She couldn't stay away from the hospital and leave Jay there alone.

''You didn't need to come back.'' Jay smiled at her gratefully in spite of his words. He didn't complain about the pain he was in, but she could see it there, behind his eyes. She was glad she'd returned. She could do something to distract him.

''I'm staying a bit. How are you feeling?''

''Better, but the doctor said I can't leave until tomorrow. Then I'll need to get a housekeeper, or something, for a few days.'' He gazed ruefully down at his bandaged hands. ''You should see these. I won't be able to do anything for quite a while. I can't even hold a book, so I guess that leaves television.''

"I'll read to you."

"You don't need to do that."

"Be quiet and listen," Valerie told him sternly and again was rewarded with a smile. As Jay leaned back against the pillow, she picked up the book she'd brought from his house and found the folded-over page. Settling in beside him, she read out loud.

"'Steve vaulted over the high fence. He wasn't winded, but then, Cyril wouldn't be, either. A spy, if he was worth anything, kept himself in good shape. You never knew when you might have to get out fast. Steve felt for his gun, reassured that it was in its shoulder holster. He sped down the concrete walk, knowing he had to narrow the distance between them. He was a great marksman, but if he shot from this far away, he might hit a woman or a child. Not even catching a master spy was worth that risk. Before his eyes, a car screeched to a halt and a door swung open. He saw nothing but the semiautomatic....''' She stopped and glanced toward the bed. "How can you enjoy something like this?"

He grinned. "It's just male fantasy."

"This is male fantasy? Chases and shooting and—''

"Wait till you get to the part where they struggle over the gun."

"You've read this before?"

Jay laughed out loud. "No, but they always struggle for the gun. It's—''

"Male fantasy," she finished for him, laughing along with him.

"*One* male fantasy," he corrected softly.

Valerie squirmed. "Shut up, Jay, and let me read."

He lay back in the bed, half closing his eyes, a faint smile lingering on his lips. Valerie returned to the book. When the nurse came in to change his dressings and check his hands, Valerie continued to read out loud. She didn't think she could bear to look at his hands. When she heard his sharply drawn breath, she faltered.

"Go on, Valerie," Jay whispered.

She read on and on. By the next chapter, she had to stop for a sip of water from the pitcher by Jay's bed.

"Thanks, Valerie. You don't have to read anymore."

"What, stop before I see how Steve gets his man?" She flashed him a comforting smile and began again. "'Steve dragged the filthy curtain from the window. It was hard to wait for nightfall, but a lifetime of training—'"

"Excuse me." A nurse strode briskly into the room. "Mr. Westcott? Mr. and Mrs. Canfield are here. They're Jimmy's parents, and they want to talk to you about their son. If you're up to it, they want to say thank you."

Jay frowned. "I don't know," he started to say.

"It's important to them," the nurse told him.

"Well, okay." He waved his hand as if to say it was nothing, but Valerie saw two deep spots of color, evident even on his wind-reddened cheeks. She'd never seen him blush before.

Mr. and Mrs. Canfield were ushered in, both looking awkward but determined. They introduced themselves and Jay introduced Valerie.

She tried to ease the tension. "How's Jimmy?" she asked.

Mr. Canfield answered, "He was semiconscious for

a few minutes this morning. He's responding to pain stimulus, which the doctors say is a good sign.'' He paused, looking pained. "Right now, that's enough.''

"That's very good,'' Valerie said softly.

Mrs. Canfield approached Jay, eyes brimming. "Mr. Westcott, can I call you Jay? I just wanted to say thank you—'' Her voice broke. "I can't shake your hand, but I thought maybe you'd let me touch your arm for a second....''

Valerie fled. Outside Jay's room she wandered the halls uncertainly. She was supposed to be good at this, at soothing others' pain. So why did she feel overwhelmed by confusing emotions, so shaken and needy herself? She couldn't stand the raw emotion she'd left behind in Jay's hospital room, couldn't bear the gratitude and worry on the faces of the little boy's parents.

Most of all, she couldn't bear to think again of Jay out on the ice, or imagine the sickening cracking sound it had made when it had nearly given way under him. He'd almost died out there, she thought, and as it was, he'd been seriously injured. Jay had lain with half his body in freezing water and saved a child's life. Although she'd been thinking about that fact for almost twenty-four hours, for the first time, the reality of it hit her. And shook her to her core. For a few seconds—she was unsure how long—she pressed against the wall, wondering if her legs would hold her.

As always when control threatened to leave her, she looked for something to do. She located a telephone and arranged for a housekeeper and a visiting nurse to come by Jay's house to care for him. Then she called her mother. It took only a few minutes for her mother to grasp the situation and realize she was needed.

By the time Valerie hung up, Ginny was planning a week's menus, designed to make sure Jay kept up his strength during his recovery. She'd mapped out a schedule with Valerie to guarantee that someone would be at his house in the evenings to keep him company.

"Whoa, I don't think he'll need us in week two," Valerie said into the receiver. "Let's just play it by ear at the end of the week." If she didn't put some limits on these ministrations, her mother would move in with Jay. She hung up the telephone, relieved. Between the two of them, Jay would be taken care of, and her mother's call to arms had lightened her heart considerably.

By the time she got back to Jay's room, the Canfields were gone and he was standing by the window.

"Thanks for staying with me through all that," he greeted her sarcastically.

She chose to ignore his tone. "What did they say?"

"I suppose the usual things a parent says to someone they think saved their child's life."

"Well, you did save his life, and it's natural that they're grateful and want to thank you. For heaven's sake, what's the matter with that?"

He sank into a chair. "Nothing. You're right. It's how I would feel if it were my kid. But, Valerie, I don't feel like a hero, like everyone's making me out to be. The reporter from the *Amsden Journal* came, and the Columbus television stations are sending crews. What will I tell them? I just went out there without thinking about it." He averted his eyes. "It's embarrassing, and I feel like a...a fraud."

She tried to understand. "Do you think a person makes a conscious decision to save someone?"

"I don't know, but I didn't, not really."

She crouched before him and put her hands on his shoulders—the only part of him she could touch without hurting him. She made sure he was looking at her. "You did an extraordinary thing, Jay. Believe it." He didn't say anything, so she added softly, "I know it's scary to think someone had to count on you that much. But you were up to it, weren't you? You didn't let anyone down and I'm so proud of you." Reaching out, Valerie put a quivering finger on his cheek and stroked it lightly.

Unexpectedly, he gave her a smile as dazzling as the sun on open water. "Thank you, Valerie. You're right. Maybe for once, I did okay."

IT WOULD BE BETTER if Jay were here, Valerie thought. She had come to count on sharing their differing perceptions about Roberta's complaint, even arguing about them. But there was no help for it. Jay would be out of commission for at least the rest of the week and she didn't want this investigation to drag on any longer than necessary.

Getting a very nervous Brenda a cup of coffee, Valerie put cream in the brew, the way she knew Brenda liked it. So far, beating around the bush, asking general questions, had gotten her nowhere. She was going to have to get more specific, but she made sure to keep her voice soft and reassuring. "Why would Roberta say she thought you were afraid of Judge Haskins?"

Brenda looked away. "I have no idea."

"You didn't tell her you were afraid of Judge Haskins?" Valerie persisted.

Brenda shook her head emphatically. "No."

"You didn't give her papers to give to the judge so you wouldn't have to see him yourself?"

"Maybe I gave things to her. I don't remember what I did every time."

This felt like cross-examining a reluctant witness, Valerie thought. She and Brenda had never been close, but they had a pleasant relationship, professional and mutually respectful. Yet now, it seemed Brenda didn't want to confide in her.

"Brenda," Valerie started again, keeping her voice gentle, trying not to show her frustration. "Forgive me, but you don't seem to be acting like yourself here. Are you or are you not afraid of Judge Haskins?"

Brenda finally turned to face her. "He's the judge, Valerie."

"I know that. I don't like having to ask any more than you like answering." She put her hand on the other woman's arm. "Please, Brenda, if you know anything, you need to tell me."

"You're his friend," she protested.

Valerie stood, good intentions evaporating in her mounting frustration. "So I keep hearing. For heaven's sake, he is my friend. I'm not going to deny the fact. I never would have made it through law school without his help. But even if he is my friend, do you really think I'd let him molest women?"

Unexpectedly, Brenda started to cry a little. "No, I guess not. I'm sorry, Valerie."

It was good to know that Brenda didn't completely distrust her, but Valerie's heart sank at the tears. Was there going to be another allegation?

Brenda looked away again, and there was silence for a full minute while Valerie waited, her lower lip between her teeth. "He gives me the creeps," Brenda said at last.

"What has he said to you? What has he done?"

She shook her head and wiped her eyes. "Nothing."

"Nothing?" Valerie repeated, nonplussed. She had braced herself for the worst.

"Well, nothing in particular," Brenda hastened to add. "It's just that he stares at me like he knows what I look like without my clothes on. Do you know what I mean?"

"Do you mean he leers at you?"

"Yeah, something like that."

Valerie sighed. "That's not real specific, Brenda."

She straightened, her eyes brimming over again. "Does that mean I'm not in trouble?"

Valerie reached for the woman's hand. "You're not in trouble, no matter what you say about him. You work for me, and I'm very happy with how you do things. And after all, Roberta hasn't lost her job."

"Yes, that's true," Brenda acknowledged, finally smiling a little. She hesitated. "I've been in Amsden for ten years, though, and I know what a big shot the judge is. He knows everyone, and a lot of people got their jobs from him. He practically *is* politics in this town. Sooner or later, he'll get Roberta for this."

Valerie sighed again. "The judge wouldn't do that."

"Oh, right." Brenda looked out the window.

It was useless to argue with her, and she didn't have any real information, anyway. Valerie stood to signal that their interview was over. The meeting had been a dead end, after all.

Brenda was almost to the door, when she turned.

"You know, if the judge picked on Roberta, isn't that especially weird?"

"Why weird? Jay says it's typical for a harasser to pick on someone who works under him, someone who seems especially vulnerable."

"Well, I suppose so. I just meant, with Roberta's problems, and all."

Valerie was suddenly alert. "What problems?" she asked quickly.

Brenda looked flustered. "I thought it was common knowledge. You know how people gossip."

"For heaven's sake, Brenda, what are you trying to say?"

Brenda licked her lips. "I thought you knew. I don't break confidences, but really, all the office people talked about it. Roberta started the tongues wagging herself, when she told Kay in the records department."

Valerie stood with her hands on her hips, waiting.

Brenda shrugged a little, still looking embarrassed. "It's just that she hates men, absolutely hates them. When she and her husband split up, she was mad at the whole lot of them. And when they were married, apparently they had sexual problems. During their divorce, it all came out." She paused, but Valerie said nothing. Finally, Brenda went on. "So, what I meant was, isn't it ironic that Judge Haskins is supposed to have made all these comments about wanting to have sex with a woman who can't stand to be with a man?"

There was another pause, longer this time. "Yes," Valerie said softly. "It is very, very ironic."

"I'M HAVING a party tomorrow night," Jay confided, and his voice sounded positively gleeful, even over the telephone. "A dinner party, and guess what? You're invited. I may even make you the guest of honor."

"Isn't this a little soon?" Valerie asked, knowing she sounded overly solicitous, but unable to help herself. Jay had only gotten the bandages off yesterday, and the idea of a dinner party was absurd.

"Look, Jay, I know you're bored, but it's been less than a week and you should rest. Your body took a beating on that ice and your hands are still healing. When you're back to work on Monday, you'll be so busy you won't believe it. The phone rings off the hook here all day with people wanting to talk to you, arrange an interview or give you awards, and I keep putting them off."

"Good," he said briskly, obviously unwilling to be deterred. "Bob and Meg are invited, and you have to come. After all, you're bringing the main course."

"I am?"

"Why sure, didn't I tell you? Pepperoni pizza. If you're dead set on having vegetables at your dinner parties, tell them to put some mushrooms and green peppers on it."

She loved to hear his laugh, so rich and deep, and she joined in gladly. Things had been a bit easier between them since Jay's injury. Part of the reason, Valerie supposed, was that she was always most comfortable when people needed her to do something for them.

"Jay, about tonight." Valerie glanced at the big appointment calendar that lay on her desk. She was busy this evening, as usual, but she ought to stop over and see whether he needed anything. "I'll come over after the Safety Advisory Board meeting if you want, but it'll be after nine. Is that too late?"

"Well, I think you can count on my staying awake for you. I don't exactly feel...lethargic...when you sit by me," he assured her.

At the new seriousness in his voice, she felt a jolt of tension, right in the pit of her stomach, delicious and scary at the same time. It was typical of the comments he'd been making all week, whenever the opportunity presented itself. It was getting hard to parry them, pretend the banter was all lighthearted fun between two very good friends.

Finally, Jay spoke again. "Just come over, Valerie. We'll listen to a disc or two, that's all."

"Okay," she agreed. They talked for a few more minutes before wrapping up the conversation.

When she set the receiver gently in its cradle, Valerie realized she was actually smiling. Sometimes, Jay just seemed to affect her that way. She should remember the past, she thought. That, of all things, should wipe the smile from her face, still her hammering heart and banish the images of those glinting pale blue eyes and that wry grin. Lord, how could he come back and insinuate himself into her life again so quickly, even now when she was older and supposedly wiser?

She wanted to remember how he had hurt her, leaving Amsden. Her memory of his defection helped her keep up the barriers against him, and she had to do that. She didn't think of herself as a passionate woman, but Jay aroused feelings in her that were difficult to understand, much less control. And she needed to control them.

He said he'd changed, and in some ways he had. He was happier, more open, but he was a restless spirit and blatantly ambitious. He was turning out to be a great trial lawyer. He had a snapping intellect coupled with all the right instincts, and he had already decided to leave the prosecutor's office. He was opening his own office, or so he'd said. But the town wasn't large enough for there to be many of the really big cases, the kind that got your name in the papers and won huge verdicts. How long would a small-town practice with a quietly earnest partner last, before it, too, began to pall?

She remembered the sensation she had felt at his house Sunday night, when she'd gone to pick up his clothes. He hadn't even unpacked. Obviously, he was keeping his options open.

Jay was attracted to her. He liked her. She could take what he offered, and not plan a future, but that wasn't her style. Practical, understanding Valerie still believed in love-ever-after, and if she'd learned anything at all, it was not to expect too much from Jay Westcott.

Her light, happy mood had fled. She picked up the phone and pressed the intercom button, waiting for Brenda to answer.

"Did you finally get to talk to the court reporter on the Preddy divorce?"

"Yes. She said she'd start transcribing the trial for you tomorrow. She sounded pretty curious about why you'd want it, though."

Valerie bit her lip. "I hope you didn't tell her anything."

Brenda sounded a little injured. "I told you, Valerie, I don't break confidences."

"I'm sorry," Valerie said automatically, already lost in thought. Would the transcript from Roberta's divorce trial shed any light on the woman or her accusations?

CHAPTER NINE

MEG LIFTED her glass of beer. "You give great dinner parties, Jay."

"Thanks," he said, inclining his head in a lofty acknowledgment that caused them all to crack up.

"No, I mean it," Meg insisted, a big smile on her face. "You chilled the mugs. Not every host would go to so much trouble."

The laughter was good, Valerie thought. She hadn't seen Meg so lighthearted in months. She had expected sadness from her, but that week in the office, Meg had confessed to feeling mostly relief that her relationship with Dave was over. And tonight, she seemed to be having a great time. It pleased Valerie to have her friend acting like herself again.

Jay surveyed the battered kitchen table. There was the empty cardboard pizza box, some plates and a few utensils. Valerie always insisted on eating her pizza with a fork, so he had set the table more elaborately than necessary.

"Someone's got to do the dishes for me. It's part of the way I give a dinner party."

"I'll do them," Valerie started to say, but a quick look from Jay shushed her.

"I'll do them," Meg said, so fast her voice sounded like Valerie's echo.

Jay's gaze slid unexpectedly to Bob. When he

caught the glance, he cleared his throat nervously. "I can help, too," he offered finally.

"There's not that much here," Meg protested.

Jay stood quickly. "Thanks, you two." He pushed Valerie gently from the kitchen, and as soon as they were out, Bob shut the door behind them.

That was odd, Valerie had time to think, before Jay insisted she pick out a disc. She chose some soft folk music she knew they both enjoyed and settled next to him on the sofa.

"You know, I had an unusual visitor this morning," Jay told her. "Believe it or not, Dave Grau came out to see me."

"After that fiasco at Sandy's, I never thought he'd want to see any of us again. Not socially, anyway."

Jay leaned his head back, looking thoughtful. "It was sort of weird. He said he just wanted to see if I needed anything, that he heard what I'd done. Of course, the whole town's heard by now, so that wasn't what was weird. It's hard to explain, but it was all as uncomfortable as hell. He kept looking everything over, really edgy."

"That sounds like Dave," Valerie said. "Meg says he used to be different, but most of the time I've seen him recently, he's either been totally depressed or incredibly jumpy. I think you just got his nervous side today."

"I guess. It seemed like more than that to me, but I don't know him that well. Not that I want to. I'll never be able to figure out what Meg saw in that guy." He moved a little closer and changed the subject. "Rebecca Canfield called after Dave left. Jimmy's making a lot of progress."

"That's great news." Impulsively, Valerie put her arm around him and squeezed.

He snuggled into the crook of her arm. "He'll need therapy, but it looks like he's going to be okay. Isn't that great?"

"Wonderful," she agreed, her heart full at the news, contentment seeping into her. It was the only way the story could have ended, she thought, after what Jay had done.

They were quiet for a few minutes, enjoying the music and each other's company. Finally, she spoke again. "Did you ever finish reading your book?"

"Ages ago."

"How did Steve trap Cyril?"

He laughed. "You can't want to know."

She loved those blue eyes when the laugh lines creased around them, she thought, enjoying being close to him. It was a relief to respond a little to Jay's flirting and know with certainty that she would leave at the appropriate time. After all Meg and Bob were in the next room, and Valerie had driven with Meg. Nothing could happen between Jay and her tonight.

"Actually, I do want to know," she assured him.

He sat back against the cushions, a small smile playing around his lips. "Well, Steve had been monitoring transmissions from the places that Xercon Five had already placed Cyril. When he put all his information into the computer, the computer linked the bombing of the jet to various individuals who were known to be in Bonn...." He went on at length, explaining the complicated plot twists, but after a few moments, Valerie realized she wasn't really listening. Instead, she was watching his mouth move as he formed the words. It was such a strong mouth, like the rest of him, and it would be so warm and firm if his lips touched her own.

She indulged her imagination until Jay finished his

summary, then they waited quietly for another song to start. In the brief silence that ensued, Valerie heard the sound of Meg's laughter in the kitchen, followed by a male voice joining in heartily.

She turned to Jay in surprise. "Surely that isn't Bob laughing."

He nodded, looking smug. "Meg can make him laugh, Valerie."

"Well, Meg can make anybody laugh, I guess. But Bob's so serious."

"Even serious people laugh sometimes," he reminded her. "You, for example."

"I'm not serious like Bob," she protested quickly.

"You're not as quiet as Bob," Jay corrected just as fast. "But you're as serious, and you always have everything under control." He lifted one finger to stroke her cheek lightly, and when he spoke, his voice dropped to a whisper. "Actually, I don't mind that you're serious. Basically, I am, too, even though I've learned to laugh at myself a little. And that self-control of yours makes a man wonder what it would be like if…some-thing made you lose it."

She felt a deep blush warm her cheeks. For so many days now, she had been imagining that loss of control.

"Let's dance." Jay lifted her easily to her feet.

"Watch your hands," she warned him.

He wrapped his arms around her, pulling her close. "Don't worry about my hands." As he began to move with her, he added, "Let's just enjoy the evening, and not worry about anything at all."

It was easy to do just that. As one melody melted into another and then another, Valerie followed him. Some of the songs weren't really suited to dancing, but that didn't seem to make any difference. They moved to their own rhythm, which sometimes had only the vaguest link to the beat of the song. Taking his time but moving her steadily, Jay waltzed her over to the lamp. When he leaned over and shut it off, the only light in the room came from what little moonlight showed through the small windows.

Jay danced her into the empty dining room, and in the darkness she felt as if they were in a private ballroom as he sang snatches of song softly in her ear. Conversation between them was unnecessary.

Jay turned her and she dimly realized he had done so to avoid the wall that separated the dining room from the kitchen. In the living room, the compact disc player fell momentarily silent as it prepared to load another disc. Valerie could hear music coming from the closed doorway to the kitchen. She pulled back and looked at him.

"They're taking an awful long time with those dishes," she whispered. "Have they got the radio on in there?"

"Shh." Jay's mouth nuzzled her cheek playfully and their own music started again. "Sure, they're taking a long time. Remember when your sister, Sara, tried to match us up over the dishes? Although the strategy didn't work out too well for us, I thought it wasn't a bad idea." She shot him an astonished look, but before she could open her mouth, he asked, "Are you complaining about the lack of company?"

She didn't answer, knowing one wasn't necessary. His mouth brushed her cheek again and a wave of anticipation swept over her. She looked up to find his eyes on her, the dark room making them huge and shadowed, and the expression she saw there sent shivers down her spine. When Jay swung back toward the living room, his body shifted closer to hers, and she lost her breath and the step.

Smoothly, he pressed her to him until she caught the beat again. Jay made no attempt to hide the effect holding her so close was having on him. The sensation was delicious.

When he kissed her, she felt as if she were melting. His lips moved over hers in unmistakable possession, as if he read in her body language utter submission to the sensation of being held in his arms. She began to tremble all over.

He pressed his lips into the hollow of her neck. "You like me, Valerie. Tell me so."

"Like" was an understatement, Valerie thought wildly. "Like" didn't begin to cover the multitude of emotions that ran through her body like lightning along water. Jay desired her. She desired him. How long could she keep fighting what was inevitable?

"I like you," she managed to say. It was true. It wasn't nearly the whole story, but it was true.

He made a soft sound in his throat, and she could feel his lips curling against her neck before they brushed her skin in a moist caress, then lifted again to her waiting mouth. He whispered once more, his lips touching hers as he spoke. "As soon as we can, we'll get rid of Meg and Bob. He can drive her home."

No sooner had Jay spoken, than the door from the kitchen opened, and yellow light sliced into the dark room.

"You probably thought we died in there," Meg started to say, then stopped short when she caught sight of Valerie and Jay locked together. Beyond her stood Bob. Valerie tried to jerk away from Jay just as Meg muttered an excuse and started to step back in the direction she had come.

"Come in, Meg," Jay invited easily, but he held Valerie trapped against him, preventing her from pulling away. "I'm sure my kissing Valerie comes as no great shock."

"No, not really." She smiled a little and came into the room. "It's hard to tell with Valerie sometimes, but you're an open book."

When Jay finally let her go, Valerie tried to tamp down intense embarrassment. She didn't feel very adult about her reaction, and she could feel the blush that stained her cheeks. She turned on the dining room light, and for a moment the four of them shared an awkward silence. It was bad enough that Meg had seen her make a fool of herself, but she didn't know Bob Vanette well enough to completely relax in his presence.

"Oh, my, look at the time," Valerie said at last, after an exaggerated glance at her watch. "You need your rest, Jay. Come on, Meg." She went to the hall closet and started pulling out coats.

"Let me help." The husky voice right next to her ear caused her to jump. Wordlessly, she handed the coats to Jay.

"You know, Bob could give me a lift home, if Jay still needs you here," Meg began uncertainly, trying to catch Valerie's gaze.

"No problem," Bob agreed, and he looked as if, indeed, it would be no problem.

"Jay needs to get some rest," Valerie said firmly, and practically marched out the door. Meg followed her quickly. Behind them, Jay shrugged elaborately at Bob, trying to hide his disappointment.

"Women," Bob intoned, putting on his jacket.

"Women," Jay echoed gloomily, standing in the doorway and watching Valerie and Meg settle themselves in Valerie's car. Bob walked over to Meg's side, and she rolled down the window for him. He said something to her, and Jay thought he saw her smile before she closed it against the cold night air. That part of the evening, at least, had worked out just fine.

"Well, you seem to have had a good time," Valerie said as soon as they were off. If she kept the conversation focused on Meg, maybe her friend wouldn't comment on her own activities this night.

"Actually, I did. I've always liked Bob, but I didn't realize what a good listener he is. I went on and on and he laughed in all the right places. You have no idea how good it felt to laugh."

As a matter of fact, she did know, she thought, and she was happy for her friend. "I thought I heard the radio going," she teased softly, trying to keep a broad smile from her lips.

"Well, we did dance a little," Meg said, sounding a bit defensive.

"So you didn't talk *all* the time," Valerie couldn't resist noting.

After a second, Meg laughed. "The same way you and Jay didn't talk *all* the time."

Valerie made no comment to that. She accelerated along a straight stretch of the dark road. They had almost twenty miles to go, plenty of time for a thorough grilling from Meg. She tried to think of some other subject to occupy the miles, but nothing seemed to come to her.

"You don't have to be embarrassed with me, Valerie," Meg finally told her softly. "I think it's great that you and Jay are getting together."

Valerie hoped her voice was firm. "We aren't getting together."

"Why not?" Meg posed the question in the most reasonable-sounding tone, but Valerie could hear the underlying curiosity.

Meg was her best friend, and Valerie wished she could share some of her unsettled feelings. But she couldn't tell the story of Jay without disclosing a lot about his past, without describing his father's cruelty and Jay's determination to escape. Even though everyone seemed to know quite a bit about Jay's past, Valerie wasn't about to contribute to the gossip.

Instead, she said carefully, "I don't think it's right for me to have a relationship with someone who works in the office."

Meg snorted, tossing her red hair over her shoulder in a gesture of impatience. "Valerie, forget being so noble. Jay is perfect for you, and even you ought to be able to see that." Valerie didn't say anything, and Meg added, "It's obvious he's in love with you, and he's smart and interesting, not to mention gorgeous. And I think you like kissing him, too. So what's the real problem?"

Valerie took her eyes from the road for a split second. "Jay's not in love with me, Meg. Love and Jay...well, they just don't go together."

Her reply was quick and blunt. "Use your eyes, Valerie."

I use my heart to see, where Jay's concerned, Valerie thought suddenly. *And I'm afraid of looking too hard and not finding what I want.*

They drove a few miles in an uncomfortable silence. Finally, Meg tried again. "If you're worried about office protocol, you don't have that much to be concerned about. Bob told me about them opening a practice together.''

Valerie was surprised. The plan was supposed to be a secret until the details were firmed up, after which, Bob would have to disclose the prospective partnership to every client, to prevent any claims of conflict of interest. It was important that the news not come out until they were ready. "Bob told you? It's a secret.''

"I can keep a secret, Valerie.''

"I know that," Valerie told her impatiently. "I just wondered why Bob would say something about the partnership to you, that's all.''

"I think he likes me, that's why," Meg said quietly, rushing the words.

"He must like you a lot, to tell you.''

"That was clue one. Clue two was when he kissed me.''

Valerie couldn't hide her astonishment. "Bob Vanette kissed you?''

"Yeah." Meg used both hands to self-consciously smooth her hair, then folded them in her lap. "Don't get me wrong, it wasn't like the way Jay was kissing you, all pressed together like that. It was shy and, I don't know, sort of endearing, the way he is." She looked out the window for a moment. "Do you think it was okay to kiss him? I mean, with me just coming out of that long thing with Dave, do you think maybe I'm wrong to feel so..." Meg's voice trailed off.

"So, what?" Valerie prompted.

"Happy," Meg said, so softly that for a moment Valerie wasn't sure she'd heard right.

Valerie wanted to cheer. She never would have picked Bob Vanette as the man for her friend, but as she thought about it, she realized it wasn't a bad combination. Meg could use someone steady and solid.

"I think you should do whatever makes you happy," she told her, and meant it. It was just too bad, she thought, that she was unable to use the same logic in her own life.

IT SEEMED as if the two of them had argued, every minute of the two weeks Jay had been back to work, starting when Valerie made her admittedly relieved announcement that she had new evidence Roberta could be lying about Judge Haskins. She had shoved the thick transcript of the Preddy divorce proceedings across her desk, inviting Jay to read the contents at his conve-nience.

Right now, he unceremoniously plunked it back on her desk. It was over a thousand pages long, eloquent testimony to how acrimonious the proceedings had been.

"Well?" she demanded.

His eyes locked with hers. "Well, what?"

She sighed wearily. "Don't you see what I mean?"

Jay settled into the chair beside her, slouching a little and scowling at her. "Ah, yes, the Brettinger theory of sexual harassment. All neatly laid out in this nice fat trial transcript." He slapped his hand mockingly on the cover. "Let's set the scene. Roberta hates her husband. It's not surprising, the way he sleeps around, and she is not exactly warm and willing. How am I doing so far?"

You sound like a jerk, Valerie almost mumbled. Instead, she smiled brightly. "You're getting there."

"Yes." His voice dripped sarcasm. "The guardian the court appointed to make a recommendation about custody of their two boys had a concern about Roberta, felt that she hated her husband so much, she might interfere with his visitation rights. But since the guardian recommended she get custody of the kids, anyway, you know what he must have thought of the husband. Anyway, there haven't been any further proceedings, so apparently visitation is going according to plan. The guardian's prediction, therefore, was way off base.''

''That doesn't mean he was wrong about everything,'' Valerie observed.

Jay used the fingers of one hand to stroke his chin while he thought. Valerie couldn't help noticing that his hands were almost healed. She was pleased, even if Jay was aggravating the hell out of her right now. It was time to get this business with Roberta over, she decided. She was sick and tired of the investigation. After all their hard work, they'd found no solid evidence of sexual harassment and neither of them had changed their gut feelings about the truth of Roberta's charges.

He sat straighter now, placing one hand on each lean thigh, a picture of thinly controlled patience. ''Okay, I'll assume for a minute that everything the guardian testified to is the absolute, unvarnished truth. Roberta hates her ex-husband, and she doesn't like sex. So what?''

She gritted her teeth. ''So, she's a bitter woman who is striking out at the most convenient target.''

Jay snorted, and then shook his head at her as if he didn't for a moment think she believed what she was saying. ''The county judge is a convenient target? A man with that kind of power?'' He paused for a moment. ''Besides, Valerie, this was a good job for her.'' He gestured again at the transcript. ''One thing *is* clear from that. She needed to find a paying job after the divorce was over. Why would she risk losing it?''

"Let's go over this one more time," she began wearily. "First, Roberta wasn't at work on five of the dates she alleges the judge harassed her—"

"Three of those dates she clarified, Valerie," Jay interrupted. "The other two could be flukes—inconsistencies that may never be explained."

"Whatever." She waved her hand in the air. "The judge has denied Roberta's charges several times, and frankly, I believe him. He's been a lawyer in Amsden for thirty years, and if he'd behaved irregularly toward other women in that time, I think we'd have heard about it before now."

"We might have, if we'd talked to the other women who have worked for him," Jay said, and there was no mistaking the accusation in his voice.

"We interviewed the last two, and nothing happened to them. No matter what you think I should do, Jay, I'm not going to go back any further, not without evidence. There's the judge's reputation to consider." This was old ground, and she wanted to scream at how dense he was.

"Okay," Jay said, and she could tell by the tone of his voice that he was at least as irritated as she was. "How about the evidence on the other side? Roberta's sister confirms her allegations." Valerie made a gesture of dismissal with her hand, but he went on without pause. "Our own secretary says he leers at her. He didn't actually make any comments to Brenda, but he does make her uncomfortable, which we have to consider. Then there's the most important evidence of all—the way Roberta told her story to me. It was one of the most compelling accounts I've ever heard. And she has everything to lose, and not one single thing to gain by making these accusations."

"Telling a story is not evidence. It's her word against his."

"Telling a story *is* evidence, Valerie," Jay insisted, leaning forward, his blue eyes on fire with his need to convince her. "Sometimes that's all the evidence we have. It's the only direct evidence I had in the Michaels trial. We're trial lawyers. In court, how many times has it come down to which story the jury believes? That's their job, and now it's ours."

Usually, Valerie's job was to present a case, advocate for the prosecution, and leave the verdict up to a jury, with proper persuasion, of course, to make the right decision. That this decision was now her responsibility was totally unsettling. She couldn't meet Jay's eyes.

Jay got up and strode to the window. Valerie didn't know about the judge's alcoholism. In defiance of logic, he had never told her. He didn't know exactly why, he just had a feeling that he shouldn't, that the timing wasn't right. For one thing, if she finally concluded that Roberta was telling the truth, she would be unconsciously looking for a way to excuse the judge's behavior. There was always the possibility that she might try to convince herself that he was drunk and hadn't known what he was doing.

Jay sighed in utter, complete frustration. He hated having to think of Valerie as an adversary, but in this case, she was. He knew how hard it was to change a person's mind when he or she believed something on an emotional level. If this was a trial, and Valerie was a juror, he wouldn't even try. He'd concentrate on the rest of the jury, the ones who hadn't formed an iron-clad opinion. Here he had no choice but to keep trying to wear Valerie down. And the fact of the judge's secret drinking was something he was going to keep close to his chest, to be brought out when his instincts told him the timing was right.

Staring out the window without seeing anything, Jay felt a tiredness seep deeply into his bones. For all the initial promise his return to Amsden had held, he felt his life had stagnated. The idea of his own practice was the only thing going forward. On the personal front, things were most affirmatively back to what he guessed was "normal." He didn't want normal. He wanted Valerie to come to her senses, period. In every way. Damn it, how long was he supposed to atone for his past sins, how long was he supposed to wait?

Outside, it was snowing, not the big, fat snowflakes of a warm, damp snowfall, but tiny, hard, gray flakes that promised a stretch of bitter weather. "It's starting to snow, Valerie," he commented, abruptly shifting gears. "Wind's picked up, too."

"There's supposed to be a bit of a storm," she mumbled absently, lost in thought.

He turned. "A bad one?"

She shook her head. "I don't think so, but it's been a strange winter. This morning, the radio said two inches or so."

"Yes, well," he said uncertainly, coming back toward her, "I guess I'd better get to work." What would she do, he wondered, if he just took her in his arms again and kissed her until she had no resistance left? He thought he could do it; she liked it when he touched her, whether she admitted it or not. But it wasn't the way he wanted it to be. He wanted her to come to him without that kind of persuasion. He rejected the notion. "I've got some research I'm late on. I should have been doing it instead of reading that transcript these last couple of days. Roberta's claim isn't the only thing I have to do."

Valerie looked ruefully down at her desk calendar. Lately, the big blotter-size paper had seemed like a slave driver, pushing her all the time. "I know what you mean. I've got a library board meeting tonight, on top of it all. I feel tired just thinking of it."

"You work too hard, Valerie."

She cracked a smile. She always found staying angry at him difficult, especially when he gave her the sympathy that she hated to admit she sometimes craved. "Who doesn't?"

"I don't, not anymore," he told her. He hesitated before going on. "I used to work all the time, but I realized I was just covering up for the fact that my life was empty." His voice dropped to a whisper, and he looked directly at her. "I think sometimes you're more like me than you realize. You're doing the same thing."

Jay always managed to twist what she said. Most aggravating of all was the fact that she could never separate the message from the man. She was always so aware of him, and that made her behave in strange ways. Despite herself, she managed to give him a sweet smile. "Thank you, Dr. Freud."

He bowed elaborately before letting himself out. "Anytime."

CHAPTER TEN

IT HAD BEEN a long but productive day. His research was finally finished, and now all he had to do was write it up. When Jay got back upstairs, he could hear the wind howling more fiercely. Even though it was only late afternoon, most of the office lights were on. He saw down the corridor that Meg's office was dark, but there was a light on in Valerie's.

She was standing by the tall old window that looked down on the spacious courthouse lawn, and now he could hear the icy snow hitting the window-pane, driven by the scouring wind.

"Valerie? I think we're in for a bigger storm than we thought."

She turned quickly. "It's so noisy out there, I didn't hear you come in. Do you hear that wind, moaning around the building? It's a regular blizzard." She shivered a little. "What are you still doing here? Meg's long gone, and I sent the secretaries home at three o'clock."

"I was down in the basement, doing some research in the library. Having to drive home in this is my punishment, I guess, for refusing to use the computer. While I was in the library, I could hear the wind, but I had no idea it was as bad as this." He came up beside her and followed her gaze out the window. Although the ground hadn't been white when he'd come to work this morning, it was now completely snow-covered. On the street, a lone car went by so slowly, it seemed to barely move. "You should head home, too, Valerie. Do you have any boots with you?"

"Over there," she said, inclining her head absently. In the corner was a pair of high-heeled leather boots. They wouldn't provide any protection in this weather, Jay thought. He would drive her the five blocks home.

"If you wait for me, I'll take you home on my way out of town."

"The library board meets at seven-thirty. I don't usually go home in between."

"There won't be any board meeting tonight," he told her firmly.

"No, I suppose not. Why don't you turn on the radio, please, while we get ready to leave. Let's find out how bad this is going to be."

He switched on the local radio station, then went down the hall for his topcoat. Fortunately, the camel hair was warm, and he found fur-lined leather gloves in his pocket. He was grateful for that small discovery; he often forgot his gloves, and tonight he wouldn't want to be stranded on the highway without them.

When he came back down the hall, Valerie was already in her coat, and she pulled her plaid woolen scarf from its usual place around her neck and used it to cover her head. "It's bad, Jay," she told him immediately, her wide hazel eyes concerned. "The way the wind's blowing, some of the outlying roads are already blocked with drifts, and the radio announcer said there were near whiteout conditions outside of town."

He sighed. "I should have listened to the weather forecast this morning."

"I did, remember? You know, if I'd known earlier you were still here, I would have insisted you go home. I can leave my car here and walk home, but you've got a twenty-mile drive, and on some of those narrow roads through the hills..." Her eyes seemed darker now.

"Well, no help for it." Jay shrugged. "I'll throw another log in the wood stove when I get home, and put my feet up."

"If you get home."

"I will."

"Maybe you should check into the motel."

"Valerie, this town has one little motel. What do you think the chances are there would be a vacancy in this storm? Besides, we could be stranded for days. I'm not going to spend the time in a motel."

She looked him over, then unexpectedly nodded. "Will you call me when you get home? I'm going to worry until I hear from you."

His smile lit his face. "Of course."

She smiled back. She knew he was pleased she was worried about him. She also knew he shouldn't be driving in this weather. Storms here weren't like storms in the city. As soon as Jay hit the open fields outside Amsden, the screaming wind would be sending snow across the road, obliterating every road marker, piling up unexpected drifts that a driver couldn't always see until it was too late. Blizzards were infrequent in this part of the Midwest, but they occurred once every few years, and people died in them. He was right. They should have paid more attention to the weather reports, but now it was too late, and she knew with complete certainty that she couldn't let him drive in a blizzard.

"Come home with me," she said abruptly.

"What?" He had been looking down, rummaging around in his pocket for his car keys, but his head snapped up at her words.

"Come home with me. You can stay in the guest room. I've got plenty of room, and if the storm stops and they get the roads plowed, you can head to the farm tomorrow."

For a second, Jay almost refused, a crazy macho refusal with a blunt statement about how he could drive through anything. Then his brain finally clicked on. His first thought was how foolish it would be to drive. Then the second thought hit him before the first was completely out of his head. He'd been trying to maneuver her into spending some time alone with him ever since he'd come back to work. She'd just offered him at least a day in her company, confined in her warm, cozy house, the storm howling with such fury that neither could venture out. He was struck with an inconsequential thought. She had a fireplace.

"Thank you, Valerie," he said in a soft voice.

Something in his voice warned her. She looked into his eyes and saw they were guileless, but there was still something there. Was he hoping...

"Just to sleep," she told him firmly, and was embarrassed at how presumptuous her directive sounded. What if he hadn't been thinking the same thing she was?

White teeth flashed and the laugh lines around his eyes deepened. "Do I get to eat dinner with you, or would that be taking too much advantage of your hospitality?"

She let go, then, and they shared a comfortable

laugh. It was going to be all right, she thought. She would have to govern her own emotions, that was all, and not let Jay create any situation she couldn't handle. It would be okay. It would have to be okay. She had made the offer to let him stay, and that had been the right thing to do.

"Ready to brave the elements?" he asked with his devastating grin, and already she was thinking of him, his eyes, his lips, all of him.

He hustled her down the stairs. At the door, he hesitated. Before pushing into the slate gray darkness outside, he spoke. "Wait here. I've got my gym bag in the car, and I'll go get it. That way, at least, I'll have my sweats to sleep in." Head down, he charged into the storm.

She waited for what seemed like a long time before Jay literally blew in the revolving doors. In the half-block walk to his car, he had become completely covered with snow. It coated his dark hair and whitened his coat. "Maybe I should drive us," he gasped, trying to catch his breath. "It's even worse out there than I thought."

"I don't know if a car could get through the side streets," Valerie observed reasonably. "We'll be better off walking."

"Whatever you say. Ready?" She nodded and he guided her ahead of him through the revolving door. Once they were outside in the fullness of the blizzard, there was no way they could talk. She could have put her mouth next to his ear and shouted, and he wouldn't have heard her in the noisy wind. Jay grabbed her arm as they began to plod through the heavy snow. The wind was at their backs, which was a good thing. Valerie knew she'd never be able to walk five blocks against it.

After a little while, Jay was no longer sure exactly where they were. A couple of the stores must still be open, because their windows dimly lit the snow at intervals. They should be out of the downtown area by now, he knew. They weren't making much progress against the snow, and it was all he could do to hold on to Valerie in the driving storm.

Maybe Valerie's sense of time and distance was finer than his, or maybe it was just that she had had more practice, having walked this way every day to and from work. In any event, she was finally pulling him up what must be a walkway and then he was on her open, broad porch, slightly out of the wind. She fumbled with her key, and then, blessedly, they were inside.

She switched on a lamp. "Come into the laundry room. We've got to get out of these soaking clothes before we freeze to death."

"What you need is a shower," Jay told her, eyeing her dark pink face and ears. Her scarf had not been much protection against the fierce blizzard. "You'll never warm up without one."

"You can have one, too," Valerie offered.

He nodded. "I'd like that. But you should go first."

"You're a guest."

"Valerie. Don't start an argument within two minutes of my arrival. I'm trying to be chivalrous here. Even a liberated man likes to let a woman go first sometimes. Take a shower."

Valerie suddenly decided she didn't like talking about who was showering first. The situation was going to be intimate enough without imagining him in her bathtub.

She used a smile to cover a sharp flash of nerves. "Well, I'll try to hurry."

"Take your time," he called after her, but she was already climbing the stairs. In the bathroom, she stripped out of her wet, frozen clothes, straining to hear him downstairs. It was no use. Even inside, the noise of the wind was so loud, she couldn't hear anything. But she knew he was down there, in her house, and he'd be there all night. She shivered. From the cold, she told herself.

Valerie turned on the hot water full blast, as hot as she could stand. The shower felt good, blessedly good, but she hurried. Jay must be as cold as she was. After she dried herself, she tried to decide what to wear, resisting the urge to put on something special. This wasn't a date, for heaven's sake, and she had no excuse for dressing up.

Surrendering in part to the impulse, she put on stretchy taupe stirrup pants and a finely knit red sweater. Its loose lines weren't provocative, but its silky angora wool made it the softest garment she owned, and she knew the bright color warmed her fair skin. Feeling funny, Valerie put on little earrings of pure gold, dabbed on some perfume and stroked a bit of blusher across her cheekbones.

"All yours," she called into the kitchen as she came down the stairs.

Jay appeared in the living room, gym bag in hand. "You look great," he said with a grin.

It was a mistake, he saw immediately. Her face closed and she cast her eyes down. He could see she was nervous, and he wondered if that was a good or bad sign of things to come. Whatever happened, they might be confined together for a few days, at least. He needed to avoid upsetting her.

"The bathroom's upstairs and to the right," she told him, her voice sounding small. More firmly, she added, "I've got to call my mom and dad before they send out a search party. Take your time getting warm and I'll make us some dinner."

"Thanks," he said happily, bounding energetically up the stairs.

After a moment, Valerie walked to the bottom of the stairs. Seemingly unable to stop herself, she climbed a few until she could see yellow light coming out from underneath the closed bathroom door, but of course she already knew she wouldn't be able to hear any sounds.

This was ridiculous, she thought. She was standing near the foot of the stairs like a lovesick teenager. Like the foolishly romantic girl she had been. Was that who Valerie Brettinger, ambitious prosecutor, potential political candidate, all-round independent woman, had become?

She headed for the kitchen, but once there, forgot what she intended to do next. He was up in her shower, naked. She imagined his lean thighs wet from the stream of water. That same water would soften the little lines around his eyes and mouth. She could touch her own lips to his and taste the moist heat there.

She wanted him. She knew that as surely as she knew her own name. She had wanted him almost from the time he'd come back into her life. She had been determined not to risk her heart again, and she was right, she thought. Valerie Brettinger was smart, smart enough to learn from her mistakes. But she did want Jay, and she wondered if it was possible to surrender the physical part of herself without surrendering the whole. For her, that might be impossible. She sighed and squared her shoulders.

By the time he joined her, Valerie had completed

her call to her parents and was stirring the homemade spaghetti sauce she had defrosted. "Smells wonderful," he told her, sniffing appreciatively. She held out the wooden spoon for him to taste, and his lips closed over the tip. "Delicious. This blizzard has given me quite an appetite. What can I do?"

She looked him over. He radiated a damp warmth from the shower, as if he hadn't bothered to towel off completely, and he hadn't made use of the blow-dryer she'd left out. He wore gray sweatpants and a navy blue jersey, both softly worn to threadbare comfort.

"Salad, bread, or wine duty?" she asked, matching his tone.

"I'll make the salad." She opened the refrigerator door and handed him the bag of leafy lettuce. He busied himself at the sink, and in a minute he began to sing, at first to himself, then louder.

In the bright, warm kitchen, she could hear his fine husky voice mingling with the whine of the wind and the pebbly sound of icy snow hitting the windows. He was singing a vaguely familiar ballad. She couldn't hear all the words, but the song had something to do with roses.

She put water on to boil for the pasta. Standing next to him, she sliced French bread and twisted the cork from the bottle of Pinot Noir that she had bought on impulse and had had, unopened, in the cupboard for months. "What's that you're singing?" she asked curiously. "Something about a garden? That's a strange song for a day like this, isn't it?"

He smiled to himself, drying the lettuce carefully on paper towels. "I guess so, but it's just what came into my head. It's an old, sad song about some lovers who had a spat. She wouldn't forgive him until he lay dying. You know those old songs. Anyway, their love survived in the rosebushes their families planted. The song has been around for a long time, so a lot of people must like it, but I suppose a practical woman like you thinks its sentiments are hopelessly romantic.''

''Hopelessly,'' she agreed. ''But I'm not as hard as you think, Jay, if that's what you're trying to get at. I'm more than capable of love.'' Of course she was, she thought. Perhaps it *was* time to try to forgive old hurts, at least take advantage of the opportunity the storm had brought.

''No one's as tough as they try to be, Valerie. Not my dad, not me, not you.'' He shoved his hand through his wet hair, making clumps of it stand on end. ''How did we ever get on a subject like this?'' he asked with a rueful smile.

Unconsciously reaching up, she stroked the wayward hair into some semblance of order, until his sharp intake of breath reminded her she was touching him. She froze, and for an instant their gazes locked. His eyes looked darker than usual, threatening to tug her into their blue depths. Quickly, she pulled her hand away.

''The storm is like a song itself, isn't it?'' she asked nervously, saying the first thing that came into her head in an effort to start the conversation again. ''Listen.''

He was quiet for a moment, then said, ''It's so bright and warm and safe here, and I know what would make this place really mellow. Do I have time to start a fire before we eat?''

She had another flash of nerves, stronger this time. ''Sure,'' she managed to say. ''I've got kindling set up, and there are some newspapers there. The matches are on the mantel. The old fireplace doesn't draw too well, and it can be hard to get a fire going. There are some pinecones in the copper scuttle next to the fireplace, and they can help get things moving—"

"I can handle it, Valerie."

She knew she was rattling on. "Right."

By the time he was done, she had set the round oak table in the dining room, and dinner was ready.

The meal took a long time. Valerie was hesitant to let dinner end, with the long evening stretching in front of her. A very long evening, with Jay in her living room. It was simply easier to have something to do. Jay, too, seemed content to linger. They talked about books and movies. Carefully, they avoided the subject of Roberta. In fact, they didn't discuss the office at all, even during the infrequent lulls in the conversation.

Finally, Valerie stood up. "Do you want some coffee? I don't have any dessert, unless you want some of my mom's banana nut bread. I've got some in my freezer."

Jay chuckled. "What other delights do you have in that freezer of yours? Besides, of course, homemade spaghetti sauce and homemade banana nut bread?"

"I like to cook, but there's only me, so I always freeze the extra," she replied, a touch defensively.

He nodded, the remnants of laughter playing around his mouth. "I've still got wine left, so I'll pass on the coffee, but thanks." He paused then. "Let's save the banana nut bread for breakfast tomorrow."

Oh, God, she thought, her stomach taking an abrupt dive for her feet. *He'll still be here in the morning.* He would go to sleep in this house, and he would wake up here. With her.

He saw her face, and in that moment, he knew he wouldn't be spending the night in the guest room. She was still shaky, still nervous, but it would be all right. He knew it.

He leaned over and felt her stiffen even before he touched her. Jay amended his intention to kiss her fully and settled for pecking her on the cheek. There was no need to rush, after all. "You made dinner, so I'll clean up." He propelled her gently in the direction of the living room, ignoring her faint protests.

"Well, I'll just go up and make sure everything's ready in the guest room," she said, finally wandering away.

But she didn't. Instead, she simply sat in the living room, staring into the fire. Why had she said that about the guest room? Jay wouldn't stay there, and she knew it, and she was pretty sure he knew it, too. She leaned back into the sofa and closed her eyes. She didn't put on the stereo or the television, instead listening to the wind as it sang and cried around the solid old house, looking for entry, but finding none. Valerie willed her mind to lose itself while she listened, and a very long time seemed to pass as she stayed there, unmoving.

"Can I turn out the light?" Jay's voice was soft, but so near she jumped.

"If you want."

He sat next to her on the sofa, stretching his long legs out in front of him, leaning back as she had been doing. "I like what you've done with the house." Shadowy green plants filled every nook, and in the dim light cast from the open doorway of the kitchen, soft colors glowed against the mellow old wood. Firelight patterned the room in moving bands of light and shadow.

"Thanks. When I moved in, the interior was a shambles. I did the decorating myself, even refinished the floors, and my mom and I shopped for a year for these old pieces.'' She hurried on. ''We found that lamp over there at a garage sale, then I went to the art show and got those watercolors over the mantel, and those candlesticks I found in a boutique in Columbus, of all places.'' She stopped, realizing that in her nervousness she was rambling again, trying to fill a heavy silence that seemed to be all around the edges of her consciousness.

Jay's voice was gentle and intimate. ''Valerie, don't talk. Just sit with me.''

After a while, he put his arm around her. ''You're afraid, Valerie. We can tell each other anything. Tell me why you're afraid.''

She looked into his eyes, watching the firelight play over his face. She didn't say anything.

''You're afraid of what we're going to do together,'' he said.

This time, she nodded slightly.

''We're going to make love tonight.'' It was a statement, not a question, and he was delighted when she gave another small nod, almost a quiver, of agreement.

''I'm not afraid of you, Jay,'' she whispered. What she was afraid of was herself; she was afraid of exploring again the depths of those bottomless hurts she experienced every time she let herself feel what she wanted to for Jay. He was so complicated now, going far beyond the simpler man of long ago who had seemed to need only her comfort, comfort that had always been easy to give. Now she knew he could burn with anger, laugh with infectious good humor, whisper her name in a voice thick with desire. He overwhelmed her.

She nuzzled her head into his shoulder, and his

arms tightened around her. For this small space of time, just during the blizzard, she was going to let herself go, test the limits of herself again.

She lifted her head and kissed him on the mouth. He responded warmly, but gently. He was waiting; she could feel it in him. "Jay," she whispered softly, "it's time." Valerie used the tip of her tongue to lightly outline his lips. Tonight was now. The past was over and tomorrow couldn't come until the storm was over.

He crushed her to him and kissed her deeply, his firm mouth harsh in his need for her. He didn't use his tongue lightly, as she had done. Instead, he thrust it between her parted lips, rocking it into her.

Between their bodies, he insinuated his hand, stroking the front of her sweater, moving its silky soft folds lightly across her skin. He stopped kissing her and moved slightly away, reaching up to her neck and beginning to pull apart the tiny pearl buttons that held the high collar together. She was still, watching him watching her as his fingers opened one, then another.

Jay's breath caught sharply and he pulled her to him. "I want to undress you, but this sweater has so many of these little buttons. Is this some torture you've planned for me?" A lustful smile curled the corner of his lip, exaggerated in the firelight, and suddenly she felt her own fingers on her sweater, urgent in her attempt to help him. Between them, they managed to get enough of the buttons undone to allow him to pull the red angora over her head.

She was truly beautiful, he thought, watching her breasts quiver in the dancing light cast by the fire. Outside, the ceaseless blizzard was raging, and he could hear his own voice begin a moan, softer than the storm. He bent to her, using his breath to heat the skin under her bra. She moaned, too, then, holding his head to her.

When he unclasped her bra and gently pulled it off, he took her breasts in both hands, their heavy firmness registering somewhere deep inside him, as he remembered the night they had climbed the hill for the last time. Someday, he'd tell her exactly how hard she'd made it to leave. But not tonight.

Instead, he bent to kiss her again, circling her nipples with the tip of his tongue before taking one in his mouth and suckling deeply.

At the touch of his wet, firm lips, every nerve ending came to life, starting at the tip of her hard nipple and sending their signals outward with lightning speed. Feeling the warmth hit her limbs in waves, she knew she needed more, more of this tight, hot male body against her skin. Her breath was ragged. "I want to feel...." Her voice trailed off.

"What?" he prompted softly.

She turned her head, suddenly shy. She had fantasized about Jay for a long time, but the real thing was overpowering.

He reached up and put his fingers on her chin, tugging gently so that she had to look at him. "Tell me what you want to feel. We can say anything, Valerie." His eyes were wide, and the fire gave the black, dilated pupils little leaping glints.

Her breath caught in her throat. "You," she told him. She took another breath and tried again, pressing his hand to the bare skin below her collarbone. "Like this."

"Without my clothes," Jay supplied, willing himself not to smile at her discomfort. Valerie was so independent, he wouldn't have imagined this shyness from her. For some reason, it delighted him that she could be bashful about making love with him.

"Don't tease me," she whispered. As answer, Jay's lips took hers in a searing kiss that left her breathless and bolder. Reaching out, she pushed the worn, soft jersey up over his smooth stomach, and he slipped it quickly over his head. Valerie moved against him, rubbing her breasts against his bare chest. The sprinkling of dark hair clustered in the center felt sensational against her bare skin. His chest felt good, she thought, hard and warm. Better than good. She put trembling lips in the hollow of his throat, smelling faint traces of her scented soap mingling with a scent that was his alone.

He stroked her hair with one hand. With the other, he guided her hand downward toward his lap. Her fingers closed over the bulge she found there, heavy and hard and hot under the worn sweatpants. He groaned, his lips against her cheek as she stroked him, outlining the distinctive hard length of him with her fingers. Valerie felt a rush of melting pleasure at finding him as eager for her as she was for him. The tip of his tongue darted into her ear for a heart-stopping instant, and then his hand sought hers again, this time pushing it gently away.

He stood up, and in one smooth motion managed to rid himself of both his sweatpants and briefs. The sight of him put an end to all Valerie's remaining self-consciousness. She had imagined his body before, too many times to count. But reality was so much better than fantasy. He was all male, startlingly so, with smooth broad shoulders that tapered gracefully, all the way to the triangle of black hair that started below his navel and sheltered... Quickly, she stood to finish removing her own clothes. She bent to pull off her thin stockings, and when she straightened again, he took her immediately into his arms.

The warm fire was at her back and his even-warmer bare skin pressed against the front of her body. Valerie put her arms around his waist and stroked the small of his back as Jay kissed her deeply. She moved her hands lower, caressing his buttocks and using the tips of her fingers to urge him even closer. His hardness was against her stomach and she moved slowly back and forth, wanting to feel it firmly against her skin. She was on fire, and it made her greedy for the feel of him.

"Oh, Valerie," he whispered, his voice catching a little as she moved against him. "You're so beautiful, and I've wanted you so much." She moaned softly into his neck as answer. "Lie down with me," he urged her in a voice made husky with passion.

He pulled her down with him onto the carpet in front of the fire. He kissed her for a moment, then stirred and muttered, "Wait, I'll be right back."

She waited for him in a haze of desire, feeling herself in a dreamlike state as she listened again to the blizzard that was only a wall away. Then he was back, easing himself down beside her, tossing a small packet aside. She wasn't surprised he had protection with him. This night was meant to be, and in a strange defiance of logic, she'd known he'd have what they would need.

"You've been carrying this around in your pocket, planning to seduce me?" she asked in a whisper, hoping it was true, tangible evidence that he had been wanting her as much as she'd been thinking about him.

His voice was against her ear. "Not exactly in my pocket. But I've had some at my house, and some in the car. The crazy way I've been feeling, I didn't want to take any chances.'' She both felt and heard his soft chuckle. ''I didn't just go for my gym bag when I went out to the car.''

Valerie sighed against him. In some ways, he was the same old Jay, her old friend, the man she expected to be concerned about her. But there was this potent masculinity, too, this heady attraction, and being held against his hard unyielding body was quickly crowding out anything other than raw need.

It was the feel of his hands on her. They had almost healed and were still surprisingly hard and a little roughened. Then she lost the ability to think at all as his hands caressed her. Slowly, he moved them down her body, from her throat, across her breasts, down her stomach, finally to stroke the tender skin of her inner thigh.

And then his fingers moved slightly higher, dizzying her with intimate, loving strokes, the little noises she was making telling him the best place to arouse her. She clasped his head to her breasts as he continued to caress her with a soft rhythm that made her ache somewhere deep inside of herself. But his fingers didn't soothe it. Instead, the ache got worse until she felt herself turning inside out, hoping he could reach even farther, touch and hold that place buried so deeply, she hadn't even known it existed. Suddenly, she heard herself urging him to hurry. He held her tightly as her climax came, murmuring endearments.

Afterward, he rolled them onto their sides, still clutching her gently to him. His tenderness and care wrapped around her as his arms encircled her. Valerie laid her head against his chest, listening to his rapid heartbeat, hearing his rasping breath. What he had just given her was wonderful, but it wasn't nearly enough. Jay's excitement fueled her own. "Please," she whispered, "I want to feel you inside me."

Jay lifted his head and smiled into her eyes, but the strain in his features was starkly evident in the light from the hearth. "And I want to be there, more than anything. More than you can know." He drew in a shuddering breath. "But we've got all night. I could touch you again." She was shaking her head, smiling back. "Don't you want to be held a minute more?"

"No," she whispered. "After, not now."

His eyes were lit by a blue fire that was not reflected from the fireplace but came from inside. "I aim to please," he started to say lightly, but his voice broke over the words. He couldn't be easy and teasing, not about this. He had wanted this moment, imagined the experience for so long, and he had planned for their lovemaking to be as romantic for Valerie as it was for him. But her plea changed any intention he may have had to go slowly. She wanted him inside her, joined with her.

He positioned her so that she was on her back beneath him and entered her carefully, watching her face. When he was fully inside, her lips formed a single word, said so softly it was almost a sigh. "Yes."

When he began to move within her, it was as if they had been together forever. She lifted her hips to him, wrapping her legs around him, and the heat inside her began to build almost immediately.

He thrust in her, slowly at first, and then more rapidly as he felt her response. The feelings he was arousing in Valerie were so powerful that they took her beyond herself. In a minute, she was no longer in front of the hearth, watching the firelight as it made leaping shadows over the face and body that held hers.

It was as if she were outside in the wild night, except it was hot there, the harshly blowing snow stinging with heat instead of cold, the wind howling and tossing her in blistering fury. When he urgently cried her name, she heard his voice on the wind. Then the blizzard was inside her, buffeting her as she met a last, hard thrust. Suddenly, she felt Jay exploding against her, and she joined him in a shattering release that she shared with him and with the storm outside.

CHAPTER ELEVEN

WHEN SHE AWOKE, she could still hear the blizzard. It surprised her with its noise. She had slept so soundly that she'd expected to awaken to a still world, but she was happy that it continued to storm. As long as it did, Jay would be with her. He was here now, his heavy thigh thrown across hers, pinning her to the mattress.

For a moment, Valerie watched him sleep. His face was turned toward hers, and his black hair was its usual messy, unruly mass. Thick dark lashes lay curled against his cheeks and a morning stubble darkened his heavy jaw. In slumber, the little lines around his lips and in the corners of his eyes seemed softer. Valerie leaned closer, marveling that he was really here, inhaling his scent, a warm, sleepy smell that clung to his skin.

Slipping out by inches, she managed to get out of bed without disturbing him. But as soon as she was free, Jay rolled over onto his back and began to snore quietly. Valerie smiled as she made her way to the bathroom. He had earned the rest. They had been up a good part of the night, making love. Feeling herself blush, she remembered how it was after they'd finally picked themselves up off the living-room floor and climbed the stairs to her bedroom. They'd barely hit the mattress, when they'd felt the need for each other again. And again.

She washed her face and brushed her teeth. Picking up the hairbrush, she tried to style her hair into some semblance of order. Wandering out of the bathroom, she wondered what time it was. It wasn't light outside, but of course the blizzard would make even the daylight dim.

"Valerie?" Jay called from the bedroom. Smiling, she headed there.

He was propped up on one elbow. "Oh, good, I was afraid you'd gone downstairs." He patted the sheet beside him. "I've kept your place warm. Come back to bed."

She glanced at the clock and saw it was after ten. By now, she was usually hard at work, and it would be positively decadent to climb back into bed. But when she saw Jay's slow grin, she couldn't resist, sliding between the warm, rumpled sheets.

"You're smiling like the Cheshire cat," he teased. "How come?"

"I wouldn't fan that healthy ego of yours by telling you," she retorted. "Your smile already looks smug enough."

Jay laughed out loud and pulled her into his warm arms. "God, you're sweet, even with that sharp little tongue of yours." He kissed her and tried to catch her tongue between his teeth.

She teased him with her tongue, darting it into his mouth and repeatedly snatching it away as he tried to capture it with his lips. "Enough," Jay finally said in a heavy whisper. She stopped, only to feel his fingertips under her arms. "Are you ticklish?" he asked impishly. "Ah, yes," he purred in satisfaction, watching her writhe under his touch.

Valerie's face and body felt hot. "Stop, please,

stop," she implored breathlessly, peal after peal of helpless laughter shaking her.

Abruptly, he pulled her against him. "I'll stop, but only on one condition."

"Name it," she told him, laughter still shaking her body.

"Let's see," he said lazily. "I'm sure I'll think of something. I know." He whispered something so erotic that she felt an instant blush on her cheeks. What had seemed so right last night felt funny in broad daylight.

She must have stiffened a little, because Jay propped himself up onto one elbow again. "You're embarrassed."

"A little."

"After last night? What could embarrass you now?"

"It was dark last night," she explained.

Suddenly, he was serious. "You're a beautiful woman, Valerie, and last night was the most special night of my life. I don't want you to be embarrassed with me." He smiled. "But, of course, if it has to be dark—"

She squealed as she felt him pull her all the way under the covers. He rolled on top of her, and the sheet and blanket formed a cave around them, a dark cocoon. He loved her there, firmly and possessively, kissing her hard on her yielding lips, trailing his open mouth down her body, until their gasping breath made it miserably hot. Then he threw off the bedding and Valerie found she didn't care about the light. Now she cared only about him, wanting him so much, she tried to absorb him into her own skin.

THERE WAS NO DOUBT about it, Valerie thought drowsily when she awoke before dawn early on Saturday morning. This time was special, unique. The storm had created a sense of intimacy, and she felt more secure with Jay than she ever had before. He went to bed with her, but the most important thing was that he woke up with her. The blizzard guaranteed it.

She couldn't help smiling with an unfamiliar sense of contentment as she realized how closely Jay held her in sleep. His leg and one arm were around her again, something she could easily get used to. Then she realized what had awakened her. It wasn't a noise, but the absence of one. There was no howling wind, just a stillness everywhere.

Sliding out from under him, she padded over to the window. She pushed back the curtains, and saw it was still dark. The world was pearly white, the snow so deep that it bent even the branches of the huge old trees to the ground. Some of the big drifts were as high as the shed roof on the house next door. The moon in the newly clear sky lit the whole still scene. The blizzard was over.

"No more storm." The voice from the bed sounded loud in the quiet night.

"No more storm," Valerie repeated. She shivered.

"You're cold." In a minute, Jay had come to stand next to her, putting his arm around her waist. "It's beautiful out there," he said quietly, his eyes taking in the softly sparkling scene, washed in muted white and gray-black and a few of the most delicate pastel colors.

He was right: it was beautiful, so beautiful, it made her heart ache. She felt his arm tighten around her.

"It's over, our little respite from the world," he said.

His thoughts were so exactly like her own that she swallowed heavily, and watched him for a moment, gazing at his profile as his eyes were fixed on the outdoors. The dim light from the window lit his features, highlighting the tip of his nose, his cheekbone, his strong chin. Except for the unruly mop of dark hair, he was fine, perfect. He had never looked so handsome. When he turned to her, his eyes were dark hollows in the night.

"It's too early to get up. We might as well get some sleep," he said.

They went back to her bed together, but neither slept. Instead, Jay lay stretched out on his back next to her, his fingers twined with hers. Valerie felt uneasy, despite Jay's closeness. Their time together would end very soon.

They didn't talk much, but listened to the stillness outside, instead. Occasionally, there was a muffled sound as one branch or another dropped a heavy load of clinging snow.

At six, Valerie couldn't stand it anymore. "I give up," she told him, climbing out of bed. "There's no reason for you to get up, Jay. Go ahead and lie there a little longer."

"I think I will." He gave her a lazy smile and rolled onto his side.

When he came downstairs three hours later, she had the radio on. "The plows are out. The main roads outside of town should be cleared later this afternoon."

He nodded, pouring himself a cup of coffee and coming to sit beside her. "How bad was it?"

"Bad enough, and a lot more widespread than we thought. Apparently, the radio has been covering the storm twenty-four hours a day, broadcasting all the shelter and rescue information. Both Toledo and Cleveland got hit, too. Everything in northern Ohio has been shut down since Thursday night, even the mail."

"Thanks to you, I didn't have to spend the last two nights in a shelter."

"Or worse."

"Right. You know, I haven't thanked you properly for taking me in."

Valerie cracked a smile. "Oh, I think you have."

He smiled warmly in return. "These days have been like a vacation to an exotic island."

More like a honeymoon, she thought, then quickly pushed the unbidden idea away. There had been no talk of the future. She had absolutely no reason to think about honeymoons or believe in forever afters. Quickly, she spoke.

"We were luckier than we knew. At least, we had electricity. Most of Amsden has been without any for over twenty-four hours. Without electricity, my furnace wouldn't run. No heat would have sent us to a shelter by now ourselves." But the power had stayed on. Every last thing had cooperated to give her this brief time of almost-perfect happiness.

Jay went to the refrigerator and poured a large glass of orange juice. Trying to make her voice sound casual, she asked, "When were you thinking you'll need to start for home?"

He looked at her piercingly. "Getting tired of me?"

"Oh, no."

"Well," he said slowly, "I suppose we ought to listen to the radio again, and find out when the roads toward the farm are being plowed. And I'm certainly not going to leave until I help you shovel out your walk and driveway."

Valerie tried to hide her relief. "Digging out might be fun."

It was. The snow was heavy and very deep, so they contented themselves with shoveling her sidewalk only. Then they ended up just goofing off, building an elaborate snowman in her front yard.

Finally, they were back in her warm house. When Jay went to take a shower, Valerie turned on the radio again. Over an early dinner, she told him the truth, although she dreaded saying it. "The roads that lead to the farm are apparently relatively clear."

"Did they define 'relatively clear'?" Jay asked with a frown.

"The plows went through at least once, but you'll have to be careful."

There was a long silence. "It will be dark in an hour or two." Jay raked his hand though his hair. "Do you think I should take a chance on driving those roads after dark?"

"Do you want to stay another night?"

He nodded. "If that's okay."

"Of course you're welcome to stay." She tried not to let him see how much pleasure she felt.

"Thanks, Valerie." He looked at her without smiling, but she saw a little light in his eyes. He could have left, she reminded herself as she got up to clear the table. Instead, he'd chosen to stay.

But time was against her again, and Sunday morning was inevitable. Her newspaper was delivered, signaling that the town was getting back to normal. The paper was full of news about the blizzard and its aftermath.

Still Jay made no move to go. Finally, late Sunday

afternoon, he stirred. "I suppose the courthouse will be open tomorrow."

"Yes, I'm sure it will be."

"I have to go now, I guess. I'll need another suit for tomorrow." The words came slowly. "I've got hearings scheduled in the afternoon, and I should get to the office first thing in the morning. I've finally tracked down the last one of Roberta's former employers, and I have an interview with him at eleven."

She nodded. The time had come, and she needed to be steady. "I've got a ton of food in my freezer. While you get your things together, I'll find you a carton of soup, or something, to thaw when you get home."

"You don't have to bother."

"It's no bother." She hesitated. "I've been taking care of you for three days now. Let me do it one more time."

"Okay." He seemed to be about to say something more, then stopped. Abruptly, he left the living room, and with heavy steps she headed for the kitchen.

A few minutes later, Jay was back with her, holding his coat. "I could stay the night, and leave early tomorrow morning to get my good clothes and grab a shower before I go to work."

It was so tempting, almost overwhelmingly tempting. But one more night wasn't going to ease the ache she felt. Actually, knowing he'd be slipping out of her bed before dawn would only make their parting worse. "You'd have to leave practically in the middle of the night."

"I know. That wouldn't make much sense, would it?" He fitted his broad shoulders into his topcoat. "Well," he said quietly, "I guess this is it, then."

Now that the sky was clear, it was bitterly cold,

and Valerie was concerned about him keeping warm. He'd have to walk more than five blocks to where his car was parked and shovel it out of the drifted snow before he could even begin the long drive home. Walking him to the door, she stood in the doorway as he left her porch, carrying his gym bag and a paper bag with his suit in it. Her snow shovel was over his shoulder. She'd made him borrow an old cap of hers, a warm but hideous hot-pink thing complete with knitted flowers. He'd pulled it down over his ears, the ends of his black hair sticking out every which way.

"Will you call me when you get home?" she asked, hoping there was no pleading note in her voice. Quickly, she tried to rally. "I mean, the roads are better, but I'll still worry. Call me to let me know you made it safely."

"I'll call you as soon as I get home," he promised.

Jay turned to go and she started to close the door. "Valerie," he called unexpectedly. She opened it again.

He stood on the walk looking at her with those pale blue eyes. It was a moment before he spoke. "I just wanted to tell you... I love you."

Waves of emotion crashed through her, mixing up her thoughts. She opened her mouth to speak and nothing came out. It felt as if she was silent for a long time.

"Say something, Valerie, anything at all. Whatever you're thinking, I need to hear it."

"Okay, yes." Valerie swallowed, but her throat still felt tight. Jay was standing on her walk, staring at her. The man had just said he loved her; of course she was supposed to say something. She hesitated, studying him. Jay met her gaze fully, waiting. But his words felt unreal, as unreal as the last three days already seemed.

She took a deep breath. This was going to be hard. "Jay, this has been a really intense couple of days. I mean, we've been locked together for some time. Stuck together, really. And neither one us has had a...well...a physical relationship for a long time, and..." She paused painfully. "Look, maybe you're overreacting to the moment. You know you haven't had experience with really strong feelings, with nights like the ones we've spent together..." Her voice trailed away.

He didn't move. "I love you," he said again.

If only she could believe him, maybe she could make her legs move, go down that icy path into his arms. But what did Jay know about real love—not love when the setting was romantic and snowy but love when it was hard, when there were problems, when he had to open up and share with someone?

"Jay, you'll feel differently when you get home, away from here. You might be embarrassed at maybe having said too much, you might wish nothing had changed." She desperately wished for some more reassurance.

But something seemed to die in his eyes even as she watched. "Valerie, do you feel nothing's changed?"

There was a long, strained silence as he waited for her to explain what she couldn't explain.

Finally shifting abruptly, Jay pushed the snow shovel more firmly against his shoulder and yanked his gym bag to his side. His voice was much rougher than the one he'd used a few moments ago. "I get it, Valerie. This is punishment, isn't it? My punishment for making love to you all those years ago and then leaving you. You want me to know how it feels.'' There was a heavy pause. ''Well, I'll tell you—it hurts, damn it! It hurts. Do you still wonder if I can feel things nowadays? Well, you just found out.'' Furiously, he turned on his heel and strode down the walk without looking back.

Her response was not about punishment, and she certainly hadn't meant to wound him. In a convoluted way, she had been trying to protect him, give him a chance to back away gracefully from emotions he might not be able to handle. And, of course, she was trying to protect herself from the hurt she'd feel when he took advantage of her feelings.

''Give me time,'' she pleaded softly into the empty, cold air. She needed time, time to adjust. She had gotten so used to thinking of Jay as one kind of person that she needed time to learn to think of him as another.

The telephone rang. Still she stood in the open doorway, though Jay had already disappeared from sight behind the huge drifts. The phone rang and rang, until she finally came to her senses, shut the door and went to answer it.

''How did you weather the storm, dear? Wasn't it exciting?'' It was her mother's voice.

Valerie guessed she made some sort of appropriate noise. It was all she was capable of at the moment.

Her mother was happily rattling on. ''I hadn't been to the store, so we were caught a little short. No lettuce or milk or anything, but we made do. I fixed chili and kneaded bread, and when the power went out, Dad stayed up all night to feed the wood stove. Two nights, actually.'' She sounded downright delighted about what most would regard as hardship. ''We just hunkered down and let it snow.''

At the cheerful words, the ache in Valerie's throat practically overwhelmed her. Her mom and dad had almost a lifetime of making do and doing together. Her mother could count on her dad to be there for her, and their love had comfort and contentment. Stability. She'd been raised to believe that was what love was. She knew she would never be able to accept less.

JAY WASN'T in the office right away the next morning, and she felt a stab of real fear. Although the roads had been cleared, they were still bad. What if he really hadn't made it home, after all? Of course, he hadn't called her last night. She should have known he wouldn't.

Meg and the secretaries spent the first hour or so sharing stories of coping with the blizzard. It was happy, excited talk, but Valerie had no heart for it. And she could hardly swap anecdotes with them about what she'd been doing. She could just imagine their faces if she told them she'd spent most of the last three days making love with Jay. On the floor in front of the fire, on the sofa, in her bed...making love, making love. She felt her mind wandering, reliving those erotic hours.

"What did you say?" she asked guiltily, hearing her name.

Meg's eyes were serious. "I asked if you'd heard from Jay? He hasn't come in yet. I wonder if the roads are still bad out his way."

"I haven't heard from him since—" Valerie stopped midsentence, just in time. "I know he got out of here all right Thursday night," she said hastily. "I'm sure he'll turn up soon."

She walked away, and after a moment Meg followed her. "Did you talk to Jay during the blizzard?"

she persisted. "Are you sure he made it home all right on Thursday?"

"Oh, yes, I talked to him." Part of her wanted to tell Meg something about what had happened, but she couldn't. She'd never talked about her feelings for Jay with anyone.

"The phones weren't out over his way, then?"

"Um, no, at least not at the beginning of the storm." Valerie heard herself and was ashamed. "Meg, I'm sorry, I've got work to do. I have to go out of town to a seminar later this week, and I've got a brief due."

Meg sighed. "Me, too. I mean, I've got briefs to write, too." She headed for her own office.

Valerie tried to concentrate. She did have a complicated brief to write, and if she couldn't get the document done before she had to leave for Columbus, Meg or Jay would have to finish it. She didn't want that to happen; it wasn't fair to saddle one of them with her work just because she couldn't seem to focus. She turned on the computer, but the search for the right case law didn't absorb her the way it usually did. That made her feel even more guilty, as she realized she was staring at the screen without reading anything it displayed. Computer time was expensive, and the office could ill afford it. It was costing twenty dollars a minute to sit and brood. Sighing, she began the process of logging off.

Her stomach heard him before her ears did and gave a quick flip. Jay was finally here, down the hall, making some remark to the secretaries. Her first sensation was relief, quickly replaced by the anxiety that was beginning to settle heavily in her stomach.

Then he was outside Meg's office, and Meg was asking him how he had managed through the storm.

"Okay," she heard him say briefly.

"Did you have electricity?"

"No, but I've got the stoves, so I was okay."

"I hope you had supplies laid in."

"Thanks for asking, but really, I was okay, Meg."

"Didn't you feel awfully alone, way out there for so long?" Meg asked, and Valerie felt herself stiffen.

"Well, like I said, it was okay." There was a pause. "I'm glad to be back, of course."

"I bet you are," Meg said, laughing, and Valerie heard Jay's footsteps.

Here it comes, she thought, bracing herself. They worked together, and she had no choice but to face him, endure the awkward words, the tightness between them.

Jay stepped into the office and shut the door behind him. He stood leaning against it, hands in his pockets, scowling. There was strain in the deepening lines around his mouth.

The ache grew. Nervously, she formed a smile. "Hello, Jay."

He wasted no time on formalities. "We have to talk, Valerie. I have to know, where do we go from here? Just tell me, okay?" He took a quick, determined breath. "You know, I thought I said what you wanted to hear. But you didn't want to hear those words, did you? So just say it, say what you want. Clear enough so I can understand."

She sat very still, struggling with where to begin. "You didn't even call," she accused finally. Even to her, her complaint sounded absolutely absurd.

One hand came out of his pocket to rake through his hair in a characteristic gesture of impatient frustration. "After what you said, you sure as hell didn't think I'd call, did you?"

"Well, so I could be sure you got home okay. You promised."

Still by the door, he swore in disgust. "And it's just another illustration of how I don't keep my promises, right? I was furious, Valerie. And I think I had a right to feel that way, after trying so hard to tell you how I feel and then getting that little speech about how I couldn't mean any of it. You wanted me to call you so that we could be just *friends* again, concerned about each other. That's what you can handle."

Nervously, she used a finger to trace the gold rim of the coffee mug on her desk, over and over. It was hard to look at him. "Jay," she started hesitantly. "I didn't mean to hurt you, I swear. But you've had twelve years. Now *I* need time."

There was a moment of strained silence as he rubbed the space between his eyebrows. When he spoke at last, his voice sounded utterly weary. "We've had time, Valerie. What we've had is too much damn time." There was another small pause. "I also used to think that all we needed was time. That eventually I'd get a chance to prove something to you. I was wrong."

The sadness that overlay his quiet voice made Valerie hurt all over.

Jay's hand went into his pocket and came up with a flat black box. He took three strides toward her, then tossed it onto her desk. It landed right next to her mug, making her jump.

"I was late this morning because I wanted to make one stop first." He flicked his hand, indicating the velvet box. "Last night, I lay awake thinking and I came up with this idea, you see. This...strategy, like a lawyer would use. It was the only thing I could think of, and—if you gave me any encouragement—

I was going to make this grand gesture." His mouth turned up in a grin, incredibly self-mocking. "This stupid, embarrassing grand gesture. For evidence, you know. Proof."

Wordlessly, Valerie stared at him.

"Proof," he repeated, as if she was supposed to understand. "I meant this to show...well, never mind what I meant. Just accept it now as a gesture of gratitude, for your concern about me Thursday night." He turned on his heel, and was at the door in a second. It shut quietly behind him as he let himself out.

Valerie sat there a moment, unable to move, curiously numb. Then, hands quivering, she slowly opened the box. Nestled against black velvet was a huge opal, hanging from a chain that was whisper-thin, caught in a setting of twisted gold. She ran a shaky fingertip over the stone's cold smoothness. It was frosted, pearly white, with glowing flecks of pink and red and blue in its depths. Jay didn't have to explain the gesture to her; she knew instantly why he'd chosen this gift. Ice and firelight. He had captured the storm.

And Valerie, who had promised herself never to cry again over Jay Westcott, put her face in her hands and felt her palms grow wet with tears.

CHAPTER TWELVE

SHE HADN'T TALKED to Jay again before she'd had to
leave for Columbus. She'd been back a few days now,
and wanted to see Jay, but he'd suddenly had an out-
of-town deposition that couldn't wait, according to
Brenda. Valerie sighed. He couldn't avoid her forever, and they needed to talk.

Wearily, she dressed for work. Columbus had been
hell. She'd had to sit through one interminable meeting after another. Valerie had ignored the fact that the
prosecutor's seminar was a good place to make con-
tacts, and that Judge Haskins had told her over and
over that a politician never missed an opportunity to
make an impression. Actually, she couldn't remember
a single person she had met in those four days.

All she could think about was Jay, and how maybe
she'd misjudged him. Jay said he loved her. Maybe
he did. She certainly loved him.

The realization that she was in love with him had
hit her somewhere on Interstate 270, on the way back
to Amsden. It had been a hard admission, something
she hadn't wanted to make. Love gave people the
power to hurt you, and she knew firsthand what loving Jay had done to her.

She got into her navy blue wool skirt and pulled
out her new ice blue silk shell to wear with it. She
had bought it in Columbus, on a long shopping spree
that had helped to fill an empty evening but had not

given her any pleasure. Briefly, she wondered if she would feel pleasure ever again.

Valerie smoothed down the shell and automatically reached for the conservative gold chain she usually wore. The black velvet box on the edge of the dresser caught her eye, and she opened it and stared at the opal pendant. Did Jay still want her? There had been something in his eyes when he had tossed the box on her desk, an attitude of defeat that was incongruous with his anger, and that was puzzling and scary to contemplate.

She picked up the pendant, dislodging the little pin that held it against the velvet. She put it on, and slipped her suit jacket around her shoulders.

But when she was done brushing her hair and gave herself a final once-over in the mirror, she realized she couldn't wear the necklace. Meg and the other courthouse staff would be sure to comment on such a lovely piece, and what was she going to tell them? When she reached up to undo the chain, for a second she couldn't get her fingers around the tiny clasp. She cursed, fumbling with it, and suddenly was hit with a flood of recent memories.

Most powerful of all was the image of him on the ice, holding on to little Jimmy Canfield in the water. She knew with certainty that he would never have let go. Never. And she wondered how it could have been that she hadn't realized right then that she was in love with him.

Her mind skittered to the blizzard, the torturous walk through the relentless snow. The safety and co-ziness of home. Her attack of nerves despite the right-ness of Jay's being there. God, he had been tender with her. There had been the fun time when they'd built the snowman, and midnight at her window when their thoughts had been so in tune, it had been like sharing one body. And finally, he had stood in the clear, biting cold in her old knitted cap and said he loved her, said the words she had waited half her life to hear.

Valerie's fingers moved from the clasp to the pendant itself, lifting its heavy smoothness and slipping it under the edge of the shell, against her skin. It felt almost like a promise.

LEANING AGAINST the door of the Porsche, Jay wadded up the paper from the fast-food hamburger he'd had for lunch, then thoroughly smashed the empty cardboard drink cup. He was putting off heading to the office for a few seconds more. Valerie would be back from Columbus and with no court in session this afternoon, he'd probably end up running into her at the coffee machine or somewhere else public enough to require courtesy.

Well, there was no way to avoid the inevitable, short of emptying his desk and walking out, which was tempting. Very tempting. With a pivot that would have done him proud at Wednesday-night basketball, Jay sent the paper ball sailing toward the trash barrel at the curb. Of course, he missed, so he strode over and plunked it into the can.

"Good thing you picked that up. Littering is a violation of a city ordinance."

The voice was practically next to his ear, causing him to jump.

Dave Grau stood next to him. Where on earth had the guy come from? "Dave," he said quickly. "I didn't see you there."

"No kidding. You damn near jumped out of your skin." There was satisfaction in his voice. Meg's old boyfriend was out of uniform, dressed in jeans and a ratty-looking jacket. There was an uncomfortable pause as he took a few nervous puffs from a cigarette, his eyes intent on Jay. "So, how are you doing?"

Rotten, Jay wanted to say, and seeing Dave again wasn't helping. In fact, lately, it had seemed he'd been running into the guy all over town. It was getting a little strange.

"I'm doing fine. You?"

"Okay."

Jay stood there awkwardly. Dave must want something, to be hanging around all the time. At first, Jay had figured he wanted him to put in a good word with Meg, or something, but Dave never asked. Jay wouldn't have done it anyway. Meg was very well rid of him, as far as he was concerned.

"Off duty today, I see," he finally offered.

"Not really." Dave took a long pull at the cigarette before tossing it to the pavement next to the trash barrel. "I do some private security work on the side. I'm headed there now."

"Well, I won't keep you, then," Jay said, relieved. With a quick goodbye, he shifted his briefcase to his other hand and headed down the sidewalk to the office. He walked more rapidly than usual, uneasy because he had the sensation that Dave had not moved from his position by the curb, that he was watching Jay from behind.

When he got to the office, Brenda told him that Valerie had asked to see him right away. That was a surprise. He'd figured she'd try to stay out of his way, pretend they were just colleagues. He pushed open her door without knocking, and she looked up quickly from her seat behind her desk.

"Well?" he asked in a tight voice.

Valerie got up quickly, smoothing her already smooth wool skirt, firmly pushing down an intense flare of nerves. "I need to talk to you. Can we go somewhere?"

"I don't think so. We don't have anything to discuss except work, and we can talk about that right in your office." Although he shut the door behind him, he made no move toward her.

She winced at his tone. "Jay, you have every right to be angry at me—"

"I'm not angry," he assured her in a voice that sounded anything but reassuring.

Valerie licked her lips, starting to walk toward him. Something in his eyes stopped her before she had taken two steps. Standing still, she spoke to him from across the room. "Okay. This is what I want to say. I was wrong not to accept what you said after..." For a second, she faltered, not sure what to call what they had shared. "After the blizzard," she finished lamely. "I realized I was wrong. Wrong about a lot of things."

He folded his arms across his chest and leaned against her office wall, his face unreadable. "Just what things have you been wrong about?"

"About doubting you." She took another long breath. "About saying I could never love you again."

His eyebrow quirked in a familiar gesture, but it was the only part of his body that moved. "You could?"

She nodded, swallowing hard. "I could. I do."

Valerie wasn't sure what she had expected. Maybe that he would throw his arms around her, hug her, tell her that he'd been waiting to hear her say these words. But it wasn't happening. Instead, he was looking at her with an odd, blank expression that chilled her. She had seen this look on his face before, but she couldn't remember the last time.

"I don't think so." Although he disputed her words, his voice was soft, as if he wasn't really arguing with her. "The problem isn't love, anyway, Valerie. It's trust. You can love me like you care for everyone—especially when people need you—and you can desire me, but you can't trust me." He raked the fingers of one hand through his coarse dark hair. "You could let me make love to you for three solid days—days I thought meant as much to you as they did to me—and have it mean nothing."

"That time in the storm wasn't nothing," she started to say in a whisper, but he was continuing as if he hadn't heard.

"When I was leaving your house, I said something I've never said to anyone before, not even to the woman I married. All three days with you, I was working up the courage to say those words. It was hard for me, but I told you I loved you. And yet you thought I was just responding to a few hot, sexy days and nights."

"I just thought—"

"I know what you thought, Valerie," Jay interrupted. "And that's precisely the problem." Jay brought his hands up in a helpless gesture, then let them fall again to his sides in a posture of resignation. "I knew you didn't trust me, but I thought I could show you I'd changed. Now I realize how foolish that was. A trial lawyer, of all people, should know you can't prove to somebody that something *won't* happen. I can't show you that I won't leave again, no matter what happens, no matter what problems come up. I can promise it, but I can't prove it to you before it happens. You have to take it on faith, and where I'm concerned, you can't do that, can you, Valerie?"

She couldn't look at him. She thought about the times he had left her, thought about how even now he was going off on his own to practice law, thought about his empty house. Jay was right. It had been much easier for her to believe that he didn't have staying power, than for him to prove her wrong.

"Well?" he prompted softly.

For a moment, the barest second, she couldn't say a word, and in her hesitation he had his answer. He swore softly, vehemently, and the sound seemed to echo into the silence.

Finally, he spoke again, and his voice was distant and cool. "I told you I'd wait a year or so before I left the prosecutor's office, and I'll stick to my word if you want me to. I can go or I can stay. It's up to you."

"You don't have to leave on my account." Her response was automatic, polite. She was aware of her body's numbness.

"Are you sure?" The corner of his mouth turned up in a grim half smile. "I've had to work hard to avoid you these last few days."

She brushed his concern aside, careful not to let him see how badly she was hurting. "Your new office isn't even ready yet. This is a small town. We're both lawyers, and we're going to be around each other, regardless." *If you stay,* she thought. "You don't have to avoid me, Jay. After all, we still have unfinished business."

"Roberta." His voice was weary, bleak. At her nod, he said, "I don't think I can finish the investigation with you, Valerie, even if I'm staying on. I don't think I can…work closely with you anymore."

She sank into her chair. It was over, finally over, and looking into those cold eyes of his, she knew there was nothing she could ever say or do that would make things right. It was over with Roberta, too. She had to finish it. She knew in her heart he was right. She might just be able to stand it if he stayed in his office and took care of his own cases, but she couldn't share any project with him.

"It's all right," she managed to say, trying to keep the tears bottled up. The numbness was wearing off, and she found herself begging her famous self-control not to desert her now. "There's no real evidence that Roberta's allegations are true. I believe in the judge, and I'm ending the investigation right now."

Unexpectedly, Jay strode into the room. "What I wouldn't give, Valerie, for some of that loyalty you show Judge Haskins. That man can't do anything wrong, while I was never even given a chance."

Valerie leaned back in her chair, studying him. That cold emptiness was still in his eyes, and she realized with a start when she'd last seen it. It had been twelve years ago. He hadn't looked that way since he'd come back to Amsden. That is, not until she had put that expression back on his face. She felt a fierce stab of guilt. She needed to get this over with as quickly as possible.

"I'll write a formal memo for Roberta's file, with my conclusions," she said in a voice that even to her own ears sounded small and shaky. "You'll need to sign it, too."

He said nothing, and she was overwhelmed by his presence. The power of his disapproval was all around her. Agitated, she rummaged around aimlessly in her desk drawer. She needed some gum or something sweet. Finally, her hand closed on a mint, the kind restaurants give out after a meal. She kept her eyes on the candy she was unwrapping to keep from having to look at Jay.

"Before you tell me it's all over, I think you should know that everything's not always what it seems. Judge Haskins, for example."

Her hands fell still. Something in his voice warned her.

He continued, looking grim. "I didn't tell you before, because it's not strictly relevant to the investigation, and I didn't want you to think anything excused the judge's behavior." Jay's eyes fell to Valerie's hands. "Have you ever wondered why Judge Haskins is always sucking on those damn mints?"

She looked down, confused by the turn of the conversation. "He likes them, I suppose. It's a habit."

"It's a habit, all right, but not the one you think. The man's an alcoholic, Valerie. You, who supposedly know him best of all, didn't know that, did you?"

When her face rose again, all the color had drained from it. Jay hadn't planned to tell her, but he couldn't let her simply reject Roberta's story.

"How do you know?" Her voice was just above a whisper.

Jay had a moment's small satisfaction that she accepted his assessment without argument. It was the first thing that had felt right since he'd stood on the snowy walk at her house and told her he loved her and understood what the words really meant. How long ago it seemed. "I just know."

She licked her lips. "But it doesn't mean he's sexually harassing Roberta."

He nodded, his voice firm. "I know it doesn't, Valerie. But it makes you wonder whether you know him as well as you think you do, doesn't it?''

Unwillingly, she nodded, but she was hardly conscious of doing so. All her carefully thought-out arguments were gone. What she was left with was her instinct, and now she questioned even that.

"It doesn't matter anymore." She heard the dullness in her voice. "As you say, it's not even relevant. If Roberta's charges are true, the drinking's no excuse. Is it?"

"No," he said, his face devoid of all expression.

"And if he didn't say and do the things Roberta claims, he's just another guy with an alcohol problem. Isn't that the way you see it?"

"More or less."

"So," she said with false briskness, "I'll write the memo, and when it's done, you can review the document and sign it, and then we won't have any more excuses to have to spend time together...." Her voice trailed away miserably.

Suddenly, he erupted into the silence. "Valerie, I'm not going to sign it! The judge is a criminal and I'm not going to put my name on a memo that says he isn't."

He caught her by surprise. "I didn't expect you to agree with my conclusions, Jay. I'll note your objections in the memo, and you're free to add whatever opinions you want."

He paced. "I'm not sure my *opinions* on the subject would be printable. Valerie, you're so...so stubborn...about everything." Back and forth he walked, and watching him make the turn at the wall like a caged animal made her want to scream. He tugged at his wayward hair. "You're pulling rank on me with this thing. I'm right about this. I know it as a lawyer and I know it as a human being. Just give me a little more time, let me talk to all the women who have worked for him."

"It's over, Jay," she stated. "I've told you, we're not on a witch hunt. Someone had to end this thing and I just did! Now," she said, struggling for composure, "I'm going to write it up, and you can do whatever you want."

"Whatever I want?" He stopped pacing, and there was a dangerous glitter in his eyes. "You're the prosecutor, you're in charge, and if I work for you I have to accept that."

She didn't answer.

"You'll have my resignation as soon as I can get it dictated."

She slammed the palms of her hands down on her desk blotter. "That's right," she said, her voice rising, hurt and anger overtaking her. "Leave. Go on, it's what you always do when things get tough for you. Don't worry about the promise you made. Let's see." She looked pointedly at her watch. "That promise you made again about five minutes ago."

His pacing had brought him in proximity to her desk. Now he leaned forward, his face close to hers. "Valerie, how can you expect me to stay now? My integrity is at stake. Can't you see that? You did what you had to, and now I'm doing what I have to. It doesn't have a thing to do with my promises, or my alleged lack of staying power. I'm trying to do the right thing for Roberta."

"And the easiest thing for you."

He straightened. "No! I made a promise, Valerie, to myself. A promise that Roberta could count on me. I can't sign my name to that memo, with or without my objections noted."

"You don't even have an office at your building." Her voice rose again, and the tears finally spilled over.

"I'll make a little cubbyhole in the corner, and the remodelers can keep working. They'll just have to move a little faster than I'd planned." He strode over to the door and flung it open. "Besides, I already have a big case I'm working on."

"You do?" Her shocked mind felt heavy and stupid.

"Oh, yes," he said, and his eyes bitterly taunted her. "Roberta needs a good lawyer, one who really understands sexual harassment. As soon as I can put it together, we'll be filing a lawsuit against dear old Judge Haskins, asking for money damages. The next time you see him, Valerie, you might tell him it's time to get a lawyer, after all."

THE NEXT MORNING, Jay's office was bare and neat, the only paper on his desk his terse letter of resignation. Reading it, she was almost overcome with loneliness, and she was fearful, too. This lawsuit Jay was threatening could cause tremendous pain for everyone concerned. Her only hope was that Jay would rethink his plans when he had a chance to cool off.

Over the next month, she did some things to ease the pain. Mostly, for the first time in her life, she talked about Jay. Meg was a good listener, her eyes wide with sympathy as Valerie talked for hours, telling her story from beginning to end.

"I had no idea you had any past with him," she said, pouring Valerie a second glass of wine. "It does put a different light on things. I can see why you were so reluctant to get involved with him again."

Valerie gulped air before sipping her wine. "So, you think I did the right thing, letting him go?"

Meg smiled. "This has to be a first. Instead of everyone pouring out their problems to you, you're the one looking for advice." She gently squeezed Valerie's hand. "Did you tell me what to do about Dave Grau?"

Valerie shook her head. "I told you I'd support whatever decision you made. Is that what you're going to tell me?"

"Yes, that's exactly what I'm telling you, but I'm going to add something, too. Valerie, I'm not trying to flaunt how Bob and I are beginning to feel about each other. I'm just going to say that I think real love and caring are worth just about anything. More than I used to think. Other things are fulfilling in their way, but without love they really don't add up to a whole life."

Valerie thought about Meg's words often over the next few days, especially when she was writing the letters of resignation to most of the boards and committees she sat on. They no longer held her interest, and she realized the ceaseless activity was wearing her out. The judge had so many ideas on how to further Valerie's career. She wanted that, too, but not if it engulfed her whole life. If she was to become a politician, it would have to be her dream, not the judge's, and it would have to be done her way.

She wanted time to do a good job at work and be able to live quietly again. She wanted to read and cook and have more time for her friends. Maybe she should redecorate her house again, make a clean sweep of things. It was a pleasant thought that for a moment pierced through the dull misery that was always with her these days. She was surviving, she could survive the loss of love. If only she didn't have to learn the same lesson over and over again.

A day after she'd resigned from her various posts, she went into the courtroom and let herself into Judge Haskins's chambers without knocking. Brenda had told her the judge wanted to see her right away, so she knew he was expecting her.

He sat at his big old oak desk, fiddling with some plaque he had been given, but he smiled broadly when he saw her.

"Valerie, sit down, my dear. I was just about to have some coffee and maybe some sweet rolls. Do you want anything?"

She shook her head. "Thanks, but I had lunch with Meg."

He nodded, still smiling. "I haven't thanked you for the tremendous effort you made in clearing my name."

"You've received my memo on the investigation."

"Yes, of course, and I've read it several times. You were very thorough."

She felt the smallest flash of guilt. She had been fair, she thought, as fair as she knew how to be. But Jay had wanted to conduct more interviews. "There was no proof," she explained.

"Right. I knew there wouldn't be." He picked up his mints. "I don't think I'll waste the calories on a sweet roll, after all. Want a mint?"

She shook her head and he popped one into his mouth. "I've got some great news for you, Valerie." He paused to make the moment dramatic. "It's not official yet, but the news will be coming out next week. You're going to be the party's candidate for state representative."

She was stunned. "How could that be? I thought

Brett Hardin was a shoe-in. He's older, and he has more experience than I do. The guy from the governor's office told me I'd need to wait a few years.''

"Let's just say I called in some favors.''

Valerie still couldn't believe it. "You made this happen? Why?''

He popped another mint into his mouth, and Valerie noted the familiar quivering of his hands. "I pay my debts, Valerie, as soon as I can. And as I said, I'm grateful for your help.''

He was grateful for her help. For a second, the words didn't make sense and then she was stunned anew, this time at her own naïveté. "You don't owe me a thing, Judge,'' she said, her throat tight. "Jay and I conducted a balanced investigation, and I made the finding I believed in.''

He waved her words away, his arms making exaggerated sweeping gestures. "Of course, of course. I'm only taking care of you, Valerie, like I always do. You're my protégée. I'm just glad that when the chips were down for me, you knew what to do.'' His eyes narrowed to slits, almost buried in the folds of his cheeks. "The question is, what are we going to do about Westcott?'' He paused. "There's been some talk among the lawyers. He's going to be filing a civil suit against me in the next couple of days.''

So he had heard. Nervously, Valerie moistened her lips.

"Couldn't you have kept him in the prosecutor's office?'' the judge asked. "He was causing enough trouble there, but at least he was under you.'' Viciously, he tried to pull the paper wrapper from another roll of mints, not succeeding. "He's as arrogant as his old man was, and in the end, just as stupid. He can't file that suit. Period.''

"There's nothing I can do about it, if that's what you mean," Valerie told him. "I could talk to him, remind him there's no evidence, but Jay does what he wants to do."

The judge was still wrestling with the paper on the mints, and he leaned back and appeared to concentrate fully on the task. She watched in sudden fascination. *He's not what he seems…he's an alcoholic, Valerie.* She'd believed Jay, knowing that alcoholism was something he understood too well. But she had looked carefully for signs of the judge's drinking in the month since she had learned the truth, and she hadn't seen any. Perhaps she hadn't wanted to. But today, Valerie was seeing Judge Haskins in a new light. And it wasn't a favorable one.

The judge finally gave up on the tube in his hand and just held it. "You're a smart girl, my dear, one of the smartest I've ever known. You can persuade Westcott not to file this suit."

Valerie stood up. "There's no way I could do that."

The judge laughed suddenly, a hollow sound that rang through the room. "There's the oldest, easiest way of all." His voice dropped, purring. "Don't you think I haven't seen the way he looks at you? Don't you think I know exactly what he wants? You could give it to him, persuade him to drop the suit."

Valerie's hand flew to her throat as she felt the hot blush flooding her cheeks. *Dear God.* It was all she had time to think, before he spoke again.

"Don't look at me that way, Valerie. You like him, too, don't you?" His voice was like thick silk, cloying and persuasive. "You're special, and I would never ask you to do anything distasteful."

In a weird way, he was enjoying himself, Valerie

realized with a sick lurch. She heard herself speak softly through stiff lips. "It's true, isn't it? It's true about Roberta."

His denial was immediate. "No."

She gripped the back of her chair for support. "You're a liar, Judge. And I'm a fool."

"And you're a real disappointment to me." He made a disgusted sound and threw the tube of mints viciously against the wall. His eyes were bright, fevered. "Tell Westcott I want a deal," he said desperately. "I can't have this all over Amsden, not after thirty years. I've had a long career, and maybe it's time I retired. Tell Westcott that if he doesn't file the suit, I'll resign."

Valerie was finally at the door.

"Tell him, Valerie."

She took a deep, determined breath. "I'll tell him, but not for you, Judge. I'll tell him so Roberta can decide if it's punishment enough."

JAY DROVE, concentrating on the power of the Porsche that he could command with the press of a foot. He had no destination in mind but he'd gotten little enjoyment out of the car, and tonight driving felt good, as good as anything could feel nowadays.

When he got to a stretch of road he knew was fairly straight and open, he let it out a little. It was dark and he couldn't really fly, not the way he wanted to. But he could inch it up, and he did.

He slowed for a curve he knew was there and took it smoothly. He knew these roads well.

A few minutes later, he skirted town on the north, but didn't spare it a glance, keeping his gaze focused on the ribbon of road ahead.

He must have been successful in shutting out the

world, because he didn't notice the police car behind him until the lights flashed insistently.

Instantly, he pulled over. He didn't need to look at the speedometer to know he'd been speeding, and cops seemed to take particular delight in handing out tickets to guys driving Porsches.

When the officer approached, Jay was surprised to see he wore the uniform of the Amsden police, not that of the county sheriff. Jay knew he had looped around and wasn't that far out of town, but it was unusual to see an Amsden policeman crossing his jurisdiction.

He knew most of the city cops, and he knew this one, he realized a second later. It was Dave Grau. Oh, God, not again, he thought. Not tonight. It was getting so every time he turned around, the guy was there.

He lowered the window. "Hi, Dave. I'm sorry, I know I was going too fast." By admitting right away to the speeding, he hoped to get this over with quickly.

"Mr. Westcott." Dave's voice was grim, and Jay didn't miss the formal salutation. He must think Jay was going to try to talk him out of the ticket.

Jay put his elbow on the edge of the window. "Look, Dave, I've had a rough night, but I know it doesn't excuse the speed. Give me the ticket. It's okay." He had his wallet out by this time, and he started to open it.

"Get out of the car, Mr. Westcott. Now."

For a second, Jay wasn't sure he'd heard right, then he moved to comply. He got out and stood in the open doorway of the car. The buzzer sounded, signaling he'd left the key in the ignition, but he made no move to retrieve it. The sound and the eerily flashing lights from the police car gave the scene a surreal quality.

"Why do you have your wallet out, Mr. West-cott?" Now the voice was almost a purr, although the eyes were hard.

"Well, to give you my license," Jay replied, puzzled and uneasy. "I figure you need to run the plates and the license through—"

"I think you're ready to offer me a bribe."

"No. Oh, no, Dave." He started to reach again for his license.

"I think I'll add that to the list."

"The list?" Jay repeated, feeling stupid, as if he'd somehow forgotten his lines and misplaced the script.

"The attempted bribery of an officer, the speeding ticket and the drunk driving charge."

The drunk driving charge? He was incredulous. "I haven't had anything to drink."

Dave laughed shortly, and it had a cold ring to it that increased Jay's apprehension. Jay looked around. The road was deserted, and there were no house lights visible. He knew this was a dark, isolated stretch of highway. He had a feeling Dave Grau knew it, too. What the hell was going on?

Dave was speaking again. "I've been following you for a while. You didn't notice, did you? Too drunk, I suppose. I followed you out of town after I observed your vehicle weaving from side to side."

He tried to think. Whatever was going on, he definitely didn't like it. "If you have the kit here, I'll take the breath test right now," Jay told him. "Or if you'd rather, I can follow you back to town. That would make it within your jurisdiction." Jay had little hope the suggestion would work, but he wanted more than anything to get back to where there was someone else around. He had no reason to fear Dave Grau. No reason except the coldness of his eyes and the cruel set to his mouth.

"Ah, jurisdiction." His voice drew out the word. "Now you sound like a lawyer, with the fancy talk. As you know, I can cross my *jurisdiction* if I'm in pursuit of a felon or even a drunk."

"I am not drunk!" Although Jay's brain told him to stay calm, his mouth and tongue seemed to have a will of their own. "Give me the breath test. Let's both be on our way here."

Dave's eyes narrowed. "Let's try some simple things first, Mr. Westcott. Put your arms out and close your eyes. Now, take your left hand and touch it to the tip of your nose."

Jay did as he was told, although he was humiliated and getting increasingly angry. He willed down the anger, knowing it would interfere with his judgment. Right now, he needed to stay cool.

"Now, the right hand. Touch the tip of your nose." Again, Jay complied. "Mr. Westcott, go to the middle of the road and walk along the line."

"What's going on here?"

"I'm giving you a standard sobriety test. Are you going to do what I say, *Mr.* Westcott?"

Dave was acting like a cat toying with a mouse, Jay decided. But he had no choice, so he went to the middle of the road and took a few steps along the painted strip that divided the highway.

He turned back to Dave, who stood leaning against the Porsche, arms folded. "Satisfied?"

Dave grinned. "Very. Okay, you can come back over here."

Jay came back slowly. He started to get into his car, but Dave thrust out a hand to restrain him. "Just a minute."

COURTING VALERIE 273

What now? he asked himself. In that second, Dave whipped him partway around so that Jay was belly up against his car. For a brief moment, he thought about making a run for it. But there was nowhere to go, and running might be just the excuse Dave needed. Excuse for what? It didn't matter, because before he had time for another thought, Dave had Jay's hands pinned behind him, and he felt handcuffs locking over his wrists. Jay fought down the rise of panic that the feel of the cuffs brought on, but he knew he had every reason to panic. He was being handcuffed on a dark road by a strangely threatening police officer, a man whose behavior was becoming increasingly bizarre.

"You're under arrest," Dave growled in his ear.

"On what charge?" he snapped, hoping Dave would hear no note of fear in his voice.

"Not charge. Charges, pal, as in four. Attempted bribery, speeding, driving under the influence."

"I was not—" Jay started for what seemed the hundredth time. Dave caught him by the upper arm and whirled him so the two men faced each other. "That was only three charges," Jay said, gazing defiantly into the eyes of the other man.

"Yeah." Dave took a step back, and the expression on his thin face was feral and pleased. "Resisting arrest is number four."

Jay never saw what Dave had in his hand. It could have been a nightstick or a flashlight or even a gun. But he definitely felt the blow that exploded with a white-hot flash of pain against his temple. He stumbled and tried to use his arms to steady himself, but he couldn't seem to get them out from behind his back. Of course, he thought numbly. He was handcuffed. He lurched to a halt against the side of the car, still upright, his head spinning from the blow.

Dave stood in front of him, a taunting grin on his face. "That, Mr. Westcott, was from Judge Haskins, and it comes with a little judicial instruction. Lay off this damn thing with Roberta Preddy. You got that?"

Jay got it. He drew himself up to face Dave, the pain in his head and his wrists a grim reminder that this was not the time to stand on principle. "I got it," he said from between clenched teeth. He had to calm Dave enough to get out of here, and quick.

"Good," Dave grunted. "In the next few days, you're going to be offered a deal to settle this little problem, once and for all. Make sure you take it."

He nodded, the motion of his head sending pain rocketing through him. "I got it. Come on, just get the cuffs off me and we'll both be on our way."

Instead, Dave folded his arms, regarding him with dark amusement. "You must think I'm stupid. I can't just let you go. You'll tell somebody as soon as you get to Amsden."

Even as Jay denied it, he knew it was no use. Dave was completely out of control. Quickly, he tried to think of possible escape. As he'd realized earlier, there was nowhere to run, and the cuffs would hamper him too much, in any case. If he dropped to the ground, maybe he could squeeze under the car and wait for someone to come along. No. There wasn't enough room under the low-slung Porsche. He grasped his one chance.

"Talk to me, Dave," he said softly, trying to keep panic out of his voice. "The judge must have something on you to make you do this. I know what kind of man you are. You would never do this unless you thought you had no choice. Talk to me."

Through the hard gleam in Dave's eyes, some fleeting emotion passed. "You're right, I've got no choice."

"If you're in trouble, I can help. Talk to me," Jay repeated.

Abruptly, Dave shoved him hard against the car. "I've got no choice, do you hear me? No choice."

CHAPTER THIRTEEN

WHEN THE TELEPHONE RANG, Valerie glanced automatically at the digital alarm clock on the dresser. One a.m. She hadn't been able to sleep, so she snatched the receiver before the end of the first ring.

"Valerie, it's Ellis Campbell."

"Oh, hello." Valerie was relieved. Middle-of-the-night telephone calls could mean bad news, and she was glad it was Ellis's voice, not her mom's or dad's. On occasion, Ellis needed to get in touch with her to discuss the charges that should be filed against someone he'd picked up. These kinds of calls had become almost routine. "What's up?"

Ellis spoke with an odd note of hesitancy. "I've got a friend of yours down here, Valerie, and he tells a mighty strange story. Dave Grau arrested Jay Westcott tonight on a number of charges, including resisting arrest."

She fought down a stab of fear and substituted incredulity. "That can't be, Ellis," she said quickly. "Jay wouldn't do something like that."

"Actually, I don't think so, either." Again, she heard him hesitate, and when he spoke again, his voice was soft and reflective. "I remember him coming into the hospital after lying on that ice so long he got frostbite, holding on to that kid. That doesn't sound like a person who would resist arrest to me. And Dave hasn't been himself lately."

"Dave has been really mean, Ellis," Valerie said sharply. "If Jay did anything, I'm sure Dave instigated it." She made a quick decision. "Are you keeping him in custody? I can be there in fifteen minutes."

"Yes, I think your coming down would be a good idea." Ellis's hesitant voice was beginning to grate on Valerie's alerted nerves.

"There's something you're not telling me. What's going on? What is it, Ellis?"

"Nothing, at least nothing that can't wait until you get down here. But, Valerie, I need to prepare you a little. Jay's okay, but he's been...roughed up some."

She gripped the receiver tightly. "Hurt?" she said raggedly.

"Not seriously. He's sustained a concussion, but I took him over to the hospital and the doctor says he'll be fine. Don't worry."

Valerie almost never swore, but she did now. "Ellis, if Dave hurt Jay..."

"He's all right, Valerie," Ellis assured her. "Just get down here, okay?"

She struggled into her clothes and grabbed her purse. As she drove, she tried to make her racing mind think rationally. Jay was hurt. It was the only thing that really registered. Although her mind was filled with questions, she couldn't consider them until she saw how badly Jay had been—what was it Ellis had said?—roughed up. Her fingers gripped the wheel painfully. Ellis was a kind man, and he might have been trying to spare her. If Jay was badly hurt... She started to shake with fear.

When she stopped the car, for a moment she couldn't get her trembling fingers to pop the button holding the seat belt, and then she couldn't seem to make her legs get out of the car.

Ellis met her as she was struggling, and he grasped her hand and pulled her to her feet.

"Ellis," she gasped. "Tell me the truth. Is he badly hurt?"

He put his arm around her waist, steadying her. "He's just like I told you. I don't know how bad Dave intended to hurt him, but Jay really is okay. He took a hit on the side of his head, but he was lucky. It could have been a lot worse."

She sagged against him, grateful for his solid presence. "Can I take him home?"

"Sure," he said readily. "Valerie, we need to talk before you see him. He's…well, he's mad as hell that I called you. He wanted me to call Bob Vanette."

Valerie had to look away before Ellis could see the tears that were threatening what little composure remained. Jay needed someone tonight, but he didn't want her. How ironic that she wanted to wrap her arms around him and soothe his hurt and tell him she loved him, and he wanted none of it.

Not that she blamed him, she thought. He had every reason to think that Bob Vanette would be there for him in a way that she would not. And the realization shamed her thoroughly. She had hurt him badly, more badly perhaps than even Dave Grau had.

Valerie squared her shoulders. "I'll talk to him."

He nodded and started to walk her toward the door.

"Ellis," she asked softly, "I'm glad you called me, but why did you, if he wanted you to call Bob?"

Companionably, Ellis put his arm around her shoulders. "Let's just say I know you pretty well. When I came to the hospital that day and saw how shook up you were over him, I figured you felt something for Jay Westcott, something more intense than what you used to feel for me." He smiled at her, a little painfully. "You're in love with him, aren't you? And it's the real thing this time, isn't it?"

"Yes," she replied softly. "I think I've been in love with him all my life." After so much denial, it was a great relief to finally say the words. "Thanks for calling me, Ellis. Jay and I have some problems to work out, and that's why he was difficult with you."

Ellis nodded in understanding. They had reached the door, but he put out a hand to keep her from going in right away. "Valerie, there's a second reason I called you. Jay says that Dave beat him up at Judge Haskins's instigation. Would you know the reason why?"

For the second time in less than half an hour, Valerie felt the world whirling around her. "Did Jay say how he knew it was the judge?" she whispered through stiff lips.

Ellis looked her over thoroughly before replying. "He says Dave told him. So, is it true?"

She nodded. "Yes, I believe it." It was another hard admission, but again she felt better after making it. The judge must have felt Jay needed some further "persuasion" before Valerie offered him the deal.

"Something's going on with Judge Haskins?"

Valerie resisted a crazy, momentarily overwhelming urge to laugh. "Oh, Ellis," she finally said, "something is definitely going on with Judge Haskins." She tried to get hold of herself. "I might need your help on it soon, but right now I can't tell anybody."

"Okay." He was obviously curious, Valerie thought, but true to form, he didn't push her.

"Ellis, I appreciate all your help." She took a deep

breath. "And your understanding, but, please, I need to see Jay now."

He allowed her to enter. "He's in the squad room."

There was a short hallway that opened into a large room. Although a few rows of chairs were set up, classroom-fashion, it was deserted. Except for Jay.

He was looking at a poster on the wall, but turned at the sound of the door opening. He stood rigidly straight, staring at her, holding a cup of coffee in his hand. There was an angry purple bruise forming on his temple, and she caught her breath, letting it out consciously. Then, involuntarily, her eyes sought his, and the hard bleakness she found there chilled her.

"Jay," she started, but she had no idea what she intended to say. Instead, she simply stared at him mutely. There was no answering tenderness in his eyes.

He spoke. "I suppose Florence Nightingale is here to minister to the wounded."

"Jay, please…"

"I didn't ask Ellis to call you."

She swallowed. "I know. But I'm glad he called me. You're hurt, and you need me, and I can take care of you." Oh, God, she thought helplessly, it was the wrong thing to say, all wrong. She was falling into the trap he had unwittingly set. Right now, he did need her, and she wanted to take care of him. But she wanted so much more. She wanted to be with him, laugh with him, share with him. She wanted to spend the rest of her life with him. But one more look at his stony face told her that he wouldn't listen.

"Am I free to go?" Jay's clipped question was directed at Ellis.

Ellis turned to Valerie. "His car's been towed, but you can get it in the morning. Jay isn't supposed to

be alone tonight. The doctor says he should be awakened every two hours to see if he's coherent, because
of the concussion.''

"I'll take care of it, Ellis," Valerie said.

Once more, Jay addressed Ellis, ignoring Valerie
completely. "I asked, am I free to go?"

Ellis smiled a little. "I'll release you to Valerie's
custody."

She thought for a moment he would actually refuse
to go with her, but he didn't. "Fine." Jay fixed Valerie with another hard stare. "Let's go."

Ellis went over and put a friendly hand on his
shoulder. "I've got a few papers I need you to sign.
Can you come over here?" He led Jay to a desk, then
suggested to Valerie that she retrieve Jay's wallet and
keys. "They're on the desk in my office. You remember the way, don't you?"

Without answering, she let herself into the long
hallway that led to the back of the police station. This
wing held offices, rest rooms and the lunchroom. Her
sneakers made no sound on the polished linoleum,
and the dim overhead light meant she cast little
shadow. Edgy from the events of the night, her senses
seemed more alert than usual.

That was probably why she caught the slight movement, or maybe it was a noise, that came from the
half-open doorway of the break room. She had no
reason to check it out, but an overwhelming sense that
something was wrong pulled her into the doorway.
She heard another soft sound on her left.

Her mouth fell open as she stared in silence. Dave
Grau sat hunched over a small table, one knee drawn
up. On the table in front of him was a mirror, a razor
blade and a small plastic packet of white powder. As
she watched, he laid a short straw on the table.

Valerie had prosecuted enough drug cases to know instantly what this was. The mirror, the razor and straw were what the lawyers called drug paraphernalia. Dave Grau was about to use cocaine. Suddenly, the wild mood swings and depression of the last few months made sense. Too much sense.

She must have made a sound, because all of a sudden Dave looked up and saw her. Propelling herself forward, she made a move for the packet even as his hands closed around it.

"Dave, give me the packet," she hissed.

Without a word, he snatched it up and ran toward the back of the room. Valerie yelled for help, then followed Dave. Knocking over a chair as he went, Dave made it to a wooden door on the far wall, threw it open and stumbled inside another room. She was only a step behind. Once they were both inside, the door swung shut behind them.

They were in a small bathroom. Ducking and turning to the side, she managed to slip around Dave. Valerie pushed her body between him and the toilet, blocking his access. Surprisingly, she felt no fear, only cold anger. This was the man who had abused Jay, who had treated Meg so roughly. For a long second, they stared at each other, their eyes only inches away.

"Stay out of this, Valerie," Dave warned her, his voice a hoarse growl. "You've been okay to me, and I don't want to hurt you."

For a second, there was only the sound of their breathing. Valerie fought down the fear that was now quickly replacing her anger. She was not going to let him destroy the evidence. She would fight him. She kept her eyes locked on his.

"Give it to me," she said with deadly earnestness.

Unexpectedly, his gaze wavered, and he looked almost vulnerable. It lasted less than a second. Lunging forward, he pushed her aside. As she fell against the wall with a *poof!* of escaping breath, he managed to drop the small bag into the toilet.

Valerie gathered herself and pulled away from the wall. As Dave reached over to flush away the cocaine, Valerie plunged her hand into the water. She got her fingertips around the plastic packet in the instant before the flushing action got under way. He reached for her, but she managed to elude his hand.

Clutching the bag tightly in both hands, she allowed herself to fall into a sitting position, drawing her legs up in an attempt to protect the evidence. Dimly, she heard shouts and she yelled again, as loud as she could.

Dave dropped to his knees, and for a moment that felt like a lifetime, they grappled for the cocaine, locked together. Suddenly, without warning, Valerie realized he had gone still. Slowly, he loosened his grip on her.

When Jay and Ellis burst into the bathroom a moment later, they found Valerie up against the wall, knees against her chest, clutching something tightly to her stomach. Dave Grau sat before her, his head in his hands, his sobs echoing loudly against the concrete walls.

IT WAS ALMOST FOUR A.M. before Valerie and Jay were finally on their way. Because the incident with Dave involved drugs and a police officer, there'd been a lot of paperwork. Ellis had meticulously followed procedure in arresting Dave and reading him his rights. Between choking sobs, Dave had confessed, telling Jay and Valerie over and over how sorry he was. All the fight had gone out of him and he listened quietly as Ellis told him he would be going to a rehabilitation center as soon as it could be arranged.

Valerie had never been happier to leave a place in her entire life. They drove in tired, miserable silence, with Jay staring out the passenger window.

It wasn't until they had pulled into her driveway that Jay finally spoke. "I suppose it would be asking too much for you to drop me off at the farm."

Valerie sighed. "You aren't supposed to be alone, you know. I'll have to check on you every two hours."

"Don't bother," he said briefly.

"For heaven's sake, Jay, you have a concussion—"

"And don't start with how I need you, either," he finished, before lapsing again into a stony silence that lasted until they were inside her house.

"May I have a shower before you show me to the guest room, please?" he asked with exaggerated politeness. The expression on his face told her he was remembering the same thing she was, that other night he was supposed to have slept in the guest room but had made exquisite love to her in front of the fire, instead. Had things between them sunk so low that she couldn't read any lingering tenderness in his eyes as he remembered that night?

Feeling utterly miserable, she gave him a towel and went to prepare the guest room while he showered. In the morning, they would talk. After so many years, it was worth one more try, but she had no idea how he would respond. Had she loved him so long only to finally lose him? Numbly, she lit the small lamp on the white wicker desk that served as a nightstand.

She didn't wait for him to come out of the bathroom, instead she spoke through the closed door. "I've readied your room. Feel free to get a snack if you're hungry."

He didn't answer, so she went on. "I'll check on you in two hours, but try to get some sleep." There was still no sound on the other side of the bathroom door. "Jay, give me the silent treatment if you feel you have to, but just let me know if you heard me, okay?" she asked finally. She leaned toward the door, straining to hear.

The bathroom door opened so abruptly, she practically fell into the room. Jay stood there, dressed only in a pair of jeans. He hadn't dried very well and droplets of water still glistened on his bare shoulders and chest. His face was drawn, and there were unmistakable circles of tiredness underlining his eyes. The bruise on his temple was growing more wickedly purple by the hour. She was tired to the point of numbness, but he must be exhausted. Even so, he was still the most attractive man she had ever met. She swallowed heavily, hit solidly with a vivid memory of herself exploring that hard chest with her lips.

He glared at her. "The guest room is ready. I can get a snack. You'll check on me in two hours. Do I have it all?" His words each pricked like the point of a knife.

She licked her lips. "Yes."

"Fine." He stalked off in the direction of the guest room. Her eyes followed him, but he didn't look back, instead shutting the door with a firmness that said as clearly as if he'd spoken that he didn't welcome her presence.

Valerie set her alarm clock to go off in two hours, although she didn't think she'd be able to fall asleep, her exhaustion notwithstanding. She took off her shoes and socks but lay stretched out on her bed, still fully clothed in the jeans and plaid flannel shirt she had thrown on before going to the police station.

She could think of nothing but Jay. She had already spent hours tonight berating herself for her foolish naïveté where Judge Haskins was concerned. Realizing how wrong she had been about the judge had opened her eyes to other things. Instead of blaming their failed relationship solely on Jay, she was forced to confront some uncomfortable truths about herself. She saw now that it was hard to let herself be vulnerable, to trust others. She was more at ease with friendliness than with the real give-and-take of an adult relationship. She did get tremendous satisfaction when people needed her, but she had needs of her own that were worthy of expression.

Jay was right. There was no real love without trust. She would have to trust him again. If he hurt her, so be it. But she was going to take a chance on happiness. Tomorrow, they would definitely talk. She was going to say what she had to, and the rest would be up to him. She only hoped that once he'd had some sleep, he wouldn't be as angry as he'd sounded tonight. Otherwise, she might never be able to break through all that sarcasm.

Off and on for the next two hours, she checked the clock, and about five minutes before the alarm was due to ring, she rolled out of bed. She hit the button on the alarm and went down the hall to the guest room, knocking lightly before going in.

In the predawn glow from the lace-curtained window, she could see his still form outlined on the bed. Jay lay on top of the covers, still in his jeans, his arms folded behind his head. When she moved closer, she saw with a jolt that he was wide awake. His eyes, washed of color in the gray light, were sober and assessing.

"Hi," she said softly, stopping awkwardly by the side of the bed.

"Hi, yourself." He didn't seem about to add anything sarcastic, but there was a wary stillness about him that didn't suggest any tenderness, either.

"You're definitely coherent." She tried to smile.

"Definitely," he agreed. "And wide-awake, too, I'm afraid."

She nodded. "Me, too. I've been doing a lot of thinking. Some of it is old ground for me, but it keeps replaying itself inside my head."

He looked away. "Look, I know I was pretty hostile tonight. Still shook up, I guess, so don't take it personally." There was a silence that Valerie made no effort to fill. She sensed he wasn't finished. "I was really scared out there, Valerie," he said softly a moment later, as if the admission was painful, but at least he looked at her again.

"You had a right to be. Dave definitely intended to hurt you, and you couldn't have had any idea how much."

"Yeah, but apparently, even with the drugs in him, he didn't want to do much more than scare me. There was no one around. He could have really hurt me if he'd wanted to."

A shudder went through her at his words. Jay reached over and took her hand, giving it a brief squeeze before letting it go. "Actually, I wonder if he isn't an okay person, without the cocaine in his system. All that time he was following me around. Was he just waiting for a chance to come after me, or was he trying to find some excuse not to do it?" After a moment's reflection, he answered his own question. "I guess maybe we'll never know. But I was thinking that he must have been scared himself, knowing what would happen if someone found out about his drug habit. That fear made it easy for the judge to use him, didn't it?"

She was lost in thought for a moment, remembering Dave Grau in earlier times, when he and Meg had been happy together. "I hope he gets help, Jay. Tonight was a good first step. Still, I'm really glad Meg's at least out of this. That's one good thing that happened, anyway."

He nodded in agreement. "She seems happy with Bob Vanette. And now, we're left with Judge Haskins."

There was unmistakable bitterness in his tone, and Valerie let it seep into her and mingle with her own feelings of betrayal and outrage. "He'll never take that first step and say he has a problem, Jay."

"Maybe he will," he replied in a voice that held no conviction.

"No way." She vividly recalled her own sudden certainty of Judge Haskins's guilt and his vehement denial of her accusation. "Today he offered me a deal to settle the case. It wasn't a bad one, but now with Dave's confessing that the judge put him up to scaring you off, Judge Haskins is going to go to jail, instead." She took a deep breath. She didn't have to tell him what the judge had proposed, but she found she wanted to. She needed to share it all, and receive whatever comfort he was willing to give her. "Anyway," she went on over a lump in her throat, "he asked me to convey his terms to you." She held his gaze. "He suggested I persuade you by letting you... touch me."

Jay swore softly. "I'm sorry, Valerie."

She smiled tremulously, and used her hand to smooth the bedclothes next to his body. "Don't be sorry. His suggestion made me sick, but in a way I needed to hear it. It was part of what helped me realize how incredibly blind I'd been, not just about him but about everything else, too. Because the judge helped me so much, I was sure he was a good man, and I always figured the other lawyers who didn't like him were jealous of all the influence he had." Another deep breath helped her go on. She needed to talk about what had happened, how it had felt. "I can't believe I was so wrong about another human being. He did such terrible things. To Roberta." Her voice had begun to quaver. "To you, too, Jay. Dave hit you, but Judge Haskins is just as responsible, just as guilty."

Jay was quiet, listening to her.

Valerie lifted her gaze to the window, as if staring through it would help her see the truth. "And I've done a terrible thing, too, Jay. I should have listened to Roberta, really listened, without any preconceived opinions. I was so sure I knew the judge." She sighed. "I let another woman down, one I knew and liked."

Jay's voice was very soft. "You know what Roberta said to me once about your investigation? She said you were wrong, but you were fair. You made a mistake, Valerie. It was a big one, but when it comes down to it, that's all it was. A mistake."

After everything that had happened, she knew she had no right to his understanding, but she was very grateful for it. Yes, she had made a mistake, one that she had to put right at the first opportunity.

Her hand stroked the sheets again. "I'm going to talk to Roberta as soon as I can, and tell her how

sorry I am for doubting her story. I'll try to explain
how much I really respected the judge, and liked him
as a person, the person I thought he was...." She
could not go on.

"It takes courage to admit you were wrong, that
you've done things that hurt other people." Jay
looked directly into her eyes. "Believe me, nobody
knows more than I do just how much courage it takes.
And I think Roberta will appreciate what you have to
say." There was a quiet conviction in his voice that
heartened her.

She hadn't planned to touch Jay until they had
things straight between them, but she found she was
reaching out, anyway. She stroked the bruise on his
temple as lightly as she could, then she ran her finger
along his rough, strong jaw. He watched her, unmoving, and she gave in to the impulse to smooth his hair.

"Valerie," Jay said, his voice sounding strained,
"I don't want to talk anymore. I want to hold you.
Will you let me do that?"

She lay immediately down beside him. He rolled
onto his side and held her against him, then buried
his face in the crook of her neck and rested there
quietly for several moments.

Valerie relaxed more fully into his arms, luxuriat-
ing in the feel of his hard embrace, the soap-scented
smell of his body, the sensation of his breath against
her skin. She had wondered if she would ever be able
to hold him again. The thought that she had come so
close to losing him mingled with the pure, glorious
physical attraction she always felt.

As if he couldn't help himself, she felt his arms
tightening around her by infinitesimal degrees. In an
instinctive response, she pressed her lower body to
his, arching until she fit snugly. His arousal was im-

mediate, and she felt a jolt of pleasure at feeling it against her. When he started to pull away, she used her own arms and legs to keep him with her.

"Stay still, Valerie," he implored her. "I was only going to hold you, but when you rub against me this way, I can't help responding."

"I...don't want you to be able to help it."

In a quick move, he rolled away from her, leaving her feeling bereft and alarmed. "Don't you want—"

"No," he said quickly. He sat up and faced the wall, focusing all his attention there. "I could make love with you tonight, and it would be so easy." There was a pause, and Valerie lay still, waiting with a lump in her throat. "But what wouldn't be easy is tomorrow, Valerie." Again, there was a dreadful pause. "I can't make love to you, especially to you, and have it be just a physical thing. Not now, not anymore."

He whipped around to face her then, and loomed over her body as she lay still, looking up at him. His eyes were shadowed, but she could see they were haunted and hot. "Those three days in the storm meant a lot more to me than sex, Valerie. I have never felt more connected to another human being than I felt to you. And I know I can't make love to you and go home tomorrow and let it be."

She stared at him for a long moment. "It can't be that way for me, either." He ought to know that about her, she thought; surely he would know at least that, after all they had shared. Those three days were the most special of her life, too. Surely—no, she thought, maybe he didn't understand. After all, her behavior afterward had hardly been that of a lover. She wondered what to say, how to show him that the time of the storm meant as much to her as it did to him. Suddenly, she had an inspiration.

She sat up to face him, her eyes locked with his. "Unbutton my shirt," she commanded in a whisper.

"Valerie." He groaned her name, making no move to comply.

She reached down and brought his hand up to the top button. As soon as she felt his fingers there, she began to tremble, and fought down the shyness she instinctively felt. "Open my shirt."

He couldn't help it, regardless of his intentions. His own hands were shaking as he brought them both to the task. When he tried to look down, she used her hand to tilt his face upward. Only when he had the buttons undone and began to slide the flannel from her shoulders with tantalizing slowness, did she allow him to drop his gaze.

"You're as soft as I remembered," he murmured raggedly.

A half second later, she heard his sharply drawn breath and knew he had found it. She looked down, too, then, and saw his fingers had closed around the opal pendant she always wore against her skin.

Slowly, they both raised their faces to each other.

"You're wearing it," he whispered, astonished wonder in all of him.

She smiled, a big smile that was so wide it hurt her cheeks. "I haven't taken it off, not since a week after you gave it to me."

"I never knew."

"Those three days were precious, but we can have more, Jay, so much more." She felt the tears in the corners of her eyes but they didn't hinder the smile she still wore. "I've loved you for years. I love you now."

He took her cheeks between his hands. "I can give you promises, Valerie, but I can't prove my love to you in advance," he reminded her hoarsely. "You have to let me show you, day by day." He kissed her forehead. "I will never leave you, but I can only ask you to believe that."

"I do believe it, Jay."

An incandescent smile lit his face. "No hesitation this time?"

"None." Her answer was immediate. As soon as he heard it, Jay pulled her down on top of him and locked his lips with hers.

EPILOGUE

"COME ON," he urged, leaving the dairy behind and hurrying her along the trail that led through the woods.

Valerie was out of breath by the time they climbed to the top of the long hill, Jay's hand holding hers. She hadn't been here in twelve years, but it hadn't changed much. There was still the same rough, grassy meadow at the crest, and the beautiful view of the folds of the land, finally ending in a wide valley. There were more houses visible across the valley now. She supposed the trees had grown some in the time since she had been here last, but not perceptibly. How short a time twelve years seemed out here, short compared with the life of a tree, or a meadow, or a hill.

Jay was unrolling the mysterious paper tube he'd been carrying. "I thought I'd put the house here," he told her, gesturing almost to the edge of the hill, "with the deck overlooking the valley."

"You're building a house?"

He grinned, the lines at the corners of his eyes crinkling as the light wind ruffed his hair. "It was a secret. I've been working on the farmhouse, remodeling it." For a second, the smile left his face, but almost immediately it returned. "I don't like the memories in that old house, and it's so dark inside. This area's building up fast. When the farmhouse is spiffed up, someone will pay a good price to get it and the old barn. It would be perfect for a horse farm, with twenty acres or so.''

Now Valerie finally understood why the farmhouse was so empty, but she still wasn't sure she fully understood him. ''You're selling the farm?''

''Just part of it, for enough money to build this.'' He brought the pages to her. The thin papers flapped in the cool breeze, and he used his hands on opposite corners to try to keep them taut.

Valerie saw that they were architectural renderings of a large house. It was made of wood, but her most compelling impression was of glass. The facade was broken at regular intervals with tall windows. The house was modern, but the extra gables and trim reminded her of her Victorian house in town.

''What do you think?'' Jay sounded a little nervous.

''It's beautiful,'' she said truthfully.

His voice dropped. ''When I first came back, I had a design worked up. It was cedar and glass, spare and contemporary in feel, like the houses that ring Amsden Lake. But after I saw your house, I decided I wanted something a touch more traditional. Cozier.'' His soft blue eyes twinkled, and the nervousness seemed to have left him. ''It has four fireplaces, Valerie.''

''Four?'' she repeated, and he laughed out loud.

''I think we need lots of fireplaces. But enough about the house. I want to show you something else.'' He took her hand and led her to the very edge of the hill. ''I can't really show you, but I can explain it.''

Valerie waited expectantly. Surely there couldn't be more than his wonderful house. Whatever it was, it was enough to paste a smile on his face that looked as big as the outdoors.

Jay's hand swept over the valley. "Under where the deck will go is a little fold in the hill. When I was a kid, I used to climb down there, near the boundary of the farm. There was a spring there, and it made the area muddy all the time. It was a perfect place for a kid to play, but when I got older, I forgot about it. When I was having the house designed, I remembered it, and I got someone to look at the spot. It's a year-round spring, Valerie." He glanced at her, but she didn't seem to grasp the significance of what he'd said, so he hurried on. "With a little excavation, they can dig out the spring and we'll have open water."

"A lake?" She sounded dazed.

He chuckled softly. "Well, no, not a lake, but a big pond, five acres or so."

She caught his good humor and turned it back on him with a grin of her own. "Big pond, little lake. It doesn't really matter what I call it, does it? You got your wish." She paused. "That day at Amsden Lake, I teased you for wanting your view from the hill *and* your own private lake. I thought it was an awfully big wish, but you just went about making it come true, didn't you?"

Jay caught her hands and whirled her until she was dizzy, then pulled her to him. The sky spun for a few moments, and the only things that felt solid were Jay's two warm arms.

"Take time to study the plans, Valerie, and make all the changes you want," he was murmuring in her ear. "As long as there's lots of light, I don't care. After all, the house is yours, too."

She lifted her head, still feeling slightly off kilter. Jay pulled a ring out of his pocket and slipped it on her finger. "I bought this when I chose your necklace, always hoping, I guess."

Valerie looked down to find a lovely aquamarine glittering in the sunlight. It was the color of the sky—no, the color of water.

"I wasn't sure if you liked aquamarines, or if you'd rather have a diamond." He spoke quickly, but just as quickly, Valerie cut off the words in a tender kiss.

"It's perfect."

He took her hand and held it to his cheek. "So, you will marry me?"

"Yes," she told him, and would have said more but Jay was pulling her to him with a kiss that took her breath away.

When it ended a long moment later, his mouth remained close to hers. She looked up across a few inches of space to find his eyes staring into hers. "This place holds some of my best memories. Like the last time we walked up here, so very long ago."

She was still breathless, beyond speech.

"I made love to you that night." His voice was low, rough. "Really made love, no matter what I told myself it was at the time, and I never forgot the feel of your arms around me. I'm so sorry I wasted all those years when we could have been happy together. But I swear I'll spend every night for the rest of my life holding on to you as hard as you held me that night."

She pushed her hand between them, using a finger to still his lips. "You don't have to say you're sorry anymore. The past is over, and I'm happy now. You've made everything so right."

Unexpectedly, his face softened, and a chuckle escaped him. "You know, Valerie, it should be right. After all, I've had twelve years to plan it."

HEROES
AGAINST ALL ODDS

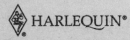 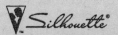

Please address questions and book requests to: Harlequin Reader Service U.S.: 3010 Walden Ave.,
P.O. Box 1325, Buffalo, NY 14269 CAN.: P.O. Box 609, Fort Erie, Ont. L2A 5X3   PAHGEN

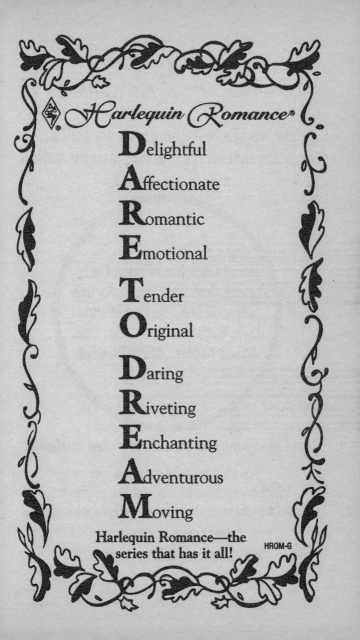

Harlequin Romance®

Delightful

Affectionate

Romantic

Emotional

Tender

Original

Daring

Riveting

Enchanting

Adventurous

Moving

Harlequin Romance—the
series that has it all!

HROM-G

HARLEQUIN ✦ PRESENTS®

The world's bestselling romance series...
The series that brings you your favorite authors,
month after month:

Helen Bianchin...Emma Darcy
Lynne Graham...Penny Jordan
Miranda Lee...Sandra Morton
Anne Mather...Carole Mortimer
Susan Napier...Michelle Reid

and many more uniquely talented authors!

Wealthy, powerful, gorgeous men...
Women who have feelings just like your own...
The stories you love, set in exotic, glamorous locations...

HARLEQUIN PRESENTS,
Seduction and passion guaranteed!

Visit us at www.eHarlequin.com

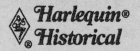

Harlequin® Historical

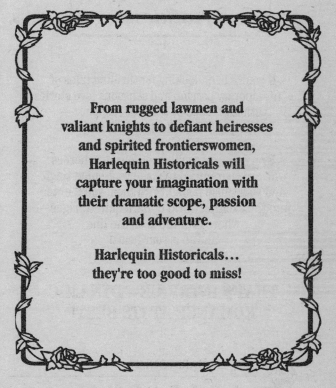

From rugged lawmen and
valiant knights to defiant heiresses
and spirited frontierswomen,
Harlequin Historicals will
capture your imagination with
their dramatic scope, passion
and adventure.

Harlequin Historicals...
they're too good to miss!

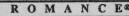